Andrew John Hamling was born in Sussex in 1951. He trained as a teacher in Devon and went on to complete a degree in psychology with the Open University. During his career as a teacher of geography he worked in Zimbabwe, Argentina and South Africa, returning to the UK in 2011. He published his first novel, *A Matter of Conscience*, introducing private investigator Bethany Gallagher, in 2013. In the same year he published a collection of poetry, *Songs for Calpurnia*. A volume of short stories, *Couplets*, followed in 2014. Since then, he has focused on developing the Bethany Gallagher series of crime novels. He now lives in Lancashire.

Also by Andrew John Hamling

Novels

A Matter of Conscience
A Family Affair
A Body on the Green
A Contract Killing
A Ghost from the Past
A Witch in Time
A Fatal Chapter

Short stories

Couplets

Poetry

Songs for Calpurnia

Andrew John Hamling

A Picture of Guilt

CONTENTS

I

VICTORIAN GOTHIC

What lay behind the smiles? The nudges and winks; the jokes and joshing? The meticulous coiffures and extravagant bonnets; the rustling dresses and neatly knotted ties? The teetering heels and guardsman polished toecaps? Internecine bickering and familial spats – and when they disassembled and reassembled into their coteries and cabals, gossip, tittle-tattle and scandalmongering. Whatever lurked behind the smiles, it was the duty of Nick Corvino to record them, to be indelibly preserved for posterity in the, as yet blank, wedding album.

Nick enjoyed weddings, especially those celebrated on a pleasantly warm, spring day, when the trees were in leaf and blossoms abounded. It made creating that requisite air of romance so much easier. True, they all followed the same script, literally and metaphorically, but each were unique in their own way; each had its element of idiosyncratic and singular interest.

Almost as much as the photography itself, he enjoyed sitting at his computer refining the results of his labours until he had compiled a visual memoir that, he hoped, the happy couple would appreciate and cherish. Thus, he was sitting on his sofa, preparing to scroll through the finished compendium, with Gallagher pressed up against his shoulder, disposed to approve, but willing to critique his efforts. Taj Mahal's *Mo' Roots* was playing on the turntable. She had been taking regular sips of her pinotage while he prepared his presentation, ignoring the glass of Old Speckled Hen which remained, untouched, on the industrial style, teak coffee table.

The wedding venue had been at Pendlehurst, on the southern edge of Barrowford. Pendlehurst had originally been a farmhouse, the majority of which dated from the 18th century, though evidence of an earlier, 17th structure was still visible. An additional wing had been appended during the 19th century. The building, now in the shadow of the motorway, was currently home to the Pendle Museum of Witches. The main focus of the museum is the Pendle Witches and the sorry events of 1612 which resulted in their hangings, but it also extends its collection of artefacts to other witch related paraphernalia from around the UK. Apart from the museum itself, there is the obligatory shop and the customary café. All that remains of the farm is the land on the opposite side of the access road, which extends as far as Carr Brook. Facing the museum, but screened from it by a beech hedge, is an ornamental garden, accessed through an arched, double, wrought iron gate. Walking through the garden the visitor reaches a lych-gate, of the type commonly found at the entrance to churchyards, which is not coincidental. The lych-gate opens out onto a courtyard surrounded by some of the farm buildings that had been relocated there and restored, to create an intimate wedding venue. Directly across the flagged courtyard, an imposing sandstone edifice, bearing the inscription 'THE ALICE NUTTER BARN' above its large plate glass doors (which lead into a room of cathedralesque proportions), is the building in which the wedding formalities take place and the happy couples exchange their vows. To the left, a slightly smaller, two-storey building, The Chattox Stables, comprises two bars, one at either end, with a dining/dancing area between them. On the right, The Demdike Smithy houses function rooms, upstairs and downstairs, and an exhibition of blacksmithing implements, including forge and anvils. Between and around the three buildings, neat lawns are laid out with beds and borders, shrubs and flowering trees. To the left of the ornamental garden is a car park with its own side access to the garden.

Nick, as was his inclination, had furnished Gallagher with all these details prior to commencing his presentation, but had declined to elaborate on the style of wedding, over and above a random, obtuse hint. Gallagher, for her part, had learned patience in these matters.

When he was ready – and having turned to Gallagher to

ensure that she was comfortable – Nick reached for his beer, took a generous slurp, as if to fortify himself, and replaced the glass on its Namaqualand wildflower coaster. The photos revealed a wedding appreciably less traditional than Gallagher had been given to expect from his previous intimations. It had not been an unduly large affair, but there had been sufficient numbers of aunts, uncles, great aunts and great uncles, nephews, nieces, cousins and friends, in addition to the requisite parents, grandparents and siblings, to fill the barn and to make the subsequent festivities (to which Nick had been invited – an offer which he had gladly accepted, not being one to turn down free food, albeit for a 'polite' couple of hours) congenial, but not unbecomingly rumbustious. The bride wore a long-sleeved silk dress, with velvet and lace flourishes, in black and burgundy, its flamboyant draping tumbling over a crinoline and its corsetry obliging a trade-off between the fullness of her figure and the fullness of her bosom – her décolletage, as Nick was not slow to point out, being the subject of much surreptitious admiration among the menfolk. The groom wore a black tailcoat with purple velvet collar and cuffs and a waistcoat of violet paisley over a cream, ruffled shirt. Her ensemble was completed by black, mid-heeled, calf-length, lace-up boots and his by two-tone brown brogues. The younger generation of guests had whole-heartedly embraced the Victorian theme, but the enthusiasm for it clearly waned with age, such that the older generation adhered to more traditional attire, with the exception of the ineluctable eccentric aunt and uncle (on the bride's side) who had gone full steampunk.

Unbeknown to Nick, at the moment he was showing off, with justifiable pride, the end result of his previous afternoon's work, the location of that commission had been transformed. No longer was it bustling with wedding guests, but was now buzzing with police officers, forensic personnel and medics and the whole venue had been cordoned off. Detective Inspector Wainwright was there, accompanied, as usual, by D.S. Bowden and D.C. Kershaw. The trio were surrounding, at an appropriate distance, the body of a male, lying supine on the lawn, betwixt the herbaceous border and a circular rose bed, that occupied the space between the barn and the stables. The pathologist, John Oldfield, with his assistant, Alice, was bent over the body, engaged in his preliminary examination and patently ignoring the threesome.

"I presume we're looking at a suspicious death." Wainwright was anxious to justify his having been called to the scene.

"I just deal in death, inspector." Oldfield spoke matter-of-factly, without interrupting his investigation. "Whether or not it's suspicious is for you to determine." At this point, he did break off and look up at the detective. "But if, by 'suspicious', you're implying that someone else might have been responsible for the untimely demise of this poor chap, then it probably is."

"Your reasoning being, John?"

"This puncturing of the chest," to facilitate his examination, Oldfield had unbuttoned the victim's waistcoat and shirt and he drew both to one side to give Wainwright a clearer view of the wound, "has, I'm guessing, been caused by some sort of metal spike and is most likely to have been inflicted by a third person." Wainwright knew very well that Oldfield's guesses could reliably be taken as fact and were only advanced as conjecture pending a conclusive post mortem.

"So he was murdered."

"It would appear so."

"You said a spike, not a blade."

"I did. The shape of the wound, being roughly circular, suggests a spike rather than the blade of a knife." Wainwright paused for a moment to assimilate the information.

"And that's the cause of death?"

"I doubt it." He turned back to the body and resumed his examination.

"Oh?" The inspector sensed a spanner about to be thrown into the works and he did not like complications.

"The amount of blood around the wound suggests he was dead before it was inflicted." He pulled back the clothing further, to reveal another wound to the lower left abdominal region, almost directly below the first one. "However, there's a greater amount of blood around this wound, caused, most likely, by the same implement."

"So he was stabbed in the stomach and then stabbed again through the heart for good measure."

"His assailant clearly wanted him dead." Bowden seized the opportunity to make his presence felt.

"Maybe." Oldfield sounded as non-committal as it was possible to sound.

"Maybe?"

"Alice." The pathologist looked up at his assistant, currently cradling the head of the deceased between her latex-gloved palms. She turned it towards the right, disclosing an ill-defined injury amid a tangle of blood-matted hair. "Penetrating trauma caused by a heavy object, delivered with sufficient force to cause a concavity in the skull." Alice returned the head to its previous position.

"So we don't know yet what actually killed him." Oldfield considered a response superfluous. Instead, he again addressed Alice:

"Can we turn him over?"

"To the right?" The taciturn, but astute, Alice inferred his intention.

"To the right." With practiced synchronicity they turned the body in the desired direction. "Hm. Can you hold it there, please, Alice?"

"What?" Wainwright intuited further complications.

"Whatever was used was driven right the way through and out the other side. And not only is there an exit wound," he bent closer and parted the grass with his latex-gloved fingers, "but it's made an indentation in the ground. He wasn't just stabbed through the heart; the spike, or whatever, was hammered through."

"His assailant wanted him very dead." Bowden continued his previous train of thought.

"However," Oldfield pointedly ignored the observation, "there's very little in the way of contusions around the wound, as one would expect if a hammer, or some other heavy object, had come into contact with the flesh, indicating that the implement was of considerable length; at least ten inches, I'd say."

"Time? Roughly." Wainwright hastily appended the rider knowing that Oldfield could become irritated if he thought he was expected to be specific at this stage." The pathologist sat back on his haunches and shrugged.

"Eighteen hours." Bowden made a quick, mental calculation.

"So, about mid-evening yesterday."

"Nick!" He had left her watching the evening local news while he tidied up the kitchen for the evening.

"What is it?" The urgency in her voice caused him to pause what he was doing and scurry into the dining area.

"Come here!"

"What's happened?" He deposited the tea towel on the dining table and joined her on the sofa.

"Pendlehurst. That's where you were yesterday."

"It is. What about it?"

"Someone's been murdered there."

"Murdered? When?"

"They discovered the body this morning. The police are treating the death as suspicious, which means they think he was murdered."

"He? Who?" Gallagher was unable to elucidate further, but a reporter was standing in front of the iron gates at the entrance to the ornamental garden, glancing down at her tablet and commencing her piece with appropriate gravitas. It was dark and there was little activity to be seen, other than a couple of uniformed police officers behind the reporter and a corner of a police car at the edge of the screen. It transpired that the deceased had been identified only as the best man at a wedding, held at the venue, the previous afternoon.

"That's the wedding you were at." She turned to him for confirmation.

"I can't remember his name off hand, but I'd have certainly photographed him. Probably several times."

"And that's not likely to be all." She turned back to the screen to garner any further information. The reporter confirmed her immediate thoughts: the police were focusing their initial enquiries on the wedding guests. "The police think the murderer was one of the wedding guests." She turned back to Nick. "That means you probably, also, photographed the murderer."

II

<u>CHATTOX AND DEMDIKE</u>

D.I. Wainwright was standing in front of his whiteboard, upon which were fixed three photographs of the deceased, taken at the scene where his body had been found, with a smattering of basic, tentative details appended.

"Kate," he turned towards his detective constable, "can you bring the room up to speed with what we know so far."

"Yes, sir." Kate Kershaw, from her desk in the shadow of the printer, drew together her notes, pushed her chair back, stood up and cleared her throat. "The body was discovered at around one p.m. yesterday. After the last of the guests had left on Saturday night, a small team of staff had gone in to briefly tidy up, check that no one had fallen asleep in a corner somewhere and lock up the three buildings: the barn, which had been used for the ceremony; the stables, which had been used for an afternoon buffet and, later, for a dinner dance, and the smithy, which had been used as a changing area, for the bride and bridesmaids and for people to freshen up, should they so wish. In the stables, one of the staff found a jacket left on the back of a chair."

"That jacket was handed to us yesterday. It seems to be about the right size, so we're assuming it belongs to the deceased. It contained a wallet, with a driving licence inside, and mobile phone and, on that basis, we can provisionally name the victim as Casey Hardacre," Wainwright tapped the name on the board with his forefinger, "pending some form of substantive identification. Casey, so the manager of the venue informed us, was the best man at the wedding." He looked back at Kershaw. "Continue, please."

"The manager of Pendlehurst, both the museum and the wedding venue, is Linda Whitehorn and she took a team of staff over to the site after lunch yesterday to clean up properly. It was only when she went to look around the gardens that she discovered the body. Being between the border and the rose garden – and the rose garden having a statue of Aphrodite in the middle of it – it wouldn't have been easily noticeable from the courtyard in front of the barn."

"Deliberately concealed there?" To Bowden, that seemed a logical conclusion.

"There's no evidence to suggest the body had been moved." Wainwright was quick to refute the suggestion. "Oldfield believes that's where he was killed. Plus, if he was killed at night, there would be no need to hide the body - and if you had wanted to hide it, surely it would have been better to hide it behind the stables." Bowden fell silent again, somewhat disconsolately. "Anything else, Kate?"

"That's about it, sir." She resumed her seat.

"John Oldfield texted me a short while ago with some preliminary findings." Wainwright took his mobile out of his jacket pocket and began scrolling through it. "He can't be certain about the cause of death just yet, but likely to be a combination of the stab wound to the lower abdomen, puncturing the left kidney, and the blow to the left side of the head. He's pretty certain Casey would have died before he was impaled through the heart. Interestingly, while the entry wounds to the kidney and heart suggest a right-handed assailant, the concavity to the skull suggests a left-handed one." He paused to allow the information to be fully assimilated.

"He was attacked by two people?" Again, to Bowden, this was a logical deduction and one that, he presumed, he had been expected to make.

"Either that, or the killer was armed with a spike of some description in his right hand and a hammer in his left."

"That would certainly indicate an intent to kill."

"It certainly would, Dean. But, both scenarios are feasible at this stage." Bowden nodded, sagely. "John's also discovered something else: two or three long, blonde hairs were found on the shoulder of his waistcoat, which definitely did not belong to Casey, and there were traces of lipstick on his mouth and neck."

15

"He'd arranged to meet someone behind the stables, or wherever." Bowden attempted to contain his fervour at the prospect of there being a salacious aspect to the investigation.

"It's possible, but this was a wedding reception and drinking, dancing and flirting are not uncommon occurrences at weddings. Or, perhaps, he couldn't wait until after the event to have a moment of intimacy with a girlfriend. However, if he had arranged to meet someone there, it would explain what he was doing wandering around the grounds after dark."

"Do you think the person he met, presumably a woman, could be his killer?"

"Without any evidence, we have to keep an open mind, Dean, but finding this woman has to be one of our immediate priorities." Wainwright took a deep breath while his officers considered the state of play. "Speaking of priorities, we need to get confirmation of the victim's identity. He wasn't wearing a jacket when he was discovered, but that doesn't prove the jacket found in the stables belonged to him. We do have an address for the jacket's owner and that's being checked out now. When we're as sure as we can be that it's Casey Hardacre, then we can notify the next of kin and arrange for a formal identification. If it does prove to be Casey, we then need to find a motive for someone wanting him dead. Meanwhile, we can make a start on interviewing possible witnesses."

"Presumably that means all the wedding guests." Bowden was not at all enthused by the prospect.

"Correct. Ms. Whitehorn is due to send a guest list over. We could have our work cut out. I'm guessing this wasn't a small, family affair. I think we're going to need to start with the bride and groom and work outwards. Have you got their names there, Kate?"

"Yes, sir." She sifted through a sheaf of papers. "Magenta Seacroft and Crispin Molyneaux."

"Thank you. Let's just hope they haven't gone on honeymoon to the Caribbean. We'll also need to speak to all the staff that were on duty throughout the whole wedding, afternoon and evening."

"And whoever officiated at the ceremony?" Bowden was beginning to see the line of interviewees disappearing over the horizon.

"Naturally."

"Do we know if there was a photographer?" Kershaw sounded thoughtful. "There's usually one and any photographs of the wedding might prove useful."

"Good thinking, Kate."

"Have we found the weapon, or weapons, yet?" Bowden did not want to be upstaged.

"A team of CSI officers are searching Pendlehurst as we speak." With no further comment from his sergeant, Wainwright scanned the room, inviting any other contributions, none of which were forthcoming. "Right. Dean, you and me are going over to Pendlehurst. Kate, call Linda Whitehorn, tell her we're on our way and ask her to assemble everyone that was on duty on Saturday."

"Sir."

"You might also ask her if there was a photographer and, if so, follow it up. Then, see if you can track down the newlyweds." Kershaw nodded and immediately began shuffling through her wad of papers before reaching for the phone. Bowden was on his feet and had donned his jacket, ready to set out.

When Gallagher walked into her office on the first floor of Sycamore Mill, it was with a measured step rather than with her usual Monday morning breeziness. Clematis Davenport was already installed behind her desk, her computer was on and her hand was hovering by the side of a mug of coffee. Her boss's uncharacteristic entry caused her to look up with a sense of apprehension.

"Morning, Ms. Gallagher."

"Morning, Clemmy." Clematis' cheery greeting was met with a somewhat subdued response.

"Good weekend?"

"Yes." Her secretary had expected further elucidation, but was left disappointed.

"Coffee?"

"Please." Gallagher lingered, uncertainly, by the desk, as if she had something on her mind, but felt constrained in expressing it. Clematis swung round in her chair, got up, walked towards the kettle, switched it on, dragged Gallagher's 'Mine's a Latte' mug and coffee jar towards her and primed the former with a spoonful of the contents of the latter.

"Something wrong, Ms. Gallagher?" She half turned her head, trying to make the enquiry sound casual.

"I don't think so." The kettle boiled, Clematis made the coffee, returned to her desk, cleared a space and set the mug down. "Thank you, Clemmy." Gallagher picked it up, absently, adjusted her shoulder bag and began to make her way towards her own office.

"Did you see there were a murder at Pendle'urst on Saturday? At a wedding." Gallagher broke her step momentarily, but did not turn round.

"Yes. I did." Though it was only three syllables, the tone of her boss's voice was sufficient for Clematis to conclude that Gallagher's pensive mood and the murder were connected.

Once safely ensconced in her own office, Gallagher took an appreciative sip of coffee, put the mug down on top of a notepad, dumped her bag on the floor, plonked herself in her chair, performed a slight, side to side swivel and switched on her computer. While she waited for signs of life she leaned her head back, caught hold of a few loose strands of hair and twirled them between her fingers. When the screen lit up, she opened up her preferred browser and typed 'pendlehurst murder' into the search box. From the sparse details reported on the news, the 'suspicious death' had, she reckoned, the potential to be interesting and, given that Nick had been the official photographer at the wedding, she saw a way of getting her foot in the door. Plus, she reasoned, with a long list of wedding guests to wade through, the police would be grateful for all the help they could get.

Before Wainwright and Bowden had reached the police station car park, the detective inspector's phone had pinged and, on checking it, he had discovered an email from Linda Whitehorn, attaching the promised guest list. First sight of the attachment had caused him to stop halfway down the steps from the rear entrance. Bowden was halfway to Wainwright's Volvo before he realised his superior was no longer by his side. He made an abrupt about turn to find Wainwright trudging towards him, with pursed lips, a furrowed brow and holding the phone at arm's length, the screen towards him, evidently inviting him to look at it. He took a couple of reluctant steps forward and peered down at the screen.

"Jesus!" Bowden's heart sank, as Wainwright's had done, when he saw two pages of names.

"I'll forward them to Kate and let her sort through them. There's no indication as to who any of these people are, apart from the best man and the bridesmaids." Bowden considered making a flippant comment about being able to cross the best man off the list, but thought better of it. "Not Ms. Whitehorn's fault." He withdrew the phone, delved into his pocket for the car keys and handed them to the sergeant. "Get the car started."

While D.I. Wainwright and D.S. Bowden were driving to Pendlehurst, D.C. Kershaw had been having a productive conversation with Linda Whitehorn. The manager of Pendlehurst had informed her that she had sent a guest list to the detective inspector and, when asked to assemble all the staff who had been involved in the wedding on Saturday, advised the detective constable that most were at the museum or the wedding venue that morning and that she would attempt to contact the odd few who were not and ask them to come in. She was also able to confirm that there had been an official photographer and Kershaw was able to write down the name of Nick Corvino, who had a studio at Westgate. Furthermore, she was able to state that the bridal couple had arranged to spend their wedding night at the Highridge Hotel, before setting out on Sunday for a honeymoon in Tintagel. That intelligence was greeted with some relief. It might have been hoped that they had not planned to go away immediately, but it was a bonus that their honeymoon did not involve a flight to the Caribbean, or some other exotic destination. However, Kershaw was alarmed to learn that Ms. Whiterhorn had received a phone call from a Mrs. Hardacre, enquiring after her son, who, she explained, had been the best man at Crispin and Magenta's wedding and who had been due spend Saturday night with his parents, but had not turned up and they had not been able to contact him since. The detective constable's worst fears were allayed, though, when, it transpired, Ms. Whitehorn had exhibited the wit and wherewithal not to mention the discovery of the body – and had not even mentioned Casey's jacket.

The crime scene investigation team had been working, methodically, through The Alice Nutter Barn, The Chattox Stables, the Demdike Smithy, the courtyard and surrounding lawns, the ornamental gardens and the car park, but, as yet, had not found any semblance of a murder weapon, or weapons.

"Not really surprising." Wainwright was standing in the middle of the courtyard, accompanied by Bowden. "If a spike had been hammered through the victim's heart and into the ground the other side, it would have taken a little bit of effort to remove it, suggesting that it was done so deliberately."

"To dispose of it."

"Precisely."

"So what now, Sir?"

"Let's talk to the staff on duty. Ms. Whitehorn has a list. Most of them were already here at the museum and she's persuaded the others to come in and kindly help us with our enquiries."

"Shouldn't we have closed the museum?" Bowden did not like to question his superior's decisions, but he was concerned.

"I know they're part of the same business, but they are separated, physically. I think it's sufficient just to cordon off the wedding venue. If we attract too many rubberneckers we may have to, but otherwise let the museum carry on."

Before they could commence their task, Wainwright's phone rang. It was Kershaw. She relayed to him everything that she had gleaned from Linda Whitehorn. He gave her a few further instructions, ended the call and peered up into the cloud-pocked sky over the stables. Bowden looked at him, expectantly.

"Our body is almost certainly that of Casey Hardacre. We'll do what we need to do here and then go and break the news to his parents."

"Sir."

The staff did not prove to be particularly helpful. Prior to – and during the course of – the ceremony, each had been assigned their duties. Two people had been posted to usher guests through the ornamental garden and into the courtyard – one at the main entrance and one at the car park entrance. Having seen all the guests safely inside, they then joined their colleagues in either the stables or the smithy. Those in The Chattox Stables had been preparing the room for the afternoon buffet, either setting out the tables, in the kitchen or stocking the bars. Once the guests had started to filter in they all claimed to have been rushed off their feet, with no time to notice individuals, a tale which Wainwright was inclined to believe – and those that were charged with clearing the seating in the barn were out of sight and earshot of the guests. After the buffet, the room had been tidied and work began on arranging the room for the evening meal and subsequent entertainment. A local disc jockey had come in to set up his equipment. The afternoon shift had gone off duty at around five and been replaced by the evening staff. The pace, as was repeatedly stated, was frenetic, though that was accepted as the norm for such events, and everyone was focused on doing their job. As the evening wore on, those that were able took the opportunity to take a time out in the back rooms of the stables, or in the barn or the smithy.

The Demdike Smithy had experienced a continual ebb and flow of guests, either seeking a little respite from the festivities, or to use the facilities therein, or in the case of the principal actors in the nuptial, to change their wedding attire for something more suitable for the evening. There had always been a couple of people on duty to keep a watchful eye over the smithy and it's display of blacksmith's tools, lest anyone should take a fancy to any of them, but none had reported any behaviour to cause concern. However, as no one was particular familiar with the exhibits, no one would have known if any had gone missing, unless they had caught someone in the act of trying to purloin one – and Wainwright gained the impression that none had been especially assiduous in their assignment. The only member of the museum staff who did have a familiarity with the display – and a vested interest in it, as he had been largely instrumental in curating it - was Terry Tebbut, who Wainwright only caught up with as an addendum to his list of interviewees. Tebbut had not been there during the course of Saturday and had only come in on the Sunday afternoon.

"So you wouldn't have had any interaction with any of the guests."

"No. I try t' stick t' the museum an' leave the social functions t'others."

"But you came in on Sunday."

"I weren't working, officially, but I wanted t' come in an' check all was OK in the smithy."

"And was it?" Tebbut hesitated with a slightly anguished expression on his face.

"No. Some bastard 'ad nicked a couple of things."

"Oh?" The assertion rekindled a waning interest. "What things?" Tebbut indicated a vacant hook on the wall, above a workbench next to the forge."

"A blacksmith's 'ammer's gone and" he stepped over a rope that, somewhat ineffectually, separated the exhibition from the main body of the smithy, and pointed to a place on the time-worn bench where a label proclaimed the existence of a 'Blacksmith's punch c. 1760', but with said punch clearly being absent "an eighteenth century iron punch."

"Can you describe it?"

"It's a punch." Tebbut evidently presupposed that everyone would know what a punch looked like. "Made of iron; about ten or eleven inches long; rounded point at one end. Used for punchin' 'oles in metal."

By the end of the day there had been several significant developments. Having interviewed Terry Tebbut, Wainwright was convinced that he knew what had been used to kill the victim, presumed to be Casey Hardacre. He had informed the CSI team of his belief and requested that they search Carr Brook with a reasonable expectation that they would find the implements missing from the smithy. He and Bowden had concluded, together, that it was unlikely that the murderer would have risked walking out of the wedding with such heavy – and presumably bloodstained - objects, while conceding that he or she must have concealed them about their person immediately prior to the killing. Waders had been procured and it did not take a couple of officers too long to locate the hammer and punch on the bed of the relatively shallow watercourse, a little way downstream, whence, logic dictated, they had been thrown.

During the course of the afternoon, Kate Kershaw had taken a call from Mrs. Seacroft. Having learned of the events immediately subsequent to her daughter's marriage to Crispin Molyneaux, from the Sunday evening news, she had debated with her husband as to whether or not they should contact Magenta and break the news to her. Mr Seacroft had put the case for not telling them, arguing that the couple would, no doubt, have already reached Tintagel and that it would be a shame to spoil their honeymoon, given that, although it occurred at their wedding, the death of the, as yet, unnamed individual had nothing to do with them. Mrs. Seacroft had argued that, as the death was 'suspicious' and that it had occurred at some time during or after the ceremony, the police would necessarily want to speak with Magenta and Crispin. Furthermore, she felt morally obliged to tell them and let them decide how they wished to proceed. Mrs. Seacroft's view had prevailed against little more than token resistance. When she had phoned the police station and was put through to D.C. Kershaw, it was to tell her that Mr. and Mrs. Molyneaux were on their way home.

After they had wrapped up their interviews at Pendlehurst, Wainwright and Bowden returned to the station. There, Wainwright was able to collect the deceased's wallet, with a view to returning it to his parents. The mobile phone, which had also been recovered from the jacket, he retained as a potential source of evidence. He and Kershaw then set out for the home of the Hardacres. As is often the case in such circumstances, Mr. and Mrs. Hardacre were disposed to clutch at straws, suggesting that driving licence photos usually looked nothing like their subject and, therefore, the police could not conclude that the body that had been found was that of their son. However, when asked if they had other photos of Casey, they were able to produce several, from which it was possible to establish, beyond all reasonable doubt that the deceased was Casey Hardacre. The Hardacres were invited to attend a formal identification process at their own convenience.

Gallagher and Nick had tuned in to the late evening news on Monday specifically to see if there had been any developments in the Pendlehurst murder case. When it was revealed that the deceased was the best man at the wedding and had been named as Casey Hardacre, Gallagher was unable to contain her appetite for involvement. She sat up straight and turned to Nick.

"You'll have photos of the best man."

"Of course." He attempted to sound disinterested, guessing the track along which Gallagher's mind was running.

"And those surrounding him."

"Yes." He continued to focus on the television screen.

"One of which could be his killer."

"Possibly."

"We need to look at your photos."

"Beth…" He took hold of her hand.

"Yes?" The look in her eyes challenged him to dissuade her. He smiled and shook his head with an air of resignation, knowing that remonstration was futile.

III

COFFEE INTERRUPTED

As had been agreed, Mrs. Molyneaux had called Wainwright the following morning, having spent the previous evening, along with her husband, interrogating her parents about the events that had transpired after they had left for Tintagel. The detective inspector, accompanied by D.C. Kershaw, immediately set out for Crispin and Magenta's home at Golf View, having submitted a request for the complete guest list and contact details of all those that had attended their wedding to be made available. Meanwhile, D.S. Bowden had been dispatched to Westgate to interview Nick Corvino at his studio and procure all the pictures the photographer had taken at the wedding. Having been forewarned of the imminent arrival of Bowden, Nick had collated the photos in readiness and then called Gallagher to arrange to meet her as and when the detective departed. He had, at least, managed to dissuade Gallagher of the necessity to trawl through the photos late the previous evening and had suggested she come to his studio the following morning where they would be able to peruse the images with, he opined, a greater degree of alertness. No sooner was Bowden out of the door, armed with a flash drive containing the photos, than Nick had called Gallagher to inform her that the coast was clear. Within fifteen minutes, Gallagher, having charged Clematis with finding out what she could about Casey Hardacre, Crispin Molyneaux and Magenta Seacroft, walked into her partner's studio, only to find him engaged with a customer.

Once the, evidently satisfied, patron had left, Nick guided her into a back office, where he performed most of his photographic magic. Their scrutiny of the photos proved somewhat disjointed as he frequently had to break off to attend to customers coming in to have their digital photographs printed, to buy picture frames and other sundry items, and including one woman who wanted a calendar making up from photos of her dogs in readiness for the following year. Gallagher needed to summon all her patience to accommodate the interruptions. Nevertheless, her forbearance proved productive. Nick explained that he did not know the names of most of the people at the wedding, or their relationship to the Molyneauxs, but had only been introduced, as a matter of courtesy, to the main protagonists. After a few pictures to give some idea of the scale of the wedding and, coincidentally, the geography of the venue, he brought up a picture of the bridal group.

"The bride and groom, Magenta and Crispin, are in the middle, as you can see. This is Casey Hardacre." He pointed to the man standing on Crispin's left. "He was Crispin's best man." This was the first time Gallagher had seen the victim of the murder. He had been named on the news, but there had not been a photo. She estimated him to be about the same age as Crispin, slightly shorter, but with an equally well-kept frame. "This," Nick pointed to the woman standing on Magenta's right, "is Carmine Seacroft, Magenta's younger sister and maid of honour to the bride." She had clearly fully embraced the theme of the wedding, wearing a long, silk or satin ultramarine dress, pinched at the waist, long black gloves and a purple, lace shawl. "The two littluns in front are Crispin's nieces; twin daughters of his older sister, Vivienne. They were Magenta's flower girls."

"Well, we can probably rule them out."

"I think so." He returned the screen to his array of thumbnail images, peered at them, allowing the cursor to float over them at will, before settling on the one he wanted. "This is a photo of the immediate family." He brought the selected picture up onto the screen. "Magenta and Crispin again in the middle. The couple to the left of Crispin are his parents, David and Vanessa. The pair to the right of Magenta are her parents, Warwick and Laura. In the back row we have…"

"Carmine." Gallagher used her powers of observation to correctly identify the woman standing between and behind her parents, before Nick could point to her.

"Well done. You ought to be a detective."

"Thank you."

"At the other end," he pointed to the woman standing between Crispin's parents, "we have Crispin's sister, Vivienne Appleton." He broke off and sat back in his chair abruptly. "Appleby?" He turned to Gallagher as if he expected her to know. "Appleton? Appleby? No, definitely Appleby." He returned to the screen, leaving Gallagher silently shaking her head. "In the middle, here," he pointed, somewhat superfluously, to the male figure looking away from the camera from between the bride and groom, dressed in a sky blue, window pane check suit with navy velvet collar and lapels, matching navy velvet waistcoat and royal blue bow tie, "is Crispin's younger brother, Rupert." At that juncture someone entered the studio and Nick made his excuses. Within five minutes, he was back and seemingly oblivious to Gallagher's pensive demeanour.

"A young lass wanted to print some photos, so I just had to sit her at a computer and show her what to do."

"Crispin didn't ask his brother to be best man?"

"Evidently not. Don't ask me why. I'm just the photographer. I only know that Crispin and Casey have been best mates since school and that they play tennis together. Or did."

The blacksmith's hammer and punch had been sent, first, to John Oldfield's pathology laboratory where he had been able to ascertain that the shape of the punch was consistent with the wounds inflicted on Casey Hardacre's torso and, further, the shape of the hammer head matched the wound to the deceased's head. The two implements had then been forwarded to the forensic laboratory, with a realistic hope, notwithstanding that they had been in Carr Brook for the best part of 48 hours, that blood and/or skin tissue samples could be extracted from the two implements and that such samples would generate sufficient DNA evidence to prove that they were they were the murder weapons. While always hopeful, Wainwright was less optimistic about finding fingerprints. Nevertheless, he was working on the assumption that there would be a positive forensic outcome linking the tools to the victim and had consequently terminated the search for other possible weapons. His focus was now on prioritising the interviewees - and possible witnesses – starting with the immediate family and working outward. He was also keen to establish a motive for the killing which would help give direction to his investigation. Meanwhile, following a cursory examination by Bowden, Nick Corvino's photos had been handed to the forensic psychologist for more stringent analysis.

Gallagher returned to her office with a large envelope stuffed with all of the photographs Nick had taken at the wedding, the rejected photos outweighing, in number, those that had been used to compile the final album.

"Anything yet?" Clematis was engrossed in her research when Gallagher bounced into the office.

"Not yet, Ms. Gallagher." She finished reading what was on the screen before her, then looked in her boss's direction and sat back in her chair. "Just the usual sort of social media stuff."

"Keep digging. And, to keep you busy, I've got some more family names for you. Murders that take place at family gatherings, usually do so for a reason."

"Because it's a family affair?"

"Exactly."

"But there were far more friends than family there."

"Don't complicate matters unnecessarily, Clemmy. Let's start with the family and we'll come on to the friends later." Gallagher breezed her way towards her own office.

"Ms. Gallagher." Clematis swivelled round in her chair to follow her boss's trajectory.

"Yes?" Gallagher stopped, turned and smiled, disconcertingly disarmingly.

"Forgive me, but this is not actually your case, is it?"

"Not yet." She resumed her path, entered her office, closed the door and left Clematis to continue her research, a little reluctantly.

Once safely within her sanctum, Gallagher dumped her bag

on the floor, placed the envelope on her desk, made herself comfortable in her chair and reached for the phone.

"Danny!" She attempted to sound innocently cheerful

"Beth." Wainwright, on the other hand, sounded suspicious.

"I see you've got another murder on your hands."

"Let me guess." The faintly audible groan gave Gallagher cause to smile to herself. "You want in."

"With all those potential witnesses you're going to need all the help you can get."

"And you thought you'd give us the benefit of your assistance." Gallagher considered silence to be the most eloquent form of response. "What, exactly, do you think you can bring to the investigation, Beth?"

"I'm intimately connected to it."

"You are?" Wainwright could not avoid sounding surprised. Gallagher allowed him time to consider his own question. "Beth, being the partner of the photographer at the wedding does not constitute any kind of relevant connection, let alone an intimate one."

"As you must be well aware, Danny, there's a ninety five per cent chance that your murderer is in one of the photographs.

"Your point being?"

"Without knowing it, Nick probably noticed, heard or saw something which is crucial to identifying the killer. I'm the one best placed to winkle that information out of him." She heard a heavy, resigned sigh at the other end of the line. "Coffee at Café Cleo? I'm buying."

Having, reluctantly, agreed to meet Gallagher later in the day, preferring to keep her in sight rather than have her interfering without any constraints, Wainwright assembled his team for a briefing in the incident room. Since his meetings with Casey Hardacre's parents and Crispin and Magenta Molyneaux, his whiteboard had acquired some further annotations. He tapped it with a marker pen.

"The deceased, Casey Hardacre, aged twenty eight. Had a house in Foxhills. Financial adviser at Helen Connell Financial

Services in town. He and Crispin Molyneaux met at sixth form college and remained best friends. Casey did a B.Sc. in economics and finance at Newcastle, while Crispin went to Liverpool and studied architecture. Apparently, they met up during vacations and went on holidays together, either just the two of them, or a group. After university they both returned to Burnley. They played tennis together at Pendle Tennis Club and hung out together. He seems to have been quite a serious minded individual. Solid, dependable, affable. Enjoyed walking and hiking, which he sometimes did with Crispin at weekends, and played flute in a local folk/rock band. Doesn't seem to have had an enemy in the world."

"Maybe he gave someone some bad financial advice." Bowden chipped in from his perch on his desk.

"Possibly. We'll check with his office." He paused to allow any further comment, but none was forthcoming. "Crispin chose him to be his best man because he was sure he wouldn't embarrass him with any salacious anecdotes from their student days."

"Anything from his mobile?" Kershaw was sitting at her desk at the side of the room.

"Nothing. No calls, in or out, to arouse interest and no unusual or cryptic messages. Certainly nothing on Saturday, but we'll continue going through the records."

"Americano, three sugars." Gallagher placed the coffee on the table, offloaded a latte and cinnamon bun for herself, deposited the tray on one of the vacant chairs and seated herself opposite him. It was a pleasant enough day for sitting outside, but not without a jacket. Wainwright's black leather one was worn over a functional cream shirt, with a plain brown tie exposing the unfastened top button, in his customary fashion. Gallagher's caramel jacket was worn over a lightweight, black jumper with a floral motif.

"I can't stay long. I've got a list of possible witnesses as long as your arm to get through."

"So you'll appreciate any offer of help." Wainwright drew

his cup and saucer closer to himself and began, studiously, pouring the three sachets of sugar into it.

"Beth, a man has been killed. It's not a game you can just join in with when you don't have anything more pressing to do, though I imagine you do have plenty to occupy you." He stirred the coffee vigorously. Gallagher took a sip of her latte and a bite out of her bun.

"You should know me better than that, Danny."

"It's a police matter and, to the best of my knowledge, it's not connected to any case on your books." He took a slurp of coffee, eyeing her over the rim of the cup.

"But I'm connected to Nick and Nick could be a key witness."

"Bowden's spoken to Mr. Corvino, as I'm sure you know, and he's been very helpful in supplying us with copies of all the photos he took at the wedding."

"I'm sure he has, but has he told you everything he knows?"

"Meaning?" He was not in the mood for abstruse word games and he did nothing to disguise the fact. She took another sip of coffee.

"Nick's very observant. He pays attention to detail. It's what makes him such a good photographer. He's frequently at the centre of things, yet, being an outsider, his presence is often ignored. It's an ideal situation from which to catch people when they're off guard and to notice things without being noticed."

"What's your point, Beth?"

"As you're well aware, people can often see and hear things without realising they've seen or heard them. Being his partner, I'm in an ideal position to tease out some of those hidden nuggets, which could prove crucial to making an arrest and getting a conviction."

"And when you do, I'm sure you'll do your civic duty and inform us."

"Naturally, but first it would be useful to be able to corroborate anything he may tell me, before I start sending you on a wild goose chase." Before he could respond his phone rang. He took it out of his pocket and looked at the screen.

"I have to take this." Gallagher acquiesced by taking another bite of her bun and brushing a few stray crumbs from her jumper. Wainwright leaned both his elbows on the table. "Wainwright." Whatever the speaker at the other end of the line said, it caused Wainwright to furrow his brow. "When?" There was a short pause. "Where?" Another, slightly longer pause. "I'm on my way." He switched off the phone, slid it back into his pocket, pushed his chair back, grabbed his coffee cup and took another long draught and rose to his feet, all of which actions in seemingly one movement. "Sorry, Beth, I have to go. Something's come up." Gallagher swallowed her mouthful.

"What is it?"

"I don't know until I get there." With that, he turned and hurried away, before Gallagher was able to remonstrate. Instead, she was left to muse on the fact that his coffee had only been half drunk, from which she deduced that whatever had called him away, must have been of great importance.

"Have you got Magenta and Crispin's address there?" After Wainwright had abruptly upped and left, Gallagher had contemplated her next move while finishing her coffee and bun. She was in something of a quandary as to how to proceed, not having any legitimate reason for involving herself other than a tenuous link by way of Nick, but proceed was what she decided to do. Hence her phone call to her partner at his studio.

"Beth, are you sure this is a good idea?"

"Ask me that later. Meanwhile, do you have their address?" He could have persisted in trying to dissuade her from whatever course of action she was intending but, instead, she heard him shuffling through some papers.

"Got a pen?" Before calling she had prepared herself with pen and notepad from her bag. He dictated the address.

"Thanks, Nick."

"Don't do anything reckless, sweetheart."

"As if." She ended the call, returned the pen and pad to her bag, checked her jacket and jumper for crumbs, pushed back the chair, with a baleful scraping sound, stood up, hooked the tan bag over her shoulder and set off for her car, parked in the supermarket car park, with a spring in her step and a self-satisfied smile on her lips.

Within twenty minutes she was bringing her grey Peugeot 308 to a standstill opposite 45, Brindley Leas in the Golf View area on the western extremity of the town. It was a modern, bay-fronted, chalet-style house, with integral garage. On the brick-paved drive stood a black, 3-year-old BMW X3. The other half of the frontage was laid with unadorned lawn. She took a deep breath. During the short journey her confidence had ebbed considerably. Once composed, she got out, locked the car and made her way across the road. She paused in front of the ubiquitous brilliant white door with a small, obscure-glass window and extracted her ID from her bag before pressing the bell push. She was about to try again when the door opened and she was confronted by a woman of approximately her own height, in her mid-twenties with long, wavy, honey-blonde hair that she instantly recognised as Magenta Molyneaux, née Seacroft.

"Mrs. Molyneaux?"

"Yes?" She sounded comfortable with her new name, but irritated by the disturbance.

"Bethany Gallagher." She thrust her ID forward. "I'm a private investigator." Mrs. Molyneaux peered forward to read the document, then up at Gallagher, then down at the photo again.

"So I see. What do you want? Now's not a good time…"

"I understand that, Mrs. Molyneaux, but I'm here about the death of Casey Hardacre."

"Casey? What's that got to do with you?"

"I'm assisting the police with their investigation into the cause of Casey's death." Mrs. Molyneaux gave her a mystified scowl.

"Do they need assistance?"

"The police have, as you will appreciate, a lot of potential witnesses to interview: all those that made up your wedding party, the staff at Pendlehurst. In an effort to progress their investigation as quickly as possible in such circumstances, they often employ a private investigator to help them." The woman continued to stare at her, albeit with a slight softening of her expression, but said nothing. "You're very welcome to check with Detective Inspector Wainwright who is the senior investigating officer on the case." The addendum was a calculated risk, but experience informed her that the offer would not be taken up.

"Wait here, please." She closed the door such that it remained ajar. Gallagher assumed that she was going to consult with her husband. Two or three minutes later the door reopened and she was met with both Mr. and Mrs. Molyneaux.

"You're helping the police with Casey's death?" Crispin Molyneaux seemed taller than in Nick's photos, but it was patently him. He was broad-shouldered with shaggy, shoulder-length tawny hair and stubble that may or may not have been by design.

"Yes."

"The police were here this morning."

"I know." This was not true, but Gallagher reckoned that ignorance would not be a good look. Molyneaux seemed to be in two minds. He glanced at his wife, whose reciprocal glance suggested she was leaving the decision to him, which, Gallagher assumed, was why she had gone to confer with him in the first place.

"You'd better come in." Molyneaux stepped back and his wife stepped aside, holding the door open, allowing Gallagher to step inside. All she noticed about the small, neat hallway was the stripped pine banister and door leading into the lounge. She was more acutely aware of being sandwiched between Crispin, in the vanguard, and Magenta, bringing up the rear. The lounge, however, assaulted her senses. It was the antithesis of the exterior. A port wine carpet covered the floor. Three walls were almost magnolia, but with a distinct hint of pink, while the fourth, feature wall, was plum. A tan, velvet chesterfield faced the television in the corner, with gold, floral brocade wingback armchairs either side of it. In the centre of the plum wall hung an oval, black-framed, gothic style mirror, flanked by two, large, art nouveau prints. She was invited to sit in one of the armchairs, an invitation which she accepted, while the Molyneauxs seated themselves, side by side on the sofa. She took the notepad and pen from her bag, balanced them on her knees and placed the bag, carefully, on the floor.

"You'll have to forgive me if I repeat some of the police's questions, but you'll appreciate this is a fast-moving investigation and you'll understand that D.I. Wainwright and I don't have an opportunity to compare notes every step of the way." The opening statement was greeted by no more than an impassive, expectant, possibly curious gaze. She launched into the standard line of questioning regarding Casey Hardacre's character, whether they knew of anyone who had born him a grudge or anyone who would have wished him harm, and about his relationship to, particularly, Crispin.

"The police asked us all these questions this morning." Magenta's intrusion appeared symptomatic of her more pronounced agitation.

"I'm sorry, Mrs. Molyneaux, but it's better to cover ground twice than to leave a stone unturned." She glanced at her husband, then gave a little shrug. "You have a brother, Rupert, I believe." Crispin looked surprised.

"How did you know that?" Gallagher contrived an awkward smile.

"My partner, Nick Corvino, was the photographer at your wedding. That's why D.I. Wainwright specifically asked me to help them." The seemingly reluctant confession had the desired effect of easing the couple's apprehensions.

"Nick? He took some wonderful photos, didn't he darling?" Magenta turned to her husband with a clearly delighted smile.

"He did indeed, Madge," Crispin gave her hand a squeeze, "but Ms. Gallagher is not here to talk about our wedding photos." He turned back to Gallagher with a less frosty expression than he had presented before her admission. "You were going to ask about Rupe."

"I was wondering why you asked Casey to be your best man rather than your brother." Molyneaux smiled a little ruefully.

"I did ask him."

"And he refused?" From what Gallagher knew of such matters, a man would not refuse an invitation to be best man at his brother's wedding. At least, she reckoned, not without good reason. Crispin glanced at his wife.

"Not exactly." Gallagher waited. "Crispin doesn't do well in social situations. I asked him out of courtesy, knowing that he would most likely refuse. I'd have been over the moon if he'd accepted, but it wasn't to be expected."

"Could you explain?"

"Rupe gets very anxious in social situations. He finds it hard to talk to people. He gets very self-conscious. Even if he'd had a script, he'd have been very embarrassed standing up in front of all those people and giving a speech. He'd have become tongue-tied and then he'd have got flustered… You understand what I mean?" Gallagher nodded. She had gleaned the information for which, primarily, she had come.

"One last thing. I know you'll have given a detailed guest list to the police, but perhaps you could let me have a copy? Just to speed matters along." She was trading on her new-found goodwill and hoped they would be amenable to the request. Her hopes were duly fulfilled.

When Wainwright arrived at Thornby Gardens it was already a hive of activity. On the circle at the entrance to the gardens, an ambulance, John Oldfield's Skoda Kodiaq, two police cars and a vehicle which he assumed had transported Bowden to the scene, had assembled. A uniformed police officer was doing his best to keep the inevitable gathering of morbid onlookers at bay. The detective inspector parked his blue Volvo such that it blocked the pavement and effectively covered the entrance such that, either deliberately or unwittingly, it deterred further spectators. Kershaw strolled across the grass to meet him.

"What do we have, Kate?"

"A body, sir. On the canal towpath." She turned away and led Wainwright towards the steps that led down to the towpath.

"Oldfield's already here."

"Yes, sir." She trotted down the steps and, at the bottom, turned to her right. Wainwright followed her along the path until they were under the bridge that carried Colne Road over the

36

Leeds & Liverpool Canal. On hearing their approach, Bowden turned round, hands in pockets, looking disgruntled. His superior intuited that Oldfield had declined to entrust him with any information about the body. The pathologist remained focused on his examination, his back to Wainwright. His assistant, Alice, looked up from her position on the other side of the body and gave Wainwright a half smile, then looked back at her boss.

"D.I. Wainwright's here."

"About time. What kept you, inspector?" Wainwright ignored the comment. When Oldfield was in one of his more irascible moods, he had learned it was best not to provoke him further.

"What do we have, John?"

"Female. Mid-twenties."

"And why am I here?" Oldfield appeared not to hear him, but then sat back on his haunches and peered over his shoulder.

"She died from multiple stab wounds. One to the stomach" he indicated the entry wound with his index finger "and three to the chest, near the heart."

"There's, what appears to be, blood on the ground, just there, sir." Bowden pointed to an area near the victim's feet.

"And there's blood underneath the body." Oldfield had resumed his study. "You'll see it when we move her out."

"So she was killed here."

"That would be the logical conclusion."

"Do we have an approximate time of death?"

"Rigor mortis hasn't set in, and from the temperature of the body, I'd say she died little more than an hour ago."

"Do we know who she is?"

"We found her bag by the wall." Bowden stepped gingerly to one side, taking care not to incur Oldfield's wrath by disturbing the blood stain, picked up a plastic bag containing a black leather shoulder bag and offered it to Wainwright. The inspector gave it no more than a cursory glance.

"Anything in it?"

"Everything you'd expect. Nothing seems to have been

taken."

"So robbery wasn't the motive."

"Doesn't look like it, sir." Wainwright turned his attention back to Oldfield.

"Any sign of sexual assault, John."

"Doesn't appear to be. Her clothing's undisturbed."

"So not sexually motivated, either."

"A targeted killing." Kershaw voiced her conclusion based on the evidence.

"It would seem so." He considered the hypothesis for a few moments. "Who found her?" The question was posed to no one in particular.

"A couple of young lads who should probably have been in school." Despite the fact that the lads in question had reported a possible murder, Bowden clearly did not condone truancy. Wainwright simply nodded.

"Anything else you can tell us, John?" Oldfield, satisfied that there was no more he could do at that juncture, stood up and addressed the detectives encircling him.

"My thoughts are that the victim was facing her attacker when he or she struck. They stabbed her in the stomach and then when she fell – or was pushed, having been incapacitated – to the ground, stabbed her thrice through the heart, using a round, narrow-bladed tool; not a knife. Contusions around the heart wounds suggest that the weapon was thrust in up to the hilt while she was on the ground. The contusions are roughly circular. All in all, I'd take a guess that you're looking for a screwdriver." Kershaw glanced towards the murky water flowing less than a yard away from them.

"Possibly disposed of in the canal?"

"Possibly, Kate. Get a dive team down here. See if they can find anything."

"Yes, sir."

The evening local news, which Gallagher was wont to watch, was headlined by the report of a second murder in Burnley within the space of three days. The police had named the deceased as

Carmine Seacroft.

IV

MYSTERY WOMAN

"Nothing?" Gallagher was slumped on the oxblood tartan tub chair in the corner of her secretary's office. She had called Wainwright first thing in the morning, but the detective inspector had proved to be evasive, unable to provide her with little more information about the second murder than she had gleaned from the previous evening's news. She had hoped that Clematis might be a more profitable source of information.

"Not yet, Ms. Gallagher. No dark secrets, shady dealings, skeletons in the cupboard, or disputes. Two, boringly ordinary families, with fairly dull, conventional friends."

"Except that the wedding doesn't appear to have been conventional."

"Very true."

"Casey hadn't been robbed. Carmine had been neither robbed nor sexually assaulted. The killings were personal. Someone had a grudge against both of them."

"Someone 'oo were at the wedding?"

"Certainly. If you intended to kill someone, you wouldn't gate crash something as public as a wedding to do it. It must have been one of the guests – and all of the guests are in Nick's photos. He always makes a point of ensuring he never leaves anyone out."

"But why take that chance?"

"Opportunity?"

"But if 'e murdered Carmine elsewhere, couldn't 'e 'ave murdered Casey elsewhere? Somewhere where 'e'd be less likely to be seen."

"Good question, Clemmy. Perhaps our killer planned to kill Casey and Carmine was an afterthought. But what's the connection? Casey was Crispin's best friend and Carmine was

Magenta's sister. Other than that they may have met, there doesn't seem to be anything to connect them, apart from Crispin and Magenta. So, having killed Casey, for whatever reason, what motive could there have been for killing Carmine?" Clematis adjusted the shiny blue scrunchy holding in place the high ponytail of her pink and purple streaked dark hair, unsure as to whether she was expected to provide an answer. "Clearly, the killer must have been connected to each of them is some way, but they must, presumably, have been connected to each other; there must be a common thread to compel the killer to murder them both. They must both have slighted the killer in some way and it seems unlikely that they would be individual and unrelated offences."

"Unless 'e's drawn up a list of 'is enemies and 'e's decided now's the time to bump them off."

"Possibly." Gallagher was not prepared to dismiss the theory, but neither was she persuaded by it. "And it's just coincidence that two of them just happened to be at the same wedding." Clematis was well aware that her boss invariably rejected the notion of coincidence. "And then there's our mystery woman." The police had made public their belief that Casey Hardacre had met someone before he had been killed and, during their press briefing the previous evening, they had appealed for that person to come forward. One of the extra titbits of information Gallagher had managed to elicit from Wainwright earlier that morning was further details about the identity of that person.

"Mystery woman?" It was the first Clematis had heard of it.

"Wainwright thinks Casey may have met with a blonde woman before he was killed."

"Perhaps you need to look through Nick's photos again and pick out all the blonde women there."

"I think I do."

"We've recovered what we believe to be the second murder weapon. Needless to say, John Oldfield couldn't resist gloating over the fact that he'd correctly postulated it to be a screwdriver;

41

a Phillips screwdriver, to be precise. Forensics have confirmed that the blood traces found on it are a match for Carmine Seacroft. But, again, the killer's left no DNA."

"Same MO then." Bowden was sitting, leaning forward, forearms resting on his thighs, hands clasped together, eyes fixed on his superior officer; a coiled spring, waiting for release. "Kills the victim by stabbing, for reasons unknown, but certainly not robbery, no sign of sexual assault, and chucks the weapon into a river or canal."

"You don't normally go out carrying a screwdriver." Kershaw was perched on the corner of her desk. "That suggests the murder was premeditated. But the tools used to kill Casey were taken from the venue, suggesting it was opportunistic; the killer hadn't gone to the wedding intending to murder him."

"That's a good point, Kate." Wainwright's tone, while not being patronizing, hinted at him already having considered the possibility. "We're working on building up a profile to get a better picture of who we might be looking for."

"Why a screwdriver?" Bowden did not intend to be outdone in meriting praise for intelligent reasoning. "Wouldn't it have been easier – and potentially more effective – to carry a knife? A screwdriver's something you pick up when you don't have a knife to hand."

"Another good point, Dean." Bowden nodded, appreciatively.

"And why choose that spot?" He was determined to press his advantage. "By the canal, in broad daylight? Isn't that a bit risky?"

"Not necessarily." The unexpected response clearly took the wind out of Bowden's sails. "That particularly section of canal – and especially under that bridge – is a known haunt of drug dealers. Many people avoid it."

"Which suggests familiarity." Kershaw was first to verbalise the natural conclusion.

"The killer picked their spot." Bowden unintentionally expressed his musing aloud. Wainwright did not consider it necessary to respond to either of his colleagues' comments.

"How are we doing with our guest list?" Before anyone could answer, a uniformed officer injected himself, unceremoniously, into the incident room proceedings.

"Sir!" Wainwright twisted round, displeased at the unwarranted intrusion, and impaled the middle-aged sergeant with a glare.

"What?"

"There's a young woman downstairs." Wainwright immediately thought that Gallagher had taken it upon herself to make an impromptu visit to the station. "She claims to be the person that were with Casey 'Ardacre on the night 'e were killed." The inspector's look softened considerably.

"Is that so? Does she have a name?" The officer consulted his notebook.

"Tez Garrity."

"Show her into an interview room. Thank you." He turned to his detective constable. "This one's for you, Kate."

"Sir." Kershaw grabbed a notepad and pen and skittered towards the door through which the sergeant had disappeared as abruptly as he had appeared.

The young woman with long, straight, blonde hair falling about her shoulders and framing a lightly made-up oval face, was sitting on one of the hard, utilitarian chairs positioned on the far side of the equally spartan table, fidgeting nervously. She looked up, almost startled, when Kershaw entered the room.

"Ms. Garrity?" The woman gave the impression of having to think about the question before confirming her identity in a strangled whisper. "I'm D.C. Kershaw. I understand you have some information about the night Casey Hardacre was killed." She seated herself, at a slight angle, so as not to appear confrontational, on the chair directly opposite to the woman.

"Yes."

"You can relax." Kershaw smiled her most reassuring smile. "This is not a formal interview. You're not under caution or anything."

"It's awkward. But when I heard about the second murder…

I couldn't really keep quiet." She looked as anxious as she sounded.

"I understand." This was not a platitude; Kershaw had encountered, what she assumed to be, this situation many times before. She waited for Tez to say what she had to say. Ms. Garrity waited to be prompted. "What is that you have to tell me, Tez?"

"I met Casey before he was killed. At the wedding."

"OK. Would you like to start from the beginning?"

"Casey and me had met on a couple of occasions before. I mean, we moved in similar social circles. I'm friends with Madge and Casey was a friend of Crispin's. I don't mean we'd met, like we'd gone out together. We just vaguely knew one another. He wasn't a stranger, that's what I mean."

"I get the picture. Madge?"

"Magenta." Kershaw nodded. "Well, it was a wedding. We'd all had a few drinks; danced a bit. I was there with my boyfriend, but Casey was between relationships. I think he'd broken up with his last girlfriend about a month ago. Anyway, we were chatting and it was obvious he fancied me. I don't know where my boyfriend was. He was somewhere else. He asked me to meet him behind the stables. He was a good-looking feller and I suppose I was a bit tipsy. I thought it would be a bit of a giggle."

"I'm not here to judge you, Tez. As you say, it was a wedding and the drink was flowing." The woman took a moment to weigh up the veracity of the assertion.

"He said we should split up and in about ten minutes he'd slip out of the room and wait for me behind the stables. He said I should slip away just after. I said, what if Finn's with me – Finlay, my boyfriend – and he said to make an excuse. Tell him I was going across to the smithy to freshen up. Anyway, that's what I did."

"What time was this?"

"About nine."

"You sound very sure of that."

"I looked at my watch so as I'd know when ten minutes was up and I'd know when to follow him." Kershaw nodded, with a hint of a smile. "Casey was waiting and we, er…"

"Had sex." It was Ms. Garrity's turn to nod, with a somewhat rueful smile. "I don't need the details."

"It was only a quickie, but it was fun. And no one was ever going to know."

"Where, precisely, did this encounter take place?"

"Behind the stables."

"What happened then?"

"Casey sent me back inside. Said he'd hang around for five minutes and then come in. He didn't want to risk us being seen going back in together."

"So, you left him there."

"Yes."

"And that would have been, what time?" Tez shrugged.

"About quarter past nine. We didn't waste time."

"On your way back into the stables, did you notice anyone else about?"

"Not really. I wasn't looking. I suppose the guilt kicked in and I was in a hurry to get back to Finn."

"You're sure?"

"I think there were a couple of people outside the stables, getting a bit of fresh air, but that's all."

"Thank you. Is there anything else you can tell me?" She shook her head.

"That's it. I just thought I'd better come in and tell you."

"You did the right thing, Tez. Tez?" Kershaw gave the woman a quizzical look.

"Short for Theresa."

"Aah. We'll need to take a statement from you later." The woman nodded and Kershaw concluded the interview before she could ask about having to give evidence in court.

"Clemmy?" Gallagher was swaying, perplexedly, in her maroon office chair, curling a lock of hair repeatedly between her fingers, attempting to disengage herself from the taunts of the sheet of paper on her desk, which she had divided, *de facto*, into two columns. At the top of the left had column she had written 'Carmine Seacroft – maid of honour to the bride' and at the top of the second column 'Casey Hardacre – best man to the groom'. Carmine and Casey were the chief attendants to the bride and groom respectively. Gallagher had determined that was the main point of significance.

"Yes Ms. Gallagher?"

"What do we know about Carmine Seacroft?"

"Not a great deal."

"Do we know where she worked? She was killed in the middle of the day. Presumably she should have been at work." She heard her secretary shuffling through a series of papers.

"I 'aven't got anything written down, but I can try checking 'er Facebook page again; see if there's anything on there."

"Do that, please."

"I'll get onto it now."

"Thanks." Gallagher replaced the receiver. The back and forth swivelling in her chair became increasingly staccato and the twisting of her hair increasingly tetchy.

She was not sure, precisely, how much time had elapsed before the buzz of the phone interrupted her cogitations. The flashing green light indicated that it was Clematis demanding her attention.

"Have you found something, Clemmy?"

"I checked Carmine's Facebook page and there's a link to Thornby Veterinary Clinic. I checked out their website and Carmine Seacroft is listed as a veterinary nurse there." Gallagher ceased her chair swivelling and hair curling, rolled closer to her desk, picked up a pen and added a note to the column on her sheet of paper headed 'Carmine Seacroft'.

"Is that anywhere near Thornby Gardens?"

"Right next to it, Ms. Gallagher."

Many of the more prominent buildings in Burnley date from the second half of the nineteenth century, are built of a beautiful yellow sandstone and often exhibit flourishes of Victorian-Gothic architecture. They are all imposing structures, reflecting the wealth of the town during its cotton-weaving heyday. In contrast, Thornby Veterinary Clinic is housed in a redbrick art deco building, possibly the only significant building of its period in the town. The clinic manager's office was on the first floor, a welcoming space, without being opulent; buff-coloured walls, ochre carpet tiles and modern wood furnishings, the chairs with padded, sepia fabric seats. A very animal inspired colour palette, Gallagher mused, as she seated herself on one of the chairs on the opposite side of the desk to Jenny Braithwaite, the clinic manager. Even the filing cabinets and shelves had an oak effect finish. On the walls were photos of family pets and farmyard animals, together with a couple of veterinary-related posters. The requisite pleasantries were exchanged and, in Gallagher's case, sympathies expressed.

"You'll be aware that Carmine's body was found underneath the bridge spanning the canal, not more than a couple of hundred metres from here."

"Yes. In a way, that makes it worse; the fact that she was so close."

"Was it normal for her to be walking along the canal in the middle of the day?"

"It was her lunch break. If the weather was fine she liked to walk along the canal to Bellevue Park and have lunch there."

"So it was something she did regularly."

"As I say, if the weather was fine and we weren't unduly busy."

"And it would've been common knowledge that she did that." Mrs. Braithwaite gave a little shrug.

"I imagine so."

"To what do I owe this unexpected pleasure, sweetheart?" He sounded genuinely delighted to hear from her.

"I need you to do something for me, Nick, if you will."

"If I can. What is it?"

"I want you to make an appointment to see Crispin and Magenta Molyneaux this evening."

"OK." He drew out both syllables as if he thought he was expected to understand the rationale behind the request. "Why?"

"I don't think they were too pleased about me following in

the footsteps of the police after Casey's murder; they'll be even more irritated to find me following in their footsteps after Carmine's murder."

"So where do I come in?"

"You were their wedding photographer. You have a relationship with them. And, as their photographer, you have all the pictures from the wedding. They'll surely know that the police want to interview a woman who was thought to have met Casey before he was killed. That woman was a blonde. I'd like you to ask them to identify all the young – I'm assuming she would have been young – blonde women in the photos. I've looked through them and there's only three or four possible candidates."

"Is that it?"

"Not quite."

"I suspected as much." The comment was made with teasingly good humour.

"I'll come with you and when you've got the information you want, I'll casually continue the conversation, making it appear incidental. I want to know more about Carmine and what the connection was between her and Casey that might have resulted in them both being murdered. The police will already have asked these questions, so they'll probably be reluctant to have me intruding on them and asking the same questions again - directly."

"So, basically, you want me to soften them up."

"I wouldn't put it quite like that, Nick, but yes."

Between them, Gallagher and Nick Corvino had identified four possible women, from the latter's wedding photos, to whom the blonde hair found on Casey Hardacre's jacket could have belonged. They were still in ignorance of events earlier in the day at the police station, as were the Molyneauxs. Consequently, Magenta and Crispin were quite happy to cooperate with Nick in his quest to put names to those four individuals. Having done so, Gallagher broached the subject of Carmine Seacroft, reiterating her condolences. While not wishing to press Magenta too hard, she was determined to establish a connection between her sister and Hardacre that might shed light on why they had both been murdered. During a lull in the discourse, occasioned by Magenta's reticence, Gallagher veered away from her line of questioning:

"You and Carmine were close." The observation caused tears to well up in Magenta's eyes, which she fought, unsuccessfully, to control.

"Yes. I won't say we did everything together – we weren't joined at the hip – but we did a lot of things together. We had similar interests and similar friends." She managed to force a smile. "It was Carmine that brought me and Cris together." She glanced at her husband, placed her hand over his and gave it a squeeze.

"Oh?"

"We had known one another for a long time. Since we were teenagers. Me and Carmine, Cris and Rupert and Viv. After we left school, we kept in touch; met up during the holidays. We all landed up back in Burnley after we'd finished our studies and we got together regularly. Between us, we always found something to celebrate. We were more like family than friends. Cris and Rupert were more like brothers to us. Viv not so much."

"How so?"

"Vivienne's the oldest of us." Crispin took up the narrative. "She was always that little bit further ahead of us, if you know what I mean. And when she got married and had the twins... We still all get on well, but she has her own life now, with different priorities."

"You said Carmine brought you and Crispin together." To Gallagher it did not seem as if they needed bringing together. Again, Magenta smiled a sad, reflective smile.

"As I said, Cris was more like a brother than a friend. I'd never thought of him in a romantic sense – and" she glanced across at him again "I don't think he thought of me in that way, either. Nevertheless, Carmine got it into her head that Cris had a bit of a pash on me. She would find any excuse to drag Rupert away and leave me and Cris alone, and, of course, when your

49

sister insists on something like that, you automatically start giving him furtive glances to see if he's eyeing you up in that way."

"And when I kept catching her looking at me like that, I started to think that, maybe, Madge had a secret crush on me." They both managed a chuckle.

"To cut a long story short, Carmine's matchmaking worked and the rest is history."

V

CONJECTURE

When Gallagher had called Wainwright the following morning, it had been with the expectation that he would not know the identity of the woman who had met Casey Hardacre at the wedding. She had reasoned that, had he studied Nick's photographs, he, like her, would have been able to narrow down the number of possibilities to four and would subsequently have followed those up. Hence, when she had offered up those four, she had been considerably chagrined to discover that Theresa Garrity had already come forward. Her disappointment had emanated not so much from the fact that Wainwright was one step ahead of her, but that she had lost a bargaining chip. She had expected that she would be able to use the information as leverage to elicit more details of the case from the inspector.

"Trouble at mill, Ms. Gallagher?" Clematis sensed her boss's mood even before she saw her. In reply, Gallagher crossed the room behind her secretary and Clematis heard the sound of the kettle being re-boiled. It was highly unusual for Gallagher to have two cups of coffee within half an hour of entering the office, from which Clematis drew her own conclusions. Considering discretion to be the better part of valour, she continued typing up an invoice for a client whose case had been satisfactorily concluded the previous day. Gallagher made her coffee, ambled towards the tub chair in the corner, pausing to glance out of the window at a canal devoid of any activity, sat down and placed her mug on the table to the side of it.

"Do you have the addresses of the immediate family, Clemmy?" Clematis finished a sentence before looking up.

"Of Casey?"

"No, Clemmy; of Crispin and Magenta Molyneaux. If any of

51

Casey's immediate family had wanted to harm him, I'm sure they could have found a better time and place than a wedding at which he was playing a prominent role." Clematis was inclined to argue that a similar rationale could be applied to Carmine Seacroft's murder, but felt that it would not be prudent to do so, given her boss's apparent mood.

"Yes, Ms. Gallagher." She began shuffling, busily, through the paperwork strewn across her desk.

"I suppose they'll all be at work during the day." Ignoring her coffee, she got to her feet again, mooched across to the window, peered out in time to see a cyclist disappear from view along the towpath on the opposite bank, then turned around and wandered back to her own office.

With the door closed behind her, she eschewed her chair, bent over her desk and retrieved the guest list, with contact details, that the Molyneauxs had provided for her (a copy of which she had made for her secretary) and stood, gazing at the names at the top: the bride's parents, the groom's parents, the groom's brother and sister and the bride's sister, now deceased. She dropped the stapled sheets of paper back on to the desk and picked up the office phone.

"Nick?"

"You're getting to be my most regular caller."

"Can you get away for an hour or so?"

"I'm a bit tied up…"

"I need you to meet me at Pendlehurst."

"Well, I suppose…"

"I know it's awkward when you're on your own there, Nick, and I do appreciate that your job's just as important as mine, but I do need your help."

Not having any formal involvement in the matter, Gallagher had not had a valid reason to visit Pendlehurst while the police still had a presence there, Now, however, the work of the police was done and the venue had reverted to its natural state, apart from a few wisps of police tape still clinging to trees, shrubs, gates, pillars and anything else to which it could be attached.

Persuading Linda Whitehorn that she had good justification to inspect the site proved appreciably easier than trying to cajole her way past officious, uniformed constables would have been, especially when she could not have guaranteed the support of D.I. Wainwright. Consequently, she and Nick were now standing in the middle of the courtyard, surrounded by the three constituent buildings of the wedding venue.

"I presume this is where most of your photos were taken." The plate glass doors, with the unmissable legend 'THE ALICE NUTTER BARN' above them provided a useful reference point.

"Correct. The barn is where the wedding took place. The stables" he pointed to their left "is where the reception was, and that's" he indicated right "is the smithy."

"From which the tools that killed Casey were taken." She looked around as if to take her bearings. "And over there" she nodded towards the gap between the barn and the stables "is where his body was found." As the corner of the stables very nearly overlapped the corner of the barn, that particular area was not directly visible from where they were standing.

"What are you thinking?"

"I'm not really thinking anything at the moment, Nick. Wainwright hasn't given me much to go on." Nick felt inclined to comment on the gripe, but thought it best to hold his counsel. Gallagher looked skyward and about her. "There's no lighting here."

"Not apart from the lights above the doors and the bollard lights surrounding this space."

"Sufficient to be able to see if anyone was out here, but probably not enough to be able to identify them."

"There would've been lights in each of the buildings."

"True." She paused to consider the possibilities. "Let's go and take a look at the crime scene." Before she had finished speaking, she was heading towards the gap between the barn and the stables. Nick was forced to jog a few steps to catch up with her. "Did you come round here?"

"Didn't have any cause to. All the formal photos were taken in the courtyard. I just hung around there awaiting orders. A few of the guests had their own cameras and some wandered off in this direction, but having reconnoitred the site beforehand, I pretty much knew what was where." Once around the corner, they were confronted with the rose bed and the statue of Aphrodite.

"That's where he was found – behind the statue." She led the way across to the spot. "And this is where he met Theresa Garrity."

"He probably took her behind the stables and had his wicked way with her there." She wandered around, behind the stables, though what she was expecting to find, she knew not.

"There's a door there."

"Probably the back entrance to the kitchen."

"Interesting. Perhaps I need to have a chat with the kitchen staff on duty." With that thought in mind, she performed an about turn and strode, purposefully, back to the courtyard, through the ornamental garden, across the road and in to the museum, explaining her thinking to Nick as she went. There were several people in the gift shop, but the attendant behind the desk was unoccupied.

"Did you find what you wanted?"

"I'm not sure yet. I need to clarify a couple of things. Could you get Linda down here again?" When they had first arrived, Mrs. Whitehorn had needed to be summoned from her office on the first floor and a similar process had to be undertaken again. The woman reappeared, her irritability at having been disturbed a second time., tempered by the gratitude that Gallagher had not taken it upon herself to snoop around her domain at will.

"Is there something else I can help you with?"

"Would the lights have been on in the barn and the smithy during the evening, after the wedding?" For a moment Linda was taken aback by the apparent banality of the question.

"Most of the lights in The Alice Nutter Barn would have been switched off once everyone had vacated it. They'd be no reason for anyone to go back in. We only had minimal lighting on in The Demdike Smithy, just so as people could find their way to the facilities."

"Thank you."

"Anything else?"

"Are the kitchen staff that were on duty at the wedding here now?"

"Most of them."

"Do you think I could have a word with them?" Mrs. Whitehorn glanced at her watch.

"They shouldn't be too busy now." She smiled, affably. "I'm sure they could spare you a few minutes. Through here." She eased herself between Gallagher and Nick and proceeded towards the museum kitchen, assuming that the pair were following. The kitchen was compact, but designed for efficiency. Three extra bodies in it created untenable congestion and work rapidly ground to a halt. Mrs. Whitehorn introduced Gallagher and Nick. A couple of the staff recognised Nick as having been at the wedding, but only one recollected him as the photographer - and she seemed tickled to discover that he was the beau of a private detective. "All four of you were at the Molyneaux wedding on Saturday, weren't you."

"We were." A tall woman in, Gallagher estimated, her mid-thirties, leaning against a worktop, spatula in hand, took it upon herself to speak for all of them.

"Who else was there? There were five of you, weren't there?"

"Freddie."

"Oh yes." She turned to Gallagher. "Freddie's not in today. It's his day off."

"That's fine. I'm sure these good people can tell me all I need to know. I shan't keep them long."

"I'll leave you to it, then." Mrs. Whitehorn inferred, as was intended, that she was no longer required and made a reluctant exit.

"There's a door at the back of the stables." Gallagher addressed no one in particular. "I presume that leads from the stables' kitchen."

"It does." The tall woman was nothing if not taciturn.

"Was it open while you were working on Saturday?"

"Of course."

"It gets 'ot in the kitchen." A slightly younger woman in a spotless white apron, her brown hair swept back and tied in a short ponytail, was a little more forthcoming. "We all need to go out and get a breath of fresh air occasionally."

"And you all went outside at some point?" They all nodded. "Did any of you see anyone behind the stables while you were out?"

"I went out for a fag, when it 'ad calmed down a bit." A young man in a similarly pristine apron, leaning against the sink, seized his opportunity to contribute. "Saw a couple goin' at it, 'ammer and tongs, further down the stables; near the end." The younger woman tittered as she pictured it.

"Did you recognise them?"

"Nope."

"Weren't you interested?"

"Not really."

"Oh."

"This is a weddin' venue, Ms. Gallagher. We also do corporate junkets. Spontaneous bonkin' comes with the territory. I'd 'ave bin surprised if there 'adn't bin anyone goin' at it." Gallagher permitted herself a hint of a smile. The explanation sounded reasonable.

"What time would this have been?"

"Like I say, when things 'ad calmed down a bit." He shrugged. "Nine-ish. Somethin' like that." Gallagher nodded. The kitchen staff waited for her response.

"The police think that the man involved was Casey Hardacre. They'd like to know who he was having sex with immediately before he was murdered. It's likely that she – assuming it was a she – was the last person to see him alive."

Once outside and safe from prying ears, Nick submitted to his curiosity:

"What was that all about, Beth?"

"What was what all about?"

"Don't be obtuse, sweetheart. You know who Casey was having it off with."

"But he doesn't know that and if he thinks he may have seen

Casey's murderer, it might help focus his mind on anything else he may have seen."

"Clever." He turned to return to the car park, having assumed that their work was done, but Gallagher continued on, across the road, back towards the barn. "Now what?"

"We need to try and reconstruct the events of last Saturday night and there's no better place to do it than the place in which they occurred." Wainwright was not one to gloat, but when he had sensed her dismay at him already knowing the identity of Casey Hardacre's paramour that evening, he could not help adding insult to injury by relating the details of the assignation in their entirety. Knowing Hardacre's movements and with the knowledge gained that morning Gallagher felt she was in a position to figure out how he was killed, if not, yet, by whom.

They were, once again, standing in the middle of the courtyard. A gardener, pushing a wheelbarrow, laden with horticultural implements trundled past without so much as a glance and disappeared between the barn and stables, in the direction of Aphrodite's rose bed.

"Now what?"

"It would help if it was dark, so we could see what the lighting was like, but we can't have everything." It hardly answered the question, but Nick did not pursue it. "Unless there's something Wainwright hasn't told me – and he seemed keen to give me every last detail – Casey, probably a little inebriated, asked Theresa to meet him during the course of the evening celebrations. He left the stables at about nine and told Theresa to follow him." Gallagher was staring in the direction in which the gardener had been last seen. "They go behind the stables for a quick shag; she returns to the stables and the next we see of Casey, he's dead."

"You think she killed him?"

"Why? Why there, at the wedding? What motive? And wouldn't she have had blood on her clothes when she returned inside?" She looked at the door to the stables and then over her shoulder at the smithy. "It's possible that she could have run across to the smithy and collected her chosen weapons before going to meet him, but how would she have concealed them while they were engaged in intercourse?"

"Maybe she went to the smithy after they'd had sex, if she knew he was going to hang around for a few minutes."

"But this has all the hallmarks of it being planned and she didn't know he was going to be there until a few minutes before it happened. Assuming she's telling the truth - and we can't, unfortunately, get Casey's version of events to corroborate her story, or otherwise. Even if it was opportunistic, she couldn't rely on him still being there when she got back. And if the same person that killed Casey, killed Carmine, what could her motive have been for that? Theresa's the obvious suspect, but it doesn't make much sense."

"Which means there must be a third person."

"Yes, Nick, but…"

"But?"

"If this was an impromptu assignation, no one else could have known he would be there, any more than Theresa could. Casey didn't even know he'd be there."

"So where does that leave us?"

"Someone wanted to kill Casey Hardacre and chose the wedding to do it. Why somewhere with so many potential witnesses around? It seems to me unnecessarily risky."

"Maybe they didn't plan to do it at the wedding."

"Which implies something happened during the wedding to precipitate it. That's perfectly plausible." She mulled the idea over for a few seconds. "Let's run with that. Something happens to trigger the killing there and then. We'll consider what that might have been later. It must have been earlier in the day, because the weapons they used don't appear to have been random. They appear to have been carefully selected, so they must have had the time to go into the smithy and choose them, more or less at leisure. No one would have thought it odd if they'd seen someone taking the opportunity to look around the display in the smithy. So far, so good. But now comes the problem."

"They couldn't have known that Casey would make himself available."

"Exactly. Unless they slipped away from proceedings and lay in wait, in the hope that Casey would come out."

"If they were away for any length of time, wouldn't they be missed?"

"Not if they'd made an excuse to leave the party altogether."

"True."

"They lay in wait – possibly in the smithy, from where you've got a good view of the entrance to the stables - and, fortuitously for the killer, Casey emerges and walks towards the garden. The killer makes his move."

"But then Theresa appears."

"And follows in Casey's footsteps."

"Pretty obvious what's going on there."

"So, our killer delays. If I was him, I'd go around the back of the barn and take up a position there." She pointed to the far corner of the barn from where a view of the garden would be available. "He waits, sees Theresa leave, sees Casey hanging back and takes his chance. I doubt Casey would've had any suspicions about someone else taking time out for some air."

"All well and good, Beth, but supposing Casey hadn't appeared?"

"The killer would have waited for another opportunity." Nick had been on the point of repeating the question when Gallagher pre-empted it with a distinct air of absent-mindedness. "He's very patient. He was prepared to wait half the night for an event that may or may not have occurred and, presumably, if thwarted would simply have gone home and put together another plan. The same with Carmine. The killer must have been aware of her routine and waited for her near or under the bridge, not knowing for certain if she'd make that walk on that particular day. If she hadn't, he'd have come back and waited his chance again."

VI

FAMILIES

Gallagher had established that all of the Molyneaux family, together with Magenta's parents, were working, which was not conducive to getting to see them. However, she reckoned that, following the death of their other daughter, Mr. and Mrs. Seacroft – or, at least, one of them – would be at home during the afternoon.

The Seacrofts lived in a stone-built cottage on the way out of Wellgate, separated from the Todmorden Road by a somewhat unruly blackthorn hedge. The slate roof was speckled with moss. Hard standing to the side of the property had been constructed of traditional stone setts, possibly, Gallagher surmised, original and which provided ample room for two cars, the present occupants being a metallic purple 1960s/70s Volkswagen beetle (she was uncertain how to date vehicles from registration plates of that era) and a silver Saab convertible from the end of the 1990s. The narrowness of the road had required her to drive her own Peugeot a further quarter of a mile down the road until she found a disused farm gateway in which she could park.

They had exhibited a large degree of reluctance to grant her admittance, with an agreement to talk to her, but had been persuaded by their desire to find the killer of their daughter, as quickly as possible and by whatever means available. The room into which Gallagher had been shown was spacious in dimensions, but cosy in ambience. Pitch pine doors, leaded glass windows and walls painted in stone-coloured, textured paint gave it a rustic feel. A wood-burning stove stood in the fireplace, with a stack of logs beside it. Upon the mantelpiece an onyx, art deco clock, with recumbent dog garniture took pride of place. The wooden floor was covered by a red, oriental rug which was starting to show its age around the edges. The burnt umber, leather sofa was well worn, as were the capacious floral-patterned armchair and the snug wingback chair covered in a wild fruit design fabric. The window seat appeared to have seen less use. A glass-topped trunk that bore the scars of extensive travel, as well as the remnants of various labels, served as a coffee table. An eclectic mix of art nouveau, impressionist and twentieth century prints adorned the walls while elsewhere the room was a cacophony of candles, artefacts from exotic places and representational and abstract sculptural pieces in a variety of woods. The only concession to modernity appeared to be the elaborate hi-fi system, with CD racks jostling for space with the bookshelves. Although she could see none burning, the room had the unmistakable aroma of incense. She had been invited to make herself comfortable on the sofa.

Following appropriate expressions of sympathy, Gallagher attempted to ease into her purpose with compliments about aspects of the décor.

"The woodcarvings are beautiful. Where did you acquire them from?" Laura produced a wan smile. She was sitting on the edge of the floral armchair. Gallagher estimated her to be in her late fifties. She was tall, about the same height as her husband, and slim, with long, ash blonde hair which, under other circumstances, might have been described as mischievously unruly, but was more likely to be the result of a lack of attention. She wore a flowing, cream, cotton dress with lace trim and open-toed sandals. Several rings of various shapes, sizes and colours adorned the fingers of both hands, her left wrist was a jangle of bracelets and a pair of jet, teardrop earrings hung from her ears. Around her neck she wore a pentacle on a leather thong. Her face was unmade up apart from a dab of pale pink lipstick.

"Warwick made them. He's a very skilled woodcarver. As you can see."

"It's really only a hobby." Mr. Seacroft was slumped in the other chair. He looked exhausted. Gallagher reckoned he was in his mid-sixties with soft, wavy, collar-length, sandy hair and a rugged, Viking beard. His jeans were faded, his trainers scuffed and his plaid shirt had the cuffs rolled up to the elbows revealing tattoos on both arms. "I sell a few pieces; keep others. By trade I'm a furniture restorer." Gallagher nodded.

"What do you do, Laura?"

"I make jewellery. I have an online shop." She paused, weighing up whether or not to continue. "I also offer an astrology service online – natal charts, horoscopes – as well as doing tarot readings at Pendlehurst and by Zoom." Gallagher nodded again.

"I wanted to ask you about the wedding." This time, Laura's smile was rueful.

"The wedding. The ill-fated wedding."

"Ill-fated?"

"Magenta and Crispin love each other very much, but they come from very different families. The Molyneauxs are… how shall I say? Conventional? I don't intend that pejoratively. There's nothing wrong with being conventional, but we're more… bohemian is probably the best word. David and Vanessa didn't really approve of the match."

"More David than Vanessa." Warwick chipped in as much, Gallagher thought, to let her know he was still there, rather than because he had anything pertinent to contribute. She was not making physical notes, not wishing to appear unnecessarily intrusive, but she made a mental note of that revelation.

"Did anything happen at the wedding?"

"Happen?" Laura sounded puzzled, as well she might have.

"From the circumstances of Casey's death, I'm thinking that something may have happened during the course of the wedding to precipitate the fatal attack. Did Casey say or do anything that upset anyone?"

"Not that I know of. He seemed to be the sort of guy that gets along with everyone. In his capacity as best man, he was the model of propriety. His speech was a catalogue of all Crispin's finest qualities and attributes. Never a hint of betraying any past indiscretions, if indeed, there are any to betray."

"I didn't see any cameras around the wedding venue." After she had returned to her office, Gallagher had called D.I.

Wainwright to share the observations and thoughts emanating from her day's activities, with the ulterior motive of hoping to garner information about any fresh developments in the case.

"No." He sounded despondent. "They only have CCTV around the museum, which hasn't been of much help."

"Any new leads?"

"I've got every available officer working on it." Gallagher noted that he had avoided answering the question.

"And you're still working on the premise that both murders were premeditated."

"They have to be. They must have known that there would be tools available in the smithy that could be pressed into service as weapons and they went to Thornby carrying a screwdriver. Intent is clear."

"And planned."

"That's what premeditated means, Beth."

"Not necessarily."

"Your point being?"

"Casey's murder may well have been premeditated, but the killer couldn't have planned to do it at the wedding. They couldn't possibly have known that Casey would be where he was, when he was. They couldn't possibly have anticipated an opportunity at the wedding. Same with Carmine. The killer may have been watching her movements and come prepared with a weapon, but they couldn't have known for certain that she'd be walking along that stretch of canal on that particular day. The intent may have been there, but it couldn't have been planned for that time and place." There was a brief silence.

"I think you're splitting hairs, but I take your point. But, if they hadn't planned to kill Casey at the wedding, why do it, with all those people about and the risk of being seen?"

"I think something happened at the wedding that caused the killer to act there and then. Casey must have done or said something that sent the killer into meltdown. I also think that, having killed Casey, they were impelled to kill Carmine. I think one led directly to the other."

* * * * *

The Molyneaux property in Helvellyn Court, Padiham could not have been more different from the Seacroft residence. It was a modern, detached property, the frontage being divided into a tasteful, grey brick drive leading to an integral garage and a very suburban garden consisting of neatly cut lawn and shrubs. The roof supported an array of solar panels. One of the few facts that Clematis had been able to unearth about either of the families was that David Molyneaux was the owner and managing director of Molyneaux Construction, which appeared to have a high profile in the area. The garage door was open, revealing a red Mercedes, while on the drive, behind it, stood a red Audi A3. Gallagher could not help feeling that the two reds clashed horribly.

Inside, the through lounge was light and airy, helped by the French doors at the rear that opened out into a spacious conservatory. The plain, ecru carpet complimented the olive green, linen weave wallpaper, creating a somewhat ascetic ambience. The furnishings were classically mid-century, from the sideboard and coffee table to the apple green three-piece suite. On the sideboard were a pair of lava lamps. The wall shelves seemed to have been themed. A corner set supported a selection of, to Gallagher's mind, clunky, 1970s, German ceramic pots and vases. Another triplet bore an assortment of trailing plants, while another was home to a collection of porcelain animals.

Given a free choice, Gallagher had elected to seat herself in one of the armchairs. The Molyneauxs took their place on the sofa. They were, Gallagher reckoned, both in their late fifties or early sixties. David was around 1.80 metres in height, not muscular, but fit, with silver hair, receding at the temples and trimmed in an unimaginative regulation cut, which could not be said to warrant the appellation 'hair style'. He was dressed in a tangerine sports shirt, with an indiscernible logo on the breast, light brown chinos and comfortable tan shoes. Vanessa was about the same age, but appreciably shorter, of medium build, with glossy cinnamon hair, coifed in a wavy bob with a central parting. Her dress bore testament to her having just returned home from the office: a fitted, copper-coloured blouse with wide lapels, burgundy trousers with sharp creases and black, medium-heeled shoes. At the end of the day her make-up, while not extravagant, was still impeccable. Dark-framed, oblong glasses gave her a no-nonsense air. Unlike the Seacrofts, they had not lost a child in violent circumstances, but they could not have been, Gallagher surmised, unaffected by the events of the past five days. Nevertheless, life had to go on.

"How did you feel about Crispin and Magenta's wedding?" Gallagher had already dealt with, albeit to little benefit, matters relating directly to Carmine and, in particular, Casey.

"Feel about it?" David's tone suggested that he considered the question to be an impertinence.

"From what I understand, it wasn't your typical wedding."

"It wasn't a traditional wedding, if that's what you mean."

"Were you happy with that?" The Molyneauxs looked at one another before Vanessa took it upon herself to respond.

"We'd have preferred something more traditional. Not necessarily a white wedding – I think those are out of fashion these days – but a church wedding and a... well, something a little more formal. Something more memorable, if you know what I mean."

"It was a bit like a fancy dress party." David expressed his wife's meaning a little more succinctly.

"We get on very well with the Seacrofts, but they have a different lifestyle to us."

"It was what Laura and Magenta wanted." Again, Mr. Molyneaux was less subtle than Vanessa.

"And you went along with it."

"We'd have preferred something different, but it wasn't our wedding and we weren't going to impose our preferences on them. Crispin was happy with it." For Vanessa, that was all that mattered.

"Magenta persuaded him." Gallagher nodded. She had formed a picture in her mind.

"You own Molyneaux Construction, I believe."

"Yes. Built it up from scratch. Very proud of it."

"It certainly has a good reputation." Gallagher had no idea whether it had a good reputation or not, but she was aware that a little flattery could go a long way. "And Crispin's an architect, I believe."

"He is. And a very good one. He'll go a long way."

"A formidable combination." David smiled, as if he had heard the comment many times before.

"We don't tend to work together. It doesn't look good."

"And what do you do, Vanessa?" Mrs. Molyneaux hesitated before answering.

"I work for a hospice trust."

"She's the accounts manager. Keeps a firm grip on the finances."

With the aid of her trusty A-Z, Gallagher had threaded her way through the backstreets of Padiham and made her way over the canal and motorway to the far end of Hinton, eventually arriving outside the house of the Molyneauxs' daughter, Vivienne Appleby. It was an appreciably more modest home than that of her parents; a 1970s semi-detached, with an asphalt drive extending alongside the house and a conifer hedge screening a neat lawn, rockery and ornamental trees from the road. The obligatory two cars stood on the drive: an eight-year-old Ford Mondeo and a slightly younger Ford Focus, the former in dark grey, the latter in dark blue. Vivienne and her husband had not extended the warmest of welcomes, but it was no more than she could expect when she arrived unannounced.

Their lounge was contemporary, with three pale apricot walls and a brick red feature wall. The geometric red, brown, orange, black carpet appeared to have been inspired by Mondrian. Wooden Venetian blinds took the place of curtains. The twins had been dispatched to their bedroom, but the floor was still littered with toys, books and other child-oriented paraphernalia. A pile of exercise books with, seemingly, a business studies textbook on top of them and a larger, accounts-type book, with a Waddington College crest embossed on the cover, on top of that, took up most of a side table near the door. Gallagher deduced that one of the Appleby's was a teacher. A blue, plastic shoulder bag on the floor, beside the table, indicated that the teacher was most probably Vivienne. The evidence made for a useful icebreaker as she sat down in the corner of the orange tuxedo sofa.

"You're a teacher." Vivienne had sat herself in one of the matching armchairs. She was dressed in jeans, a green paisley smock top and flat, black shoes. Gallagher could not be sure if that was her work wear or her casual wear. Her light brown bob rested, pertly, on her shoulders, occasionally revealing discreet hooped earrings. The morning's make-up had all but faded and, like her mother, the only jewellery on her hands was an engagement ring and wedding band.

"Yes."

"Business studies?"

"Head of."

"And you, Mr. Appleby? What do you do?" Lewis Appleby was standing, legs apart, hands thrust into his jeans' pockets, looking down at her. A short-sleeved, denim shirt and trainers completed the ensemble.

"Is it of any relevance?"

"None whatsoever." She smiled benignly.

"Retail. Procurement." It was clear that neither of the Applebys was inclined towards small talk.

"I wanted to ask you about Casey." Neither of them said anything. "Did Casey argue with anyone at the wedding?"

"Argue? No." Vivienne sounded surprised by the question.

"You're sure?"

"I can't be sure, but if an argument had broken out, I'm sure we'd have noticed."

"Did he do or say anything that may have upset anyone?"

"Not that I heard. Why?"

"What are you getting at?" Lewis did nothing to disguise his irascibility.

"If someone had planned to kill Casey – and the police believe, as do I, that it was premeditated – a wedding, with all those people around, would not be the best place to do it." Gallagher reckoned that seeming to take them into her confidence might be a more productive strategy. "I'm thinking that was not the plan. After all, it would have been difficult to get him on his own. It was only misfortune that caused him to wander off around the stables, enabling his assailant to seize their chance. And if they had not planned to murder him there, then something must have happened to trigger it. Casey must have done or said something."

"From what Cris said, he was a very easy-going kind of guy. Not the sort of person that would upset anyone." Vivienne's tone had softened considerably. She even managed a hint of a smile. "Cris chose him to be his best man because he was a safe pair of hands."

"More so than his brother?"

"I think Cris asked him, out of politeness, but standing up and talking in front of a lot of people is not really Rupe's thing. I think he was frightened of cocking it up"

"I see."

"Casey was very good. His best man's speech contained nothing embarrassing or contentious. Just the opposite; it was a glowing testimonial highlighting all Cris's best qualities."

"How well did you know Casey?"

"Hardly at all. He was Cris's friend." Lewis instinctively shot her a glance that he was unable to retract. Gallagher looked from one to the other and a momentary stand-off ensued. "Casey was a financial adviser. We had a little money to invest and Cris recommended him. I didn't know him personally."

"The investment went down the pan." Lewis was not disposed to be as circumspect as his wife. "We lost the money."

"That must have rankled."

"It did. For a while." Gallagher gained the impression that it still did, at least with Lewis, if not with Vivienne.

The journey back to Burnley, along Accrington Road and Western Road, allowed her to neatly bypass the town centre and arrive at Sutcliffe Road without undue delay. It was mid-evening, but it was still light and, as such, Gallagher had felt justified in making one further call. Immediately after leaving the Applebys, she had texted Nick to tell him of her intentions and that she expected to be home within the hour. Sutcliffe Place was one of Burnley's imposing, sandstone edifices from a bygone age. As to its original function, she was completely ignorant, and it had latterly fallen into disrepair, but more recently developers had seen its potential and had converted the building into flats. Being close to the centre of town and with views, she supposed, over Bellevue Park, she assumed it must be a sought-after location, commanding a relatively high price. She found herself a parking space in the car park at the rear; a relic, she was inclined to assume, of its previous incarnation. According to the directory in the foyer, Rupert Molyneaux's flat was on the first floor.

Not for the first time, she was received cooly. It seemed that Molyneaux's prime quibble was not that she had arrived unannounced, as might have been expected, but the time of her arrival. Nevertheless, she eventually gained an invite to enter. The light, spacious, open-plan ambience of the flat belied the rather austere, Gothic façade of the building. As she had supposed, she glimpsed a view of Bellevue Park. The walls were painted in magnolia and the high ceiling in a dark beige, which had the effect of lowering it. A fitted, mushroom carpet covered the floor. A contemporary, bronze three-piece suite was arranged, precisely, around a low, marble-topped coffee table with chunky, light oak legs. An equally spaced row of four coasters were set out along one side of the table. Two pens and a pencil were aligned in close proximity with one another and perpendicular to the long edges of the table. A neatly folded copy of the Guardian was the only other accessory. On a long oak side table, a bowl, with fresh fruit in it, occupied the centre with two classical figurines arranged, symmetrically, either side of it. On one end, a stack of four books created a pyramid, the largest forming the base and the smallest the apex. On one wall, four rectangular, framed watercolour prints were composed in a perfect square.

Rupert extended a perfunctory invitation to sit down, the implication contained therein being that he anticipated her stay would not warrant her doing so. She thanked him, cordially, and duly availed herself of his hospitality. He remained standing, nervously shifting his weight from one foot to the other. He was

69

slightly shorter than his brother, with the same tawny hair, but neatly groomed, medium length, with a slightly rakish quiff. His grey trousers and pale blue and grey striped shirt were, she supposed, his office wear. He had simply removed his tie and kicked off his shoes.

"You keep a very orderly house, Mr. Molyneaux. I wish mine was this tidy." He shrugged.

"It's what I do. I'm an archivist. At the university." He smiled, almost apologetically, as if he considered being an archivist at an academic institution not to be a real job. "I guess I bring my work home with me." They exchanged a few further pleasantries, Gallagher hoping that, doing so, would encourage him to sit down, but he remained resolutely standing. Eventually she conceded defeat and broached the subject of his brother's wedding.

"I understand that you declined to be Crispin's best man."

"I did."

"Any particular reason?" He looked over her head, at the wall behind her, then back towards her, but not directly at her.

"I'm not comfortable in those sorts of situations. Social situations. It was Cris's big day. I didn't want to embarrass him. I didn't want to ruin it." Gallagher inferred that what he really meant was that he was scared of getting tongue-tied and embarrassing himself.

"I understand." She paused to consider her next question. "We – the police and I – believe Casey left the stables at nine p.m.; maybe just to get a bit of fresh air. We think someone must have followed him and taken their chance to kill him, for whatever reason. Did Casey become involved in an argument with anyone during the course of the evening?" Molyneaux shrugged again.

"Not that I saw."

"Was there anyone at the reception that might have wanted to do Casey harm?"

"I doubt it. Casey was one of those guys that gets along with everyone."

"Did you see anyone, other than Casey, leave the stables at around nine."

"No."

"You seem very certain."

"I am. I'd already left. I left about eight."

"Oh? How so? Your brother's wedding and you left early?" He pursed his lips, again looked over her head, heaved a sigh and returned his gaze to the chair in which she was sitting.

"Like I said, I'm not comfortable in social situations. I get very tense. When it all gets too much I have to walk away. I stuck it out until eight and then I just had to get out."

"I presume there'll be people who can confirm that."

"I doubt it."

"Oh? Why? You must have said goodbye to everyone. Or at least Crispin."

"No." She waited for an explanation. "When I get wound up like that, I just have to walk away." He began twisting his hands together, then stuck them in his trousers pockets. "If I try and say 'goodbye', people inevitably ask me why I'm going and try and persuade me to say. I never know how to explain. I can't explain. It's easier just to slip away without saying anything." Gallagher nodded and let the matter rest.

VII

PHONE CALLS

While Gallagher was criss-crossing Burnley and its environs, seeking out the families of Crispin and Magenta Molyneaux, Wainwright was sifting through the evidence he had accumulated thus far. It was not looking promising. John Oldfield, the pathologist, had not been able to furnish him with any more information than he already had. All the weapons used in the two killings exhibited traces of the victims' blood, but no fingerprints, not even partial ones, or DNA traces that were not related to the victims. From the entry wounds of the primary weapon, Oldfield had been able to ascertain that the killer was probably about the same height as Casey Hardacre and taller than Carmine Seacroft, and was, most likely right-handed, albeit with the blow to Hardacre's head being delivered with the left hand. Meticulous examination of each crime scene had not elicited any footprints that might further the investigation. The lawned area at Pendlehurst, around where Hardacre's body had been found, had been well-trampled by a multitude of people and, by accident or design, the killer had not, it seemed, gone down to the water's edge to discard the hammer and punch. Similarly, the grassy areas on the approach to the canal had been walked over by numerous people and the towpath itself was tarmacked. The officers Wainwright had available to him were still working through the guest list for the wedding, but it was a laborious process, yielding very little information. Everyone had been focused on having a good time and guests were coming and going from the stables throughout the evening, such that no one took any particular notice of who they might have been. The lack of CCTV at the venue was a major disappointment. Furthermore, Wainwright was still unable to attribute a credible motive for either murder, least of all for that of Carmine Seacroft.

"What about Theresa Garrity's boyfriend, Finlay?" Kershaw's question lacked conviction, but in the absence of any other suspects, it seemed, to her, worth pursuing.

"He's on the list, but I'm expecting him to confirm Theresa's story. Knowing that we will talk to him at some point, I can't imagine that she would spin us a tale that he wouldn't corroborate."

"Even so, jealousy's a strong motive."

"True, Kate, but he would have had to have followed her out of the stables and seen her and Casey together. He'd then have had to have the wit and wherewithal to go back to the smithy and find something with which to kill him. It just doesn't seem plausible. Assuming he had followed her outside and had seen them together, wouldn't he have just confronted them? Unless he's totally hot-headed and saw red."

"Not impossible." Although he did not verbalise the notion, Wainwright tacitly conceded that, at this stage, nothing was impossible.

"What about the Applebys?" Bowden had been leaning on his superior's desk, listening to the hypothesising and waiting for an opportunity to add his own considerations.

"Holding Casey responsible for losing them money?"

"Sex and money are often the two strongest motives for murder."

"Agreed, but clearly the Applebys haven't lost everything. I know losing their savings is enough, but any investment is always a risk. Would they really have held Casey accountable to that degree? And if they did, why at the wedding? That's what doesn't make sense. Maybe Gallagher's right. Maybe…"

"Gallagher?"

"I spoke to her on the phone earlier. At least, she called me." Bowden did not look appeased, but Wainwright ignored him. "Maybe Casey's murder was premeditated, but the killer didn't intend to strike at the wedding. Maybe, something happened during the wedding that precipitated it. Casey did, or said, something to someone that unwittingly led the killer to act there and then."

"And Carmine?" Kershaw sounded sceptical.

"There has to be something linking Casey and Carmine. We just haven't uncovered it yet. Whatever it is, Gallagher suggested that Carmine's murder was a direct result of Casey's. One, for whatever reason, followed from the other."

"So where do we go from here?" Bowden did not give any indication that he had an answer to the question.

"Keep digging. There must be something, somewhere to link the two murders. Even if we could just find a realistic motive for one of them, it might lead us to the other. We need to come up with something, though. The Chief Super's starting to get twitchy."

"What are we going to tell the press?" Kershaw was aware that the press were increasingly expecting to be told of some positive developments."

"The usual, Kate: investigation proceeding apace; all available officers involved; following various leads – unspecified, of course." It was unlike Wainwright to succumb to sarcasm and he checked himself. "Maybe we could say that the woman who we believed to have met Casey before he was killed has come forward. If pushed we'll neither confirm nor deny whether she's still a person of interest."

"That's bound to lead to speculation." Bowden was not sure if his superior's policy was a good thing or not.

"Which might expose any cracks. Maybe bring one or two people out of the woodwork.

"Viv! Everything alright?" It was unusual for his sister to phone him so late in the evening.

"Fine, Cris. You?"

"Bearing up. To be honest I rather wish I was back at work. It'd take my mind off things."

"There's nothing to stop you going in."

"True, but I don't want to leave Madge on her own."

"How's she coping?"

"As you'd expect. It's hard for her. And the police don't seem to be making any progress."

"That's why I was calling."

"Oh? Have you heard something?"

"Not really. Did you see the news tonight?"

"We're trying to avoid it."

"The woman they suspected may have met Casey before he was killed came forward."

"And?"

"No details. They didn't even say if she was a suspect."

"Oh."

"Do you know who she might be?"

"Me? No idea. What made you think I would?"

"You were Casey's best friend."

"As far as I know, he wasn't in a relationship. He ended the last one a few months ago. He was footloose and fancy free."

"But if he had been seeing someone, he'd have told you."

"Probably. But…"

"So, what was he doing with her?" Crispin remained silent, certain that she did not really require an answer. "I mean, I know what he was probably doing with her round the back of the stables, but who is she?"

"Like I said, Viv, he was single and this was a wedding. Romance was in the air; the alcohol was flowing. It's not unusual."

"Maybe not, but it is unusual for the bloke she met to wind up dead ten minutes later. There's got to be something there."

"David." She could see it was him, but she was surprised that he should be calling mid-morning.

"Laura."

"Is anything wrong? I mean, apart from the obvious. Where are you?"

"At the office. It's quiet at the moment, so thought I'd give you a call. How are you?"

"Struggling to focus on anything. The police don't seem to be making any progress."

"No." Molyneaux tried to order his thoughts. He knew why

he had called, but it still seemed awkward. "Is Warwick there?"

"No. He's gone into work. Sometimes it's easier. When we're together we feel obliged to talk about… well… Carmine, but we don't know what to say."

"Quite." He paused again. "I wondered if you might like to come over for dinner tonight."

"Dinner?"

"Yes. Nothing special. I thought it might be good to get together. The four of us. Just to chat. It might help. Plus…"

"We can't."

"Oh."

"Madge is coming over. It's very difficult for her. Carmine was her younger sister. And her maid of honour. She's finding it hard."

"I understand." He did understand, but his voice, nevertheless, betrayed his disappointment. "Is Cris going?"

"I don't think so."

"Oh?"

"I know they're married now, but I think he feels he'd be intruding. I think he's arranged to play tennis. It's his way of dealing with things. I can't criticize him."

"No. I think he feels a bit conflicted. Between the loss of his best friend and Magenta's loss of her sister."

"It's not easy for anyone, David."

"I know. What about tomorrow?"

"Tomorrow?"

"For dinner."

"Oh yes. Dinner."

"I really need to see you again, Laura."

"I know. I want to see you, too. Warwick's…"

"Dinner can't hurt. The four of us."

"I suppose not."

"Hi, Cris. It's Rupert."

"Hi."

"Are you busy?

"Not really. I wish I was. It's difficult being at home. We're

76

here all day, just brooding. There's nothing we can do. I think we both wish we were at work. On the other hand, we both want to be together. Where are you?"

"At work. Taking my lunch break."

"Oh yes." Crispin glanced at his watch. "I lose track of time."

"How's Magenta coping?"

"Pretty well. Considering."

"It must be very hard for her."

"It is. They were close. She and Carmine."

"I know."

"She's going over to her parents tonight. A little bit of family support."

"Aren't you going?"

"No. I don't always feel comfortable there at the best of times, Rupe."

"I think I would go."

"Maybe, but..."

"Sorry. I didn't mean to sound critical. I just meant... Don't you think she might appreciate the emotional support?"

"I think they want to be together as a family. Not that I'm not family, but it's Madge's sister and Warwick and Laura's daughter. They have their own way of dealing with things."

"Will you be OK on your own?"

"I'll be fine. She'll only be gone for a couple of hours. Anyway..." He had not intended to say any more.

"Anyway?"

"I've arranged to go and play tennis. I thought it might take my mind off things for an hour or two. I'd often do that with Casey, after work on a Friday."

"Maybe that's not such a bad idea."

Crispin and Magenta had coordinated their departure time, the time being dictated by the time for which Crispin had a court booked. As he had set out for the tennis club, so his wife of, almost exactly, one week set off in the opposite direction to visit her parents. They agreed that he would call her after he had finished his game and then she would depart her parents, expecting that they would arrive home at much the same time.

Two hours later, Crispin had called his wife and, having apprised her parents of the arrangements, Magenta had no difficulty taking her leave of them. She anticipated that Crispin would get home before her, but was not unduly surprised when she discovered she had got there first. She busied herself in the bedroom, expecting him to be back within a matter of minutes, it being less than a ten minute drive from the tennis club. When ten minutes turned into twenty minutes, she began to become irritated; it was most unlike him. Having told her he was on his way, she could not imagine what could have delayed him. When twenty minutes extended into half an hour, she became concerned. She rooted through her bag to find her phone, plumped herself on the bed and keyed his number. His phone rang the preset number of times before transferring to voicemail. Given little alternative, she left a brief message, asking him where he was and requesting he call her if he was going to be much later. When a further ten minutes had passed and he had not called, she became anxious. She tried calling him again, but still to no avail.

In the light of recent events, she began to fear the worst, and after an hour had elapsed, she attempted to call the police station, with the intention of speaking with Wainwright. She had a good idea of what he would say, but she had wound herself up into a state such that she did not know what else to do. As it turned out, Wainwright, along with the rest of his team had gone home, and the officer to whom she spoke was less sympathetic than she had anticipated Wainwright would be. She, again, sifted through her bag until she came across the card Gallagher had given her. It, at least, had a mobile number on it as well as an office number, so she was certain that she could get through to speak to her, notwithstanding that it could now be considered an unsocial hour. She needed to speak with someone who could at least reassure her and, maybe, give her some advice.

The following morning Gallagher was up bright and early, considering it was a Saturday. Nick was always up bright and early as, apart from being a normal working day for him, it was often one of his busiest days. She breakfasted on yoghurt, into which she had sliced a banana, much to Nick's disgust, and coffee and then left the house, very unusually, before Nick. She had discussed Magenta's phone call to her as they had been preparing for bed the previous evening, and had announced her intention of paying a visit to the tennis club should Magenta not contact her, as Gallagher had requested, to say that Crispin had returned. She had received no such call or text. Nevertheless, he had been surprised to see her up and about so early and ready to start the day before him. He had commented that it was probably not necessary to make her call at that hour, but she had only smiled sweetly and had whispered something about early birds and worms. While unable to refute the assertion, he was inclined to the view that her main motive was to steal a march on Wainwright.

Whatever her motivation, when she arrived at the tennis club, there were only two cars in the car park. The clubhouse was a single-storey, red brick building. The main entrance was accessed by a footpath leading directly from the car park. The reception area was functional rather than lavish. The woman behind the desk, thirtyish, Gallagher reckoned, with dark, wavy, shoulder-length hair clipped neatly behind her ears and wearing a sports shirt and green blazer with the club badge on the breast pocket, had evidently only just assumed her duties. Gallagher introduced herself, flashed her ID and stated her business, which was that a member of the club had apparently disappeared after playing there the previous evening. She asked the woman to confirm that Crispin Molyneaux had, in fact, been playing there that evening. The receptionist donned the deep red, narrow, oblong-framed glasses that had been lying on a pile of dishevelled papers and turned to her computer screen. Having found the information that she needed, she turned the monitor towards Gallagher and pointed to a listing on what was clearly a booking form.

"Crispin had a court booked from six 'til eight last night. Not sure who he was playing with. He normally played with…" Her voice trailed off, realising that to mention Casey Hardacre's name might appear tactless.

"Quite. And he was here last night?" The woman half-turned the screen back towards herself.

"Yes. Logged in at five fifty-three."

"Do you know what time he left?" The woman looked at her screen again.

"Logged out at seven fifty-eight." Gallagher nodded. Magenta, when she had checked her call log, had stated that Crispin had called her at eight o-three.

Once outside again, Gallagher surveyed her surroundings. The ungated entrance to the club car park was set in a corner. Iron railings, with fleur de lis finials extended from the entrance along the back of the clubhouse. The clubhouse itself was on the left, as one entered, and presented a blank wall, broken only by three, small, high windows. Facing the visitor, a high privet hedge screened the car park from the tennis courts. A short section of hedge continued around a corner to where the path, that Gallagher had latterly traversed, led to the front of the building. On the right, a more prosaic iron fence separated the car park from the neighbouring place of worship associated with a fringe Christian denomination. On the church side, trees of varying maturity stood at irregular intervals. On the club side, a narrow border of bedding plants was fronted by a line of decorative stones. In the corner, between the church and the privet, a shipping container, with a double door cut into the side, appeared to be the groundsman's depository.

As she leaned against the bonnet of her car, she considered the circumstances. Neither of the two cars in the car park belonged to Crispin Molyneaux, suggesting that he had left the club after logging out and calling Magenta. Clearly, it seemed, the call to his wife did not indicate anything other than that he intended to return home promptly. This raised three questions in Gallagher's mind: Why did he not return home? Where did he go to instead? Where was he now? A further question insinuated its way into her thinking: Does his unexplained disappearance have anything to do with the murders of Casey Hardacre and

Carmine Seacroft? As she contemplated these questions, she commenced a perambulation around the car park, though with no idea of what she hoped or expected to find.

What she did find may have been something or nothing. Either way, it gave her cause for concern and, rather than phone Magenta Molyneaux, she was moved to call Wainwright.

"Danny?" She was once again leaning against the bonnet of her Peugeot.

"Beth! To what do I owe this pleasure first thing on a Saturday morning?"

"Crispin Molyneaux's gone missing."

"Crispin? Missing?"

"Magenta tried calling the station last night, but, it seems, got short shrift. She'd been hoping to speak to you, but you'd already knocked off, so she called me."

"Go on."

"He went to the tennis club last night while Magenta went to her parents. He'd arranged to call her when he left the club so that she could leave her parents and arrive home at much the same time as him. Anyway, he called her to say that he was on his way, but he never got there. That's when she tried to call you and ended up calling me."

"That's all we need."

"Anyway, I'm at the tennis club now and…"

"Hold on a minute, Beth; I've got another call coming through. It's Kate. I'll have to take it." Without waiting for a response, he left her on hold. Within a couple of minutes, he returned to her. "I've got to go." The sudden urgency in his voice implied that he meant he had to go somewhere, rather than merely curtail the call.

"Go where?" There was a long pause, which confirmed her suspicion. He was, she deduced, debating whether or not to tell her.

"Campion Lake." He unceremoniously ended the call. Gallagher put her phone away, opened the car door and leaned over to the passenger seat to pick up the dog-eared A-Z that permanently resided there, preferring its wisdom to that of the satnav. Resting it on the roof of the car she opened it at the appropriate page. Campion Lake was, she estimated, little more than a kilometre and a half from the tennis club and a mere stone's throw from Crispin's home in Brindley Leas.

Gallagher did not get very far along Campion Lane, beyond what was necessary for access to the handful of houses either side of it, before she was stopped by a uniformed police officer. Reluctantly, he was persuaded to make a call to D.I. Wainwright who, himself, had only just arrived at the location – a location which the police were in the process of securing. He idled back towards her car, placed his hand on the roof, bent down to the open window and grudgingly gave her directions to the car park where, he informed her, she would find Wainwright.

The car park was already a hive of police activity. D.C. Kershaw was at the entrance, expectant of her arrival, and gave her directions as to where she should park. She exhibited uncharacteristic impatience as she waited for Gallagher to get out of her car, collect her bag and prepare herself to be led to wherever Wainwright was; she was feeling miffed at having been assigned escort duty and, thus, excluded from proceeding towards the cause of their presence.

"What's going on here? What's happened?"

"A morning dog walker reported seeing a body in the woods at the back of the car park." At that juncture, John Oldfield's Skoda rolled into the car park, promptly followed by an ambulance. Kershaw ignored them, instead giving instructions, as she marched towards the focus of interest, to a uniformed officer to direct the pathologist and the medical crew. As the two women approached, Bowden instinctively looked round.

"Oh, it's you."

"Like the proverbial bad penny, D.S. Bowden." Bowden could not conceal a resigned smile.

"It's Gallagher, sir." Wainwright uncoiled himself from his observation attitude and turned round.

"Crispin Molyneaux." Gallagher nodded. "You're not surprised?"

"I feared the worst. Having called Magenta to say he was on his way home last night, he didn't arrive. His car was gone from the tennis club this morning and I thought that, maybe, he'd decided he couldn't face going home, for whatever reason, but then I found a stone discarded by the edge of the car park there. Clearly it had been removed from a flower border and, when I examined it, I found it has, what appears to be, blood on it. Rather than leave it *in situ*, with the risk of it being tampered with, I picked it up and put it in the car." It was Wainwright's turn to nod.

"Like Casey and Carmine, nothing seems to have been removed from the body. Wallet, mobile, all intact."

"Personal, then."

"It would seem so."

"Hope you haven't disturbed anything." Oldfield's voice curtailed any further discussion. The three detectives and Gallagher stepped back to allow him and his assistant, Alice, free access to the body.

"Good morning to you, too. It'd be more than my life's worth, John."

"Correct, detective inspector." Without fuss, Oldfield settled himself down to examine the body.

"There doesn't seem to have been much attempt to conceal the body, though amidst the undergrowth it could quite easily have gone undetected for some while. He was found by a dog walker this morning – or, more correctly, it was found by the dog. The dog's owner admits that she wouldn't have noticed it hadn't been for her dog." Wainwright was recapping what Bowden and Kershaw were already aware of, for the benefit of Gallagher, pending some insight from Oldfield. Molyneaux, Gallagher had noted, lay no more than two or three metres from the edge of the car park. "The body appears to have been dragged here from the car park." Wainwright indicated the incriminating trail of flattened grass and brush between the car park and Molyneaux's feet, which his team and Gallagher, at the inspector's behest, had studiously avoided. "CSI should be able to tell us more on that when they get here. And that," he pointed to the BMW parked seven or eight yards from where they were standing, "is Crispin's car." Gallagher looked back towards it and chided herself for not recognising it as she had passed.

"Either Crispin Molyneaux drove himself to his own death," Bowden felt compelled to explain the implications of his superior's statement, "or someone else drove him in his own car."

"What I can tell you, before proper examination," Oldfield had looked up from his preliminary inspection, "is that your victim suffered blunt force trauma to the right rear of his head and, as far as I can see, three stab wounds to the chest. Probably a wide-bladed knife. Possibly a kitchen knife. I can't say at this stage which was inflicted first, or which was the cause of death. And, before you ask, plus or minus twelve hours." That, Gallagher calculated, would put the time of death at around the time Molyneaux was last seen or heard of at the tennis club.

VIII

A SIGHTING

Wainwright had taken the unusual step of asking Gallagher to accompany him when he went to break the news of Crispin Molyneaux's death to his wife. He did so on the grounds that it was her to whom Magenta had reported his disappearance and her who had followed it up in the first instance. On opening the front door, Magenta had not appeared surprised to see the detective and the private investigator there. She, herself, had looked tired. Gallagher surmised that she had been awake for most of the previous night. With little ado, she had invited them in, led the way into the lounge and slumped into one of the brocade armchairs, leaving her visitors to remain standing or seat themselves as they wished. After a brief exchange of glances, they had taken up a position on the chesterfield, from where Wainwright had delivered his solemn message. It had taken some while for it to sink in and the pair allowed her time to process it.

"Who would do this? Why? What have we done?" She looked at them, imploringly.

"That's what we're determined to find out. And we will find out. We will find who is responsible."

"Will you?" There was no suggestion of criticism, but equally there was no hint that she had any faith in their ability to do so.

"Yes. I can assure you, Magenta, we'll not rest until we've discovered who killed Crispin, and Carmine and Casey, and brought them to justice." Magenta nodded. She had neither the strength not the will to argue.

"Do you have anyone you can stay with, or who can stay with you?" Gallagher took the conversation forward in as gentle a manner as she could muster.

"My parents." The answer was mechanical.

"Would you like me to take you there?"

"Do they know?"

"Not yet." Gallagher allowed Wainwright to provide the answer.

"Can you tell them? I don't know how…" Her voice tailed off.

"We'll do that. And we'll inform Crispin's parents."

"Thank you." She suddenly looked across at Gallagher, remembering that she had asked her a question. "I'd like a little time to myself; to try and get my head around it. And I'll have to put a few things together."

"I can stay with you, if you want, until you're ready to go." Gallagher was not sure what else she could say.

"That would be good, if you could do that, Beth." Wainwright nodded, approvingly, in Gallagher's direction, then straightened himself and addressed Mrs. Molyneaux again. "I think it would be advisable if we arranged twenty-four hour protection for you, until we catch the perpetrator." Try as he might, he could not avoid engendering a sense of alarm.

"Protection? Do I need it?"

"Magenta," Gallagher cut in before Wainwright could reply, "of those at the wedding, the best man, the maid of honour and now the groom have been murdered."

"You think I might be next?"

"As things stand, Crispin's death provides us with the best opportunity of finding our killer." Wainwright was stood at his whiteboard, upon which a photo of Crispin Molyneaux had been appended, next to those of Casey Hardacre and Carmine Seacroft. "It would appear that Crispin was abducted from the tennis club last night. Whether or not he was killed there, or killed later, we don't yet know. However, the killer must have known he would be at the tennis club. Crispin's brother, Rupert, spoke to him yesterday lunchtime and Crispin told him that he was going to the club that evening. Laura Seacroft spoke to David Molyneaux yesterday." He tapped their respective photos on the board with his pen. "David had phoned her to invite the Seacrofts to dinner yesterday evening, but Laura told him they couldn't do it because Magenta was going to see them, on her own, and that Crispin was going to play tennis while she was there."

"So, Laura and Warwick Seacroft knew he would be at the club and so would David and Vanessa Molyneaux." Bowden wanted to be sure that he had understood his superior correctly."

"Precisely, Dean." He turned back to the whiteboard and tapped the photo of Vivienne Appleby. "Vivienne, Crispin's sister, said she didn't know her brother had planned to play tennis that evening but," he paused to give emphasis to his corollary, "when we checked Crispin's phone, we found Vivienne had called him on Thursday evening. He could have mentioned that Magenta was going to her parents on Friday evening and that he was going to the tennis club."

"The whole family could be suspects, then." Bowden verbalised the obvious conclusion.

"Do any of them have alibis?" Kershaw was leaning against her desk.

"Magenta was with her parents until shortly before the time that we think Crispin was abducted and killed. After Magenta left, they would have had difficulty getting from Wellgate to the tennis club before he left there. However, we don't know what time he left there."

"CCTV?"

"The tennis club are sending it over, Dean. Hopefully that should give us something." He paused for any further questions, but when none were forthcoming, he continued. "Otherwise, the Seacrofts only alibis are each other. Likewise, the Molyneauxs: their only alibis are each other. Rupert Molyneaux lives alone and he says he was at his flat, on his own, last night. As for the Applebys, assuming they knew Crispin was playing tennis, their…"

"Don't tell me, their alibis are each other."

"Precisely, Dean."

"What about this woman that met Casey before he was killed?" Bowden considered a further possible suspect.

87

"Tez Garrity?"

"She could have set him up. We only have her word for it that Casey asked her to meet him. She could have lured him out of the stables."

"Motive? I don't see any reason why she would want to kill Casey, let alone Carmine or Crispin." Bowden remained silent.

"Do we have any more from the pathologist?" Kershaw had resumed her seat, sensing the briefing was soon to be over.

"Not yet, Kate. Oldfield does things in his own time. We're also waiting for forensics to come back with an analysis of the blood – or what appears to be blood – on the stone Gallagher found in the tennis club car park, as well as whatever they get from Crispin's car." A cursory inspection of Crispin Molyneaux's BMW at Campion Lake had revealed a considerable amount of blood in the back of it, which was assumed to be that of Crispin.

When Wainwright had left Magenta Molyneaux, Gallagher had accompanied him to the front door and had extracted from him a promise to keep her informed about developments in the investigation that had now taken a new twist. He had, in her perception, shown token reluctance to do so, but had concluded that, as she had furnished the police with, potentially, material evidence, in the shape of the tennis club stone, which might otherwise have been lost, she had a reasonable claim to be kept in the loop.

Wainwright had left D.C. Kershaw in the car, not having wished to create an overbearing presence of three detectives when he broke the news of Crispin's murder. Having informed the widow, he first got on the phone to Bowden to instruct him, together with a female colleague, to inform the Seacrofts of the death of their son-in-law, and thence to apprise the Applebys, while he and Kershaw drove to Padiham to notify the Molyneauxs of the death of their son. Meanwhile, Gallagher had remained with Magenta, attempting to console the inconsolable. Her grief, on top of that for her sister, had rapidly overwhelmed her.

It had not been long before Laura Seacroft called her daughter and, after a brief outpouring of emotions, arrangements had been made for Magenta to stay with her parents. At the conclusion of the call, Gallagher had helped her pack a few essentials in an overnight bag and had then called Wainwright to tell him that she was about to take Magenta to her parents.

Gallagher did not spend too much time at the Seacroft house. She saw her safely inside, expressed the requisite words of condolence to Laura and Warwick and had taken her leave, having observed, on the way in, a police car already parked on the opposite side of the road. She had checked that they were the detail assigned to keep a watchful eye on Magenta and, when satisfied, set off back to the tennis club.

Arriving at the tennis club she was not surprised to find the car park over half full. It was, after all, the middle of the day and it was a Saturday. She had hoped it might be otherwise, so that she could make a more thorough search of the area unobstructed, but, as it was, there was nothing she could do. It was as she was turning her car around to return home that her mobile demanded her attention. She stopped, blocking the entrance, rooted through her bag for the phone and, having found it, discovered it was Wainwright.

"We've just received the CCTV footage for yesterday evening from the tennis club. Do you want to come and view it?"

"I'm on my way, Danny."

"OK, Dean, let's go." Wainwright, Kershaw and Gallagher were assembled around Bowden's desk.

"Where do you want to start from?"

"Bethany says Crispin logged out at the tennis club at nineteen fifty-eight and called Magenta at twenty o-three, so let's start from twenty hundred."

"Sir." Bowden located the spot and pressed play. The CCTV provided good coverage of the club car park, which gave Wainwright cause for optimism.

"Twenty o-three. That's when he called his wife." For wont of anything better to say, Kershaw stated the obvious. There were three cars in the car park, Crispin's BMW being parked nose to the wall of the club, but no activity.

"Probably called her from outside the building, before going to his car." Gallagher offered the hypothesis to explain, as yet, Molyneaux's non-appearance on the screen.

"OK, here he comes." Wainwright leaned, a little more intently, towards the screen."

"Twenty o-five." Bowden demonstrated that Kershaw was not the only one who could state the obvious.

"Goes straight to his car. Unlocks it. Goes to the rear. Lifts the tailgate." Wainwright, unconsciously, rendered the unnecessary commentary. "Hold it!" Bowden instinctively pressed pause. "Who's this? Play on, Dean." Bowden did as instructed. They all huddled closer to the screen. A figure, dressed in a dark, padded jacket, jeans, a baseball cap, with the peak pulled down, and, most noticeably, wearing gloves, emerged from behind the shipping container in the corner. The figure loped, head bent forward, defying identification, towards Molyneaux.

"He's carrying something." Bowden made the observation.

"Looks like the stone from the border." Gallagher added the clarification.

"He must have picked it up before hiding." Kershaw contributed the supposition.

"Crispin's preoccupied with putting his tennis gear in the back of the car." This was an assumption as the tailgate largely obscured him from view.

"I doubt if he would have heard his attacker anyway; the car park's tarmacked." Gallagher added the self-evident information. What followed on the footage was somewhat confused. Within a few strides, the attacker was behind Molyneaux. His hand, with the stone in it, appeared above the tailgate. It was tacitly agreed that the assailant delivered the blow to Molyneaux's head at that point. The stone was tossed back to where Gallagher had found it and the attacker was then seen closing the tailgate.

"Just stop it there, Dean." Bowden did as ordered. "Twenty o-seven. Less than two minutes. Crispin would have fallen forward, into the boot and it wouldn't have taken much to bundle his legs in. Go on." Bowden pressed play again. The assailant went to the driver's door, head still bowed, and got in. "Crispin probably had the keys in his hand." A few seconds later the BMW could be seen leaving the tennis club. Bowden stopped the video and leaned back in his chair.

"No chance of identifying them from that. They were very careful to conceal their face. They probably guessed there would be CCTV."

"I think you're right, Dean. Let's go back to when they entered the car park. Maybe that'll give us something." Bowden rewound the footage.

The sequence prior to the attack shed no further light on the identity of the attacker. They had entered the car park on foot, hunched forward and head lowered. It was agreed that, either they had walked to the locale or they had parked their car at some distance from it and walked from there. The attacker carefully selected a stone suitable to their purpose and then made their way behind the container to await the appearance of the intended victim. Again, all four concurred that they must have been familiar with the layout of the car park, if not the tennis club as a whole.

Having gleaned everything they could from the CCTV footage, the group dispersed, Kershaw back to her own desk and Gallagher, escorted by Wainwright, towards the door.

"At least we've established Crispin was alive and well when he was hit over the head." Wainwright attempted to put a positive spin on their viewing.

"Which suggests considerably more forethought than the other two murders."

"What makes you think so?"

"Well," Gallagher came to a halt just outside the door and turned to face him directly, "the speed with which the whole incident took place would indicate that the attacker had no intention of killing Crispin at the tennis club; that the plan had always been to knock him out, bundle him into the back of his car and drive him somewhere else to kill him. Whether that somewhere else had already been decided upon, or whether Campion Lake was a convenient, last-minute decision, I don't know, but I'd suspect they'd already fixed upon the lake."

"If they hadn't planned to kill him at the tennis club, then they must have had a good idea where they were going. Unless the intention was to kill him and they needed somewhere to dump the body, rather than leave it in the boot of the car in the car park."

"Except that they had clearly armed themselves with a knife with which to kill him. What we've just witnessed was a violent kidnap, not a murder attempt."

"Why? It's quite likely Crispin would have come round by the time they reached the lake. That would have resulted in a struggle."

"You don't know there wasn't one."

"I'll grant you that. We're still waiting for the pathologist's and forensics' reports.

"Perhaps our killer had something to say to his victim before they killed him."

"In the light of the other two killings, that's likely to have been personal." Pursed lips and a raised eyebrow indicated Gallagher's concurrence.

"Have you found the murder weapon, yet?"

"We haven't turned anything up in the immediate vicinity. The first weapons were tossed into the brook at the back of Pendlehurst; the second into the canal. I'm thinking they may have tossed the knife they used this time into the lake, but…" he paused "we don't know if they did - and if they did, where they threw it from, or how far they could have thrown it. We've got a diving team onto it, but it could be like looking for a needle in a haystack."

Gallagher was sat at the dining table, her laptop open in front of her, idly coiling a lock of hair between her fingers, when she heard Nick come in through the front door. She leaned back in her chair, listened to him deposit his gear in the hall and waited for him to enter the room.

"Hi, sweetheart." He crossed the room towards her.

"Hi, Nick." She lifted her face towards him and he kissed her on the lips. "How's your day been?"

"The wedding this morning was good. Usual familial bickering when it came to who stood next to whom for the photos, but that's par for the course."

"And the picnic?"

"It was a children's birthday picnic." His tone suggested that should be sufficient to answer the question. She grinned at him.

"You enjoy it, really." He kissed her again on the top of her head.

"How's your day been?"

"Crispin Molyneaux was found murdered this morning." After expressing his shock, Nick pulled out a chair and sat himself at right angles to her. Without further prompting she recounted the details of the day, Nick being content to listen, occasionally interjecting pertinent comments.

"The CCTV gave no indication at all as to who your killer might be?"

"None. Couldn't even tell if it was a man or a woman." Nick peered around the edge of the laptop at the screen, although he had previously noticed what she was looking at.

"You still think the answer might be there?"

"Yes." The answer was unequivocal. "It has to be someone who was close to all three victims, which means it's almost certainly someone who was at the wedding. There must be a clue somewhere in your photos."

"You've examined them in minute detail, Beth."

"I know, but I'm sure I must have missed something. There must be some tell-tale sign. Just a few hours after these pictures were taken, one of the people here murdered Casey Hardacre." Nick remained silent. He did not know what he could say. "You arrange all the photos, don't you? You decide who should be in any particular photo and who should stand where."

"Yes."

"And, knowing you, you pay attention to detail."

"Such as?"

"You make sure they're all facing the right way; they have appropriate expressions; their ties are straight; they don't have their hands in their pockets. That sort of thing."

"I do my best."

"So, there's not much opportunity for self-expression." He was about to object, but she cut him off. "I don't mean that as a criticism. What I meant was, it's all very carefully choreographed and self-expression is kept within fairly tight parameters; any disagreeable looks or gestures would be pretty much eliminated."

"That's what I'm paid for: to create the illusion of happy families, when sometimes they're not."

"Nevertheless, there must be some little sign of discord here."

Dinner had been a subdued affair. On receiving the news of Crispin Molyneaux's murder – and after the arrival of her daughter - Laura Seacroft had called David Molyneaux, firstly to offer her condolences and secondly to ask whether the Molyneauxs still wished them to visit. Molyneaux had assured her that he and Vanessa would welcome their support. Naturally, it was expected that Magenta would go with her parents. Nevertheless, the meal had been awkward. In quick succession the Seacroft's had lost one of their daughters and the Molyneauxs had lost their son – and connecting the two deaths, Magenta had lost her sister and her husband. No one quite knew what to say. Each were preoccupied with their own personal grief, yet no one wanted to appear to be making themselves the centre of attention. No one wanted to hint at being competitive in their grief; each affected party wanted to console the others. Yet, no one could seem to find the appropriate words for the occasion. They had, briefly, diverted themselves with a futile consideration of who could have been responsible, but that had soon petered out. No one wanted to be perceived as suggesting that it could have been a member of the other family.

They had adjourned from the kitchen and had settled into the lounge; the men occupying the armchairs and the women, the sofa. Laura cupped her wine glass in her hands and stared into it. The other four glasses sat on the coffee table. During a lull in the stilted conversation, David rose to his feet.

"I'd better go and fill the dishwasher." Without waiting for a response, he made his way, uncomfortably, towards the door, down the hallway and into the kitchen on the other side of it. Meanwhile, Laura replaced her glass on a vacant ceramic coaster.

"I'll give him a hand." She got up and followed in Molyneaux's footsteps. When she reached the kitchen, Molyneaux was rinsing the plates under the tap before arranging them in the machine. "I thought you might like some help." He started and turned round, the plate he was holding dripping water on the floor.

"I didn't hear you come in." She smiled, walked up to him, took the plate, placed it on the counter and squeezed his hand.

"It's a difficult time for all of us, David." With both his hands free, he grabbed her round the waist and planted his lips hard on hers. He felt her involuntary, but fleeting response before she pushed him away. "David!" The panic in her whisper transmitted to him and he glanced, instinctively, towards the door.

"No one's going to see us here." He tried to kiss her again.

"I wasn't thinking of that. This is not the time. Crispin, your son, was found murdered this morning."

"Do you think I've forgotten that, Laura? Now's the time I need you." He turned her around and pushed her backwards into the teak-topped dining island and kissed her again. This time there was no resistance, only the sensation of her tongue inside his mouth. He felt for her breasts beneath the decorous, high-necked, calf-length, bottle green dress. She clasped her hands around his neck. He hitched her dress up so that he could feel the naked flesh of her thighs. She wrapped her legs around him. "God, I want to fuck you." She smiled at him, impishly.

"Not half as much as I want you to fuck me, but we have to be patient." She was breathing heavily. "Until all this is over." She pulled his mouth towards hers again.

"I hope it's over quickly. I hope they catch the bastard soon."

"They will. And then we can get back to…" She paused. 'Normal'; just wanting to get back to normal sounded callous.

"Fucking?"

"That's not what I was going to say," she grinned at him and

95

kissed his chin, "but that as well." She shoved him away. "Come on. We'd better get that dishwasher loaded."

IX

VISITS

Everyone had wanted to give voice to their own, personal grief, but everyone had felt constrained, by everyone else, about doing so. In that sense, the previous evening's dinner had only added to the stress each was under, rather than alleviating it. It was partly for that reason that the Molyneauxs had asked their other son and daughter, together with Vivienne's husband, to lunch the following day. At least, as family, they had a common loss. The murder of Crispin had brought the events of the previous week home to them in unequivocal terms. The Applebys had not really known Casey Hardacre, other than in a professional capacity, and Vivienne had not seen much of Carmine Seacroft since she had married Lewis. Rupert had got to know Carmine through the foursomes they had enjoyed with Magenta and Crispin, but had little in common with Casey. Vanessa and David Molyneaux hardly knew either Casey or Carmine at all. However, what they all had in common was Crispin. Hence, the four of them, plus Lewis, who felt the awkwardness of the proverbial spare wheel, sat down to partake of Sunday lunch together.

"Why would anyone want to kill Cris?" Vanessa Molyneaux blurted out the question before anyone had taken a first mouthful. Tears welled in her eyes. Vivienne patted her arm, then held it while her mother sniffed and took a couple of deep breaths in an effort to restore her equilibrium.

"It's OK, mum; you're allowed to cry." Her mother forced a grateful smile.

"But why Cris? What'd he ever done to anyone?"

"What had any of them ever done?" Vivienne attempted to place her brother's murder in context. "If the same person killed all of them, what could any of them have done? It seems so senseless."

"There has to be a reason." David attempted to be rational.

"Does there?" His wife turned on him. "What possible reason could there be?"

"If there isn't a reason," Lewis was reluctant to add his thoughts, but nevertheless did so, "then the police are looking for a psychopath. Someone who kills for no reason."

"Then any of us could be next." Vanessa shot him an almost accusatory glance.

"Someone must have had a grudge against all of them." Lewis attempted to alleviate her fear, regretting that he had said anything in the first place.

"What sort of a grudge, Lewis?" His wife turned to him, not wanting to believe either scenario, seeking some alternative rationale. In reply, all she got was a shrug.

"I've no idea, Viv; I've no idea."

"They never even got to enjoy their honeymoon." The corners of Vanessa's eyes moistened again, only this time she could not prevent a tear rolling down her cheek. "It seems so cruel."

During the morning, prior to going to his parents for lunch, Rupert Molyneaux had phoned Magenta. He had assumed that his sister-in-law would be on her own and had wanted to check on her to make sure she was coping and that, if she wanted someone with whom to share her grief, he would be happy to visit her, given that Crispin had been his brother as well as her husband. She had informed him that she was staying with her parents, but that she would welcome his company, if he was inclined to go there.

So it was that Rupert arrived at the Seacrofts house on the Sunday afternoon. Laura and Warwick greeted him cordially and apologised for the inconvenience of him having to negotiate the protection officers on duty. They exchanged a few words of condolence, after which Magenta took over and led him out into the garden, where they sat themselves on a wooden seat enclosed within a trellised bower, adorned with jasmine on the two sides and honeysuckle along the back.

"I hadn't realised you were here." He looked across her, rather than at her, his hands clasped in his lap. Now that he was here, he was not sure what he was going to say to her.

"There's no reason why you should've."

"I suppose not. I don't want to intrude."

"You're not intruding, Rupert. It's nice of you to come round. My parents can get a little intense and, last night we all had dinner with your parents."

"I know. I had lunch with them earlier."

"So you said." The statement had an unintended air of finality about it, which caused Molyneaux to remain silent. "It was all a bit claustrophobic. They were all looking at things from a parents' perspective and, I have to admit, I felt a little left out, even though I wasn't, if you know what I mean." He nodded.

"It could have got like that at lunch, but fortunately I had Viv and her husband there."

"I wish I could make some sense out of all this."

"You can't make sense of the senseless, Madge."

"No. It'll probably never make sense."

"However, I thought we could try." He turned his head slightly so that he could see her profile. She was peering straight out at the garden. She half-turned towards him."

"How?"

"I was thinking, other than that they were both at your wedding, Casey and Carmine had no connection to one another. There seems to be no logic to someone wanting to kill Casey and then wanting to kill your sister. At first, I thought it might have been two different killers and that the closeness of their occurrence had been tragic coincidence, but with Cris's murder…"

"What are you thinking?" She shifted her position, to look at him squarely. When their eyes met, he instinctively looked away. Rupert invariably tried to avoid eye contact with anyone.

"Carmine and Casey might not have known each other, but Cris knew them both. That can't be coincidence."

The conversation meandered on until each had exhausted their supply of thoughts. They had not solved anything, but they had achieved a certain measure of catharsis.

"Thanks for coming, Rupert." She offered him a weary smile and stroked his arm affectionately. He returned the smile and patted her hand.

If Gallagher had had her way, she would have spent most of Sunday poring over photographs with a magnifying glass. As it was, she had not got her way; Nick had persuaded her that the clemency of the weather made it an ideal day for a picnic. She had tried arguing, somewhat lamely, that everyone else would probably have the same idea, but Nick had not been deterred. Hence, he had packed the picnic basket and a rug into the back of his Antara and they had set off for Wycliffe Forest Park.

The car park at Wycliffe did not hold good memories for Gallagher; it had been the scene of a particularly unpleasant murder in the not-too-distant past. However, as she often reminded herself, if she avoided everywhere associated with distasteful crimes, she would not go anywhere.

They had walked down the footpath connecting the car park to the hamlet nestled in the bottom of the valley, past the cluster of stone-built houses and across the packhorse bridge. A group of children had been playing in the beck and a tractor had trundled across the ford.

"That's the remains of Wycliffe Hall." The ruin was being overrun by sightseers armed with mobile phones and one woman, Nick was delighted to see, with an actual camera.

"I know it is Nick."

"But did you know Charlotte Brontë used it as the setting for *Jane Eyre*?"

"Did she?" In her previous encounter with the village, Gallagher had been acquainted with the hall, but any further details would have had no relevance to that particular case and, consequently, she had not taken the trouble to acquire them.

"Apparently so."

"What happened to it?"

"The last lord of the manor was a bit of a gambler, I think. It was split up after his death to pay his debts. The house was subsequently abandoned and, during the nineteenth century, it was cannibalised for its stone to build other things. Don't ask me what. Maybe other houses in the village. Possibly, being as this was the nineteenth century, height of the industrial revolution and all that, for building factories or mills or whatever."

"Shame." They passed the ruin and the renovated barn, now reincarnated as a visitor centre, and over a stone stile into the picnic area. All the specially constructed tables were occupied, but Nick had planned on laying out their picnic on the grass anyway. It was something of a suntrap and, for a while, Gallagher was able to forget her triple murder and bask in the warmth, Nick's prattling conversation and the culinary delights that he had prepared, accompanied by a bottle of her favoured pinotage. Having finished with a couple of individual trifles that Nick had found lurking in the fridge – and of which the 'Use By' date had just expired – they packed up the basket and lay back on the rug, Gallagher nestled in the crook of his arm, her head resting on his chest.

"Dare I ask what you're thinking?"

"Only you can answer that, Nick." He knew what she was thinking and denying it would not prevent her from doing so.

"Come on, then, sweetheart. Tell me."

"I'm thinking that, instead of focusing on motive, we ought to be focusing on opportunity." Nick anticipated that she would elucidate further without his encouragement. "If our main suspects are the family, then they were all at the wedding and all had equal opportunity to kill Casey Hardacre. It seems that everyone knew that Crispin Molyneaux would be at his tennis club on Friday evening and, it being evening, everyone would have an opportunity to drive there, abduct him and kill him, though," she peered up at his chin, "the Seacrofts might have had difficulty getting there, but it wouldn't be impossible." Nick was not sure where her argument was going as, it seemed to him, everyone, thus far in her rationale, had opportunity. "That leaves Carmine Seacroft. She was killed in the middle of the day, in the middle of the week. Who would have had the opportunity to do that?" He gave her a squeeze.

"I'm assuming that's a rhetorical question." She smiled, though he was unable to see it.

"Laura Seacroft works from home so could have gone out and returned without anyone knowing, especially if Warwick was at work, restoring furniture."

"One-man business?"

"I think so. He may have an assistant. I'm not sure."

"Either way, he could also have arranged to go out and return without anyone knowing."

"Vanessa Molyneaux is an accounts manager for a hospice trust. She would have limited time for lunch; probably not enough time to get to Thornby Gardens, wait for Carmine and get back again without arousing suspicion."

"Well, that's one relegated to the subs bench."

"David Molyneaux owns his own construction company."

"So not accountable to anyone."

"He could come and go as he pleases and for however long he pleases. Rupert Molyneaux works at UCLAN. He would've been the nearest to where Carmine was killed but, like Vanessa, how much flexibility would he have had in respect of time?" Nick was not sure if she intended that as a rhetorical question and duly made a quick, mental calculation.

"Less than five minutes' drive from the university to Thornby." He felt Gallagher shrug.

"Vivienne Appleby. Teaches at Waddington. I doubt her lunch break would coincide with Carmine's." She paused, giving Nick time to consider the matter.

"Teachers do have free periods. Actually, I think it's called non-contact time, or something like that nowadays. Free periods sounds bad."

"Get to the point, Nick."

"If she had a free period that coincided with Carmine's lunch break, she could have played hookey and slipped out for an hour."

"It's a thought. And then there's Lewis Appleby. Works in

retail. Again, the time issue - if he was in the office. He's a buyer. Procurement manager, I think he calls himself. He could quite easily have been out of the office. But, he would've had to have known that Carmine would be where she was at that time." From what he had heard, Gallagher had not, absolutely, been able to eliminate anyone on the grounds of opportunity and, consequently, he was loath to make his next statement.

"Magenta Molyneaux?" Gallagher shifted her position slightly and ran her hand up and down the inside of his thigh.

"She, of all people, would have known Carmine's routine, and she was off work – she should have been on honeymoon – so she'd have had ample opportunity. But, leaving Casey aside, that would mean she would've murdered her sister and husband. Why? What possible reason? However, seeing as I can't definitely rule anyone in, I can't definitely rule anyone out." Nick stroked her hair.

"So, just to recap – and not to put too fine a point on it – everyone, except perhaps Vanessa, in theory, had opportunity."

"We're not getting very far, are we?"

"I hate to agree with you, sweetheart, but no, it doesn't seem like it." He felt her sigh. "But there's not much more you can do about it today. Leave it 'til you get back to the office tomorrow. Maybe the police will have come up with something by then."

"Maybe." She did not sound optimistic.

103

X

DETAILS

D.I. Wainwright was, once again, stood in front of his whiteboard with his team assembled before him, eager to hear of any developments that may have transpired over the weekend.

"The diving squad were at Campion Lake all day yesterday and eventually recovered a knife that conforms to Oldfield's supposition about the weapon used to kill Crispin Molyneaux, i.e. a wide-bladed kitchen knife. It's a common enough brand, but even so, it's unlikely that more than one or two of our suspects would have it at home."

"Unless it was bought specifically." Bowden was keen to show that he was on the ball.

"True, but the weapons used at Pendlehurst were whatever was at hand and the screwdriver used to kill Carmine seems to be one that you'd find in many households – and, if you were going to buy something for the purpose, you would go out and buy a knife, not a screwdriver. I'm thinking that the knife used to kill Crispin came from the killer's home." Bowden ceded to his superior's rationale. "The condition of the knife indicates that it had been in the water for less than forty-eight hours, which tallies with the time that Crispin was killed. Forensics found traces of blood and they'll get back to us when it's been analysed. Hopefully, it'll be a match for Crispin's.

"The investigating team at the scene indicate that a struggle had taken place next to Crispin's car. The way that the ground had been disturbed suggests that it had been quite a violent struggle."

"Crispin had regained his senses during the drive from the tennis club to the lake and was fully *compos mentis* when his murderer took him out of the boot." Kershaw was sitting in a chair just behind Bowden.

"The evidence would point to that, Kate. There was a considerable amount of blood on the ground, blood splattered on the bodywork of the car and on one of the rear wheels. The conclusions are that he was stabbed once or twice while he was more or less upright and at least once when he was on the ground. The body was then dragged to where we found it."

"Shoe prints?" Bowden looked hopeful.

"Any prints are indistinct, such that they can't determine a make, or even a type, of shoe." Bowden nodded in disappointment. "The blood in the back of the BMW is definitely that of Crispin, but that really only confirms what we already know. The car's still undergoing analysis.

"John Oldfield's initial findings are that the blow to the head would only have been sufficient to render a fit young man, such as Crispin, temporarily unconscious, but we already know Crispin was still alive when he reached the car park." Wainwright broke off to consult the report he had been holding throughout the briefing. "One of the stab wounds managed to miss all major organs; another punctured the right ventricle of the heart while the third – and, in John's opinion, the probable cause of death - severed the pulmonary artery." He closed the file and looked up. "He also concludes that the assailant was right-handed, which is not a great deal of help. What is of more help is that he found defensive wounds on Crispin's hands and arms which indicate that he put up a fight, which is consistent with a struggle having taken place at the car park. He also found fibres underneath Crispin's fingernails which could, tentatively, be from the type of padded jacket the attacker at the tennis club car park was wearing. They'll need further analysis by forensics to identify them definitively."

Had Gallagher been alert to it, she would have heard the familiar double tap on the glass panel of her office door, followed by the sound of the door opening and Clematis Davenport entering with her second mug of coffee of the morning. As it was, Clematis discovered her boss swivelling from side to side in her chair, vigorously curling her hair between her fingers, apparently oblivious to her secretary's presence. A file lay open on the desk, together with a notepad, the lined page of which was littered with, seemingly, random scrawlings. A pen rested on top of the sheet. Clematis made a space and deposited the 'Mine's a Latte' mug on the back of a discarded envelope.

"Trouble at mill, Ms. Gallagher?" Clematis took the liberty of seating herself in the client chair on the opposite side of the desk. Gallagher ceased her movement and came to rest facing her, with the bemused look of someone unexpectedly confronted by a stranger.

"Sorry, Clemmy. I didn't hear you come in."

"You looked miles away."

"I'm puzzled." To Clematis, that was a statement of the obvious. She leaned forward, encouraging further elucidation. The nails on her left hand were painted in sea green, while those on her right were fuchsia. Both sets had been shaped into parabolic points which caused Gallagher to wonder how she managed to type effectively. "Casey and Carmine were killed without any evidence of a struggle. It seems the killer approached each victim, stabbed them, turned away and left, implying no interaction between them. Had they wanted, they could have killed Crispin in the same way. It wouldn't have been too difficult for anyone that knew him to find him on his own somewhere and commit the murder, but they didn't do that. Perversely, they knocked him out with, it seems reasonable to assume, no intention of killing him, bundled him into the boot of his car, drove him to another location and killed him there. From what I saw of the scene, there had probably been a scuffle, resulting in Crispin's death."

"Maybe 'e 'adn't expected Crispin to regain consciousness."

"But that doesn't answer the question of why go to all that trouble of engineering the charade of knocking him out at the tennis club, then driving him to the lake. They could've found ample opportunities to kill him in the same way as the other two."

"Dare I suggest the obvious?"

"Which is?" Gallagher took a sip of her coffee.

"That there's two murderers?" Her boss remained unmoved at the theory.

"I'd briefly considered it, Clemmy, but no. I'm convinced one person killed all three; one person who was known to all three."

"OK, but 'e still might not 'ave expected 'im to 'ave regained consciousness." Clemmy sat upright and adjusted the purple, velvet scrunchy holding her high ponytail in place.

"I think they had expected him to. That's what's puzzling me." Not having any further suggestion and not really following Gallagher's thread, Clemmy remained silent. "I think they wanted to confront Crispin, but on their own terms. They knocked him out, drove him to the lake, dragged him out of the boot, then…" She took another sip of coffee.

"Then?"

"Then, I'm supposing there was some sort of interaction. Either, they had something to say to Crispin, or they wanted to hear something from Crispin. Either way, they wanted Crispin to know that he was about to be killed. Hence the scuffle. This murder was intensely personal. The other two were simply collateral damage that occurred, contrarily, before the main event."

"So what you're saying is, Crispin Molyneaux was the intended victim all along." That, to Clematis, seemed like the logical conclusion.

"Except that there must have been a reason for killing Casey and Carmine beforehand."

"So Casey and Carmine 'ad to be killed before Crispin were killed." Clematis had the distinct sense that they were going around in circles and she was quite relieved when Gallagher's mobile rang. Her boss instinctively leaned down, set her bag upright, from where it had toppled over as a result of her previous swivelling, and plunged her hand into it to get at the insistent phone.

"Nick!" On hearing the name, Clematis immediately began to get to her feet, not wishing to trespass upon a personal call, but Gallagher motioned to her to resume her seat. Reluctantly, she complied.

"I'm always busy, Nick. …

… I can make time. …

… Give me a moment." Gallagher trapped the phone between her ear and her shoulder and began tapping away at her keyboard until she had retrieved the wedding photos. Before resuming the conversation she indicated to Clematis that she should join her on her side of the desk so that she could see the computer screen and, her secretary presumed, could hear what Nick was saying. "OK. What am I supposed to be looking at?" As was his inclination, Nick had numbered all the photos to make it easier to identify them.

"I'm not sure how useful any of this is going to be, but it's been quiet this morning and I was looking at all the photos again and made one or two observations that may or may not be relevant."

"At this stage, Nick, anything could be useful."

"Can you find…" He proceeded to list four numbers. "Got them?"

"Give me time."

"As you know, I always take several photos of any specific group and then select the best one to go into the portfolio that's sent to the client."

"I've got them all now." They were the photos of the immediate family group.

"You'll notice that, in all of the photos, while everyone else is doing as they're told and looking at the camera, Rupert is looking away."

"Rupert is very self-conscious; he doesn't like making eye contact, not even, I suspect, with a camera."

"I know; you said. That's why I didn't take much notice of it. And, maybe, why you didn't, either."

"Take notice of what?" Gallagher glanced up at Clematis and raised her eyebrows. Clematis smiled, indulgently.

"They're four separate photos. In between each shot I make little adjustments; small rearrangements. The interval is only short, but the subjects have time to take a breath and recompose themselves for the next shot." Gallagher waited for him to come to the point, knowing that it would be futile to try and hurry him. "You might expect Rupert to be looking in a slightly different direction each time, but he's not. I know he's standing immediately behind – and between – Crispin and Magenta, but you can clearly see his eyes are resolutely fixed on Magenta." Gallagher and Clematis peered more closely at the screen as the former flicked between the photos.

"You're right, Nick. He does seem fixated on her, though he could just be staring down her cleavage, which might be understandable, if not excusable."

"There are some other pictures you might be interested in, again, if you hadn't already noticed them. Some of the more informal ones."

"I'm ready." She had invariably focused her attention on the photos featuring the most likely suspects and had not given the other, less formal shots, a great deal of scrutiny.

"Number twenty seven."

"Got it."

"Right centre you can see the Applebys and Casey Hardacre apparently in conversation. Look at Lewis's body language. It's definitely hostile. And look at Casey's right hand. He seems to be trying to reason with him."

"So they were arguing about something."

"Possibly the bad investment." Clematis, quick-witted as ever, drew the inference before her boss.

"Possibly, Clemmy."

"But look at Vivienne." Clearly Nick had heard Clematis' interjection, but he continued, regardless. "She's very passive; almost embarrassed. And look at Casey's left hand." Gallagher and Clematis again leaned in towards the screen. "You probably can't see it very well, but when I enlarged that section, his fingers are touching hers. And I don't have the sense it's accidental." Gallagher and Clematis looked at one another and exchanged a tacit understanding. "Moving on. Photo thirty four." He gave her time to locate the picture.

"OK."

"In the background, on the left, close to The Alice Nutter Barn you can see David Molyneaux and Laura Seacroft. They're easily recognisable from their dress."

"I see them."

"As you can probably make out, she's leaning over and appears to be whispering something to him."

"It looks perfectly innocent." Gallagher suspected that his enthusiasm was leading him to stray into conspiracy territory.

"Possibly, but what you can't see, until you zoom in, is David's arm, the one furthest from the camera and largely hidden. You can just see it in the gap between their bodies. From the position of the arm, I would deduce, as a professional photographer, that his hand was either on her thigh or grabbing her arse."

A few further words were exchanged between Gallagher and Nick before the call was terminated and Clematis returned to the seat on the other side of the desk.

"Some interesting little details there that puts a different complexion on various matters. Nick implied that Laura Seacroft and David Molyneaux were closer than they might care to admit. When I spoke to them it was Laura who pointed out that the two families had different lifestyles and it was David who was the less subtle in expressing his disapproval of the wedding. They were the two that were most keen to distance themselves from one another. Maybe there was an ulterior motive there. Could it be that they were going out of their way to conceal an affair? I can't really see it, but maybe a case of opposites attract. But if they are having an affair, where does that leave us?" Clematis was only half listening; she was following her own train of thought. "Clemmy?"

"Sorry, Ms. Gallagher. I were listening. It's possible. We both know there's been odder couples than them. I were also thinking about Casey and what Nick said about 'im."

"What about him?"

"While Casey and Lewis were apparently arguing, Casey were touching Vivienne's 'and Nick said 'e didn't think it were accidental. Vivienne don't seem to mind – and she were staying out the argument."

"You think there's something between them?"

"From what you told me about what that woman Casey 'ad it off with at the wedding – what were 'er name? – said…"

"Hold on a minute." Gallagher shuffled through her notes until she found the relevant sheet of paper. "Tez Garrity."

"That's 'er. She said it were Casey that initiated the rendezvous."

"Yes."

"Maybe there were more to Casey than met the eye. Maybe 'e fancied 'imself as a bit of a ladies' man. Coming on to Vivienne and getting it off with Tez."

"And if he'd hit on Vivienne around the time they were discussing investments and Lewis suspected something was going on…" The two women looked at one another with meaningful expressions. "I think I need to make a few more house calls."

Gallagher was aware that schools tended to take their lunch breaks relatively early and assumed that Waddington College, at which Vivienne Appleby worked, would be no exception. Indeed, she had recollections of a previous case, involving a member of staff at that college, where that had been established. She tried calling Mrs. Appleby but, unsurprisingly, the call had gone straight to voicemail, convincing her that Vivienne preferred the distraction of work to being sat at home, brooding. She left a message, requesting, on the most innocuous pretence, to meet her during her lunch break. Lewis Appleby, she reckoned, could wait until after she had had spoken to his wife. He worked for a large, independent clothing retailer near the centre of town and, as long as he was in his office, he would, she knew, be able to make himself available at virtually any time. Vivienne duly got back to her and, having stationed herself in Padiham, in anticipation, she was able to meet Mrs. Appleby, at the bus stop, near the school gates, without unnecessary delay. She appeared wearing a short-sleeved, tie-necked, apple green blouse over black trousers, with crisp creases and black, medium-heeled shoes. Appreciating that her interviewee's time was at a premium, she wasted little time, other than the requisite pleasantries and expressions of condolence, in getting to the point.

"One of Nick Corvino's photographs, taken at Crispin and Magenta's wedding, shows you, your husband and Casey Hardacre together."

"Probably. It's what happens at weddings."

"Casey and Lewis appear to be arguing."

"Do they?" Gallagher could not be sure if the indifference was feigned or genuine.

"Can you remember what the argument was about?"

"I don't recall an argument, Ms. Gallagher."

"I have the picture. Maybe it would refresh your memory." Gallagher did not have Nick's portfolio with her, but experience informed her that human nature would justify the bluff. The pause that followed confirmed her theory.

"Yes, now I think about it, there was a little bit of a disagreement."

"About?"

"I can't remember the details."

"But I imagine it was about the investment that lost you money."

"Probably."

"In the photo you don't seem particularly engaged in the argument. In fact, you almost seem embarrassed by it."

"I was probably worried that Lewis… that they were going to cause a scene, which would've spoiled the wedding."

"Did your husband start the argument?"

"No. I mean," she quickly corrected herself, "Casey began talking shop; finance; investments. It probably wasn't the wisest thing to do. That set off Lewis."

"But not you."

"It still irks Lewis. Yes, I'm still upset about it. We lost a lot of money – a lot of money for us – but investment is a risk. Perhaps Casey should have been more judicious, but he wasn't. There's nothing we could've done about it. Casey always maintained he'd done his best for us, but we were unlucky."

"How well did you know Casey?"

"I knew him. He was Cris's friend. Cris introduced us."

"No more than that?"

"What do you mean?"

"How close were you?"

"Close?" Vivienne suddenly realised the direction the questioning was taking. "What are you implying?"

"Was there anything between you and Casey?"

"Absolutely not! What on earth gave you that idea?"

"The photograph shows you and Casey, well... not quite holding hands, but..."

"Don't be ridiculous. Look, is this really necessary? My brother was murdered forty-eight hours ago..." She let the sentence hang, not knowing how she had intended to finish it.

"I know it's hard, but I have to ask." She paused to let Vivienne recompose herself. "So there was nothing between you."

"No." The denial was emphatic, but Gallagher gave her time to reconsider.

"Casey could be a bit of a flirt."

"He flirted with you?"

"I think he flirted with all the women, but I never encouraged it. At all."

"Did Lewis notice?"

"I doubt it. He didn't make it that obvious."

"Suppose he had noticed?" Vivienne shrugged. "Suppose he did notice and suspected you of infidelity."

"Lewis knows me better. He knows I'd never be unfaithful."

"Suppose your husband thought Casey was out to steal his wife, having first stolen his money."

"Our money." The emphasis on the pronoun added to her fluster. "What are you implying?"

"I'm not implying anything, Mrs. Appleby. I'm just trying to get to the truth."

Lewis Appleby's office was on the second floor, above the two trading floors, of the clothing store located on a small retail park on the edge of the town centre. It was, Gallagher had noted,

113

little more than a stone's throw from Thornby Veterinary Clinic and the site of Carmine Seacroft's murder. The office was small, but comfortable. A grey desk with rosewood-effect top dominated the room. Three, wood-framed, blue-upholstered office armchairs were scattered, seemingly randomly about the room. Deep red carpet tiles added a modicum of warmth and welcome to the room. The window, behind Appleby's faux leather chair, looked out over the greenery that attempted to conceal the railway line. A couple of framed certificates took pride of place either side of the window. Two rails of clothes – one of ladies', one of men's - were pressed against the walls flanking the desk. Smartly dressed in a charcoal grey suit, pale blue shirt and plain grey tie, he appeared, like his wife, to be putting on a brave face.

"It's good of you to see me at such short notice."

"I can't say I'm pleased to see you" the comment, Gallagher inferred, was not intended as an insult, but rather a wish that circumstances had not required her visit "and I don't know what I can tell you that I haven't already told the police."

"I understand. I'll not keep you long. I just wanted to clarify a detail in one of the wedding photographs."

"What sort of detail?" He did not look, or sound, perturbed and Gallagher concluded that Vivienne had not contacted him between leaving her at the bus stop and entering his office.

"In one of the photos you and Casey appeared to be having an argument."

"Did we?"

"Were you?"

"Possibly."

"What was the argument about?" Appleby pondered the question, leaned forward, rested his forearms on the desk and clasped his hands together.

"I've nothing against him, but he liked to think of himself as a big shot in the world of finance, despite the fact that he was only working for a small company. He started bragging about a couple of successes he'd had recently. I reminded him that his handling of our investment had been less than stellar."

114

"Is that it?"

"That's it. It didn't amount to much. It was over as quickly as it started."

"You didn't argue about anything else?"

"Like what?"

"I don't know. I'm just trying to establish the facts."

"No."

Given that Laura Seacroft conducted most of her business from home, Gallagher had reckoned that was where she would find her. She drove slowly passed the entrance to the cottage and noted the purple Volkswagen, which she had, for no good reason, attributed to Mrs. Seacroft, parked on the drive, confirming her hypothesis. She continued on and pulled up in the same gateway that she had used previously. She sat for a moment or two, considering her plan of action, glanced at her watch, then turned and searched for her phone in the tan shoulder bag lying on the passenger seat.

"David Molyneaux?"

"Speaking."

"It's Bethany Gallagher."

"Oh." He sounded disappointed rather than irritated, which she regarded as a positive.

"I'm sorry to bother you,…"

"It's no bother." The abruptness of the interjection and the tone of voice suggested that it was highly bothersome.

"I just wanted to clarify a couple of details with you. I wonder if I could call in and see you this afternoon."

"I'm on site all afternoon." There was an air of finality in the statement.

"I'll only need ten minutes of your time. I could come round to wherever you're working." She could hear his mind trying to think up an excuse for rejecting the suggestion.

"We're redeveloping the old industrial site on Slater Street."

"In Burnley?"

"Yes."

"I'll meet you there at four." She had no idea where Slater

Street was, but she always kept her A-Z with her and was confident that would enlighten her.

"You'll have to find me."

"I will." She ended the call before he could find a reason for thwarting her plans."

Feeling satisfied with her machinations thus far, Gallagher clambered out of the car, leaned back in to retrieve her bag, slipped her phone into it, closed and locked the door and strode, purposefully, back towards the Seacroft cottage. The door was only opened at the second time of asking, but she did receive a welcome that was cordial, if not warm. Mrs. Seacroft's first question was simply to ask if Gallagher was bringing her positive news regarding the killing of her daughter and son-in-law. Reluctantly, Gallagher had to confess that she was not; that she was only there to clarify a few details. Nevertheless, Laura was happy to ask her into the lounge and, once again, invited her to take a seat on the sofa. There followed several awkward pleasantries, during which Gallagher gained the impression that they were alone in the house.

"Is Magenta not here?"

"She's gone to work. I tried to dissuade her, but she was adamant. She thought it would be preferable to mooching around here." Gallagher nodded.

"That would explain the absence of a police presence outside."

"Yes. They follow her everywhere. They're very good. They keep her in sight, but try not to be intrusive."

"Where does she work?"

"At the art shop in town. She's a picture framer. She graduated in fine art and hopes to become a qualified restorer one day." Again, Gallagher nodded. "You wanted to clarify some details."

"I was wondering how close you and the Molyneauxs were." The question clearly took the woman aback.

"How close?"

"Yes. The marriage of Magenta to Crispin threw you and the Molyneauxs together, when you wouldn't normally revolve in the same circles. Both you and them said that you live very different lifestyles."

"True, but we get along well enough. They're very pleasant people, but with different values."

"Values?"

"David especially, being in the construction industry, but also Vanessa. She lives in a world of figures, preoccupied with balancing the books. They live in a world of business and commerce; we are more the artistic, creative types. David's the epitome of the corporeal world – literally, bricks and mortar – while I'm more the epitome of the psychical world." Gallagher noted that she took the first opportunity she had to distance herself from David Molyneaux. "Chalk and cheese really." She smiled, disarmingly. "Why are you asking?"

"I've been re-examining the photos Nick Corvino took at the wedding."

"Yes?"

"There's one photo that clearly captures you and David in the background, standing by the barn."

"Quite probably. I'm sure we fraternized." The woman was, as yet, unruffled, which made Gallagher begin to doubt her interpretation of the image.

"You seemed very close."

"How do you mean?" There was a slight uncertainty in the question.

"You were standing very close together, closer than might be expected of two people merely fraternizing." She deliberately used Laura's own word. You seemed to be whispering something to him and, when the photo was blown up, he clearly had his hand on your backside." Mrs. Seacroft forced an embarrassed chuckle.

"I don't know what you're implying, Ms. Gallagher, but if you're suggesting there's something going on between me and David Molyneaux, let me categorically disabuse you."

"I'm not implying anything, Laura; I'm simply trying to clarify an observation." Laura was about to retort, but thought better of it and swallowed the words. "Of course, if you and David do have more in common than you claim, it's none of my business, but I'm just trying to get a grasp of the bigger picture."

"I've just had that private detective, Gallagher, here."
"Gallagher?"
"Yes. She's the woman…"
"I know who she is, Laura. She's just been with you?"
"Yes. Why?"
"She called me earlier this afternoon, wanting to talk to me. What does she want?"
"Said she wanted to clarify some details, but…"
"That's what she told me. I said I was working on site today, but she insisted on coming to see me."
"What did she say to you, David?"
"She's coming here at four." There was a lull while Mrs. Seacroft attempted to make sense of events. "What did she say to you?"
"I think she knows; or, at least, suspects."
"Knows what?"
"About us."
"Us? How could she possibly know? We've always been very discreet."
"There's a photo. From the wedding." This time, it was Mr. Molyneaux that caused the hiatus as he, in turn, tried to make sense of the unexpected twist.
"What did you say to her?"
"Nothing. There's nothing to say, is there?"
"Of course not."
"But she's a crafty bitch. She probably reckoned I'd be at home, but wanted to make sure she could talk to you immediately afterwards. She wants to play us off against each other. But I don't even know what relevance it has. Where are you?"
"Slater Street."
"Couldn't you make yourself scarce? Maybe tell one your guys to tell her you'd been called back to the office, or something?" Molyneaux thought about the proposal for a moment.
"That wouldn't look good. She'd suspect you'd been in touch

with me and I'd taken flight to avoid her. That'd just make us look guilty, though of what, I don't know. Anyway, she'd catch up with me sooner or later. Better to face down her questions now."

Gallagher had little difficulty finding the derelict site at Slater Street, where once had stood a cotton mill and a collection of associated factories. A high, wire fence had been erected around the perimeter, with notices attached at intervals warning people to keep out, but the access gate was open. She parked alongside the disused, overgrown and barricaded car park opposite. The site was populated with a variety of vans, trucks and heavy plant, some emblazoned with the name 'Molyneaux Construction', but only a couple of which appeared to be doing anything. She approached a hard-hatted, hi-vis suited employee and asked where she could find David Molyneaux and was directed towards a corner of the site with a distinct economy of speech. On approaching the corner, where a gaggle of men were in animated conversation, Molyneaux, having evidently spotted her, emerged from behind a truck mounted crane, painted in the company's brick red livery, and strode to meet her.

"You found me, then." He removed a glove and extended his hand. The yellow jacket and safety boots seemed almost comical worn in conjunction with a suit, formal shirt and tie – a little like, Gallagher mused, the attire sported by government ministers on location at a project about which they were expected to know everything but, in reality, knew nothing.

"I always find people I'm looking for, David." She shook his hand. "It's good of you to see me."

"Not at all, especially if it helps find my son's murderer. And, of course, Carmine's and Casey's. You wanted to clarify some details."

"I was wondering about your relationship with the Seacrofts."

"Relationship. How do you mean?"

"You hinted, previously, that you didn't have a lot in common with them." He shrugged.

"That's right. We don't. They're both very arty-farty. We're

119

more down to earth."

"How do you get on with Laura Seacroft?"

"Laura?" He waited for her to add something, but she declined, making him feel uncomfortable. "She's into all her psychic stuff: astrology, crystals and suchlike. Load of old codswallop, if you ask me." Gallagher perceived that just as Laura had attempted to distance herself from him, so he was trying to distance himself from her.

"I was examining Nick Corvino's wedding photos again. There's one in particular." He remained impassive, pointedly not prompting her to continue. Nevertheless, she went on to outline the content of that particular photo, just as she had done with Mrs. Seacroft. From his consciously restrained reaction, it was clear that he knew what she talking about, from which, she deduced, Laura had been in contact with Molyneaux, to forewarn him, after she had left Wellgate, suggesting they had something to hide and needed to align their stories.

"I think you're misinterpreting a perfectly innocent chat between in-laws."

"You think so?"

"You can read anything you want to in any photo." He was doing his best not to show his irritation at her insinuation.

"The camera doesn't lie."

"What you're suggesting is ridiculous and, quite frankly, offensive. And even if it was true, I don't see what it would have to do with the death of Crispin."

"I'm not passing judgement, David; I'm just trying to understand the bigger picture."

"I can assure you, Ms. Gallagher, there's nothing going on between me and Laura Seacroft. Now, you've had your ten minutes and I have work to do."

XI

MEETINGS

The morning drizzle kept the patrons of Café Cleo inside. Only a couple of hardy souls were huddled under an umbrella at an outside table. Wainwright returned from the counter with a tray bearing an Americano, which he set, somewhat haphazardly, on the table in front of one of the vacant chairs, tossed the three sachets of sugar onto the table and, with a little more grace, placed Gallagher's latte in front of her, together with a cinnamon bun.

"Thank you."

"You're welcome." He seated himself opposite her. His navy blue suit was complemented by a duck egg blue shirt and an indigo and buff striped tie, fastened at his throat with a half Windsor knot. The buff colour was welcome relief from the unrelenting blue with which she would otherwise have been confronted. "You said you had some information."

"More like observations, only one of which I've been able to confirm." She sipped her latte cautiously, then took a bite out of her bun. Wainwright, with an air of ritual, emptied the sugars into his coffee, stirred it vigorously, lifted it to his lips, blew across the surface to cool it and took a sip.

"Any little scrap of information could be useful at the moment."

"Not going well."

"Very little physical evidence and no real motive to account for all three murders."

"One of Nick's photos caught David Molyneaux and Laura Seacroft in the background. They weren't caught in a compromising position – they'd have had more sense than to do that – but they were, clearly, intimate." Wainwright took another sip of coffee. "I spoke to both of them. Both were very keen to distance themselves from one another, but both were rattled. What's more, after I'd spoken to Laura, she'd clearly called David to warn him. There's certainly something going on there."

"You think they're having an affair?"

"Almost certainly."

"Interesting."

"But I can't see how that connects to the murders."

"Coincidence?"

"That the mother of the bride and the father of the groom are shagging one another? Really?"

"If it's not, then you're implying that they're somehow implicated, directly or indirectly, in the murder of his son and her daughter, as well as Casey Hardacre."

"Yes. But I don't see how or why." She took another sip of her latte; Wainwright slurped his Americano.

"You said 'observations'; plural."

"Another photo shows Lewis Appleby and Casey Hardacre arguing at the wedding. Vivienne was with them. Again, I spoke to them separately and neither denied they were arguing about the investment that went bad. Vivienne played it down and that may have been because Casey appeared to be flirting with her. If Lewis thought that his wife was having an affair with Casey, coming on top of the investment matter…"

"That might give him a motive for killing Casey."

"But what motive could he have for killing Carmine or Crispin?"

"It could be worth looking into a bit deeper." Gallagher took another bite of bun. "Anything else?"

"Nick always takes several photos of the same subject and selects the best one to add to his client's portfolio. In all the photos he took of the family group, Rupert is looking over Magenta's shoulder; he can't seem to avert his gaze from her cleavage." Wainwright smiled.

"Understandable."

"Quite possibly - I think it grabbed Nick's attention – but you'd have thought he could have been persuaded to look towards the camera just once."

"You think there's more to it?"

"I don't know, but you'd have thought even Rupert could have managed to face the camera for a wedding photo." She brushed a few crumbs of bun from her apricot, keyhole top and took another sip of coffee. "Have you got anything else on Crispin's murder?"

"Not a lot, I'm afraid." Given that she had volunteered to give him some information, he was happy to reciprocate with what he knew about Crispin Molyneaux's killing. "Oldfield seems to think he put up a considerable struggle before he was killed." Gallagher, in turn, advanced the hypothesis that she had shared with Clematis Davenport. "So, you think the killer wanted Crispin alive until they could say their piece; get whatever it was, off their chest. When he realised they intended to kill him, he put up a fight, but to no avail."

"I was thinking, even with a head wound and the trauma of being bundled into the boot of a car and driven somewhere, his survival instinct would have kicked in and an athletic young man like Crispin, would have been a match for most people."

"Suggesting his assailant was as fit and healthy as he was."

"And probably a man. I don't think any of the women on our suspect list would have had the strength to overpower him."

"Unless he was still groggy and just flailing against the odds. As you say, instinct."

Her mother had made and packed, in a neat plastic container, a pastrami and avocado sandwich, to which she had added a banana. There was a kettle in the office and she had her own, William Morris inspired mug there. It was not, strictly speaking, an office; rather, a back room cluttered with frames, no two of which ever seemed to be alike, mount boarding, equally varied, plastic and glass glazing, rolls of tape and other materials requisite to the work of a picture-framer. At one end of the room was a computer that was slow and somewhat temperamental, but which sufficed for the necessary admin associated with the business. Two, much newer computers, used essentially for design work, were located in the adjoining workshop. As a rule, she liked to go out of the shop for lunch, but did not enjoy the sense of being followed, as necessitated by present circumstances. The police protection officers were, to their credit, as discreet as they could be, but she could not avoid being aware of their presence. In the past, she had sometimes met her sister for lunch and, occasionally, had arranged a rendezvous with Crispin. Those times seemed like a bygone era now, yet she still half expected her phone to ring and to hear Carmine or Crispin at the other end, ready to suggest meeting up for lunch. Thus, it came as a slight shock when her phone did ring. She balanced the barely started sandwich on the corner rim of the box, brushed off her fingers, stretched out for her bag, squashed on to one of the few available spaces on the work surface, fiddled around inside it and retrieved the phone. She looked at the screen and instinctively raised her eyebrows and let loose a little, bemused grunt. She pressed the button to answer the call.

"Hi, Rupert. This is a surprise."

"Hi, Madge. Hope it's not inconvenient to call."

"Not at all. I've just started my lunch break."

"I thought you might of done." There was void, during which Rupert tried to collect his thoughts and formulate his words, and which Magenta felt obliged to fill.

"Is everything alright?"

"Yes. How's things with you?"

"I'm coping. One day at a time."

"Yes. That's all you can do. It's all any of us can do. Have you heard anything?"

"From the police? No. They don't seem to be making much progress. Mum and dad are getting increasingly agitated about the lack of developments. And about the protection. How long it's going to be necessary for. It can get a little intense."

"Yes. I was thinking about that."

"About what?"

"About your situation. I mean, I hope the police do make a breakthrough soon. We all want to see the killer caught. You don't want to have to have protection forever. I was thinking it might be getting a bit claustrophobic for you. Staying with your parents and you all being on edge."

"It is, but they prefer me to be there, where they know I'm safe. They don't worry as much." There was another pause in which Rupert battled to arrange his thoughts.

"I was wondering if you might like to come for a drink tonight. At a pub, or something."

"A drink?"

"Just to get out of the house for a couple of hours. I mean. I know the police will be there, but I thought getting out of the house for a couple of hours…" He was going to say 'might do you good', but thought better of it; in his head it implied that it would be good to forget about the murder of her sister and husband for a couple of hours, which he realised she would not want to do, even if she could.

"It's a nice thought, Rupe, but I'm OK. Really."

"I just thought escaping for a couple of hours might… help."

"I'm not sure…"

"It's OK if you don't want to, Madge, or you don't think it's appropriate. There's no pressure. I just thought it might help. I know I'm finding it difficult to process what's happened." He sensed her mulling over his proposition, but did not want to press his case too hard lest doing so should prove counterproductive.

"I guess an hour or so wouldn't hurt – and I would be quite glad to get away from the house. It's a bit of an emotional roller-coaster."

"It'll probably do us both good. Just to share stuff." He paused, realising that the onus was on him to suggest a venue. "Somewhere near you, perhaps?" He gave her time to propose a suitable meeting place, close to her parents' house.

"The Coachman? On the corner? I can walk there."

"That sounds good. Seven o'clock?"

"That's fine."

"I'll see you there."

"Tez Garrity would like to speak to you."

"Tez?" The name was familiar, but she did not quite have a context for it. "Put her through, Clemmy." There was the usual hiatus as Clematis Davenport transferred the call from the outer office to Gallagher's inner sanctum. "Ms. Garrity."

"Bethany Gallagher?"

"Speaking. What can I do for you?"

"I wondered if I could come in and talk to you."

"In connection with?" Gallagher had a recollection of Garrity's name cropping up in connection with the recent spate of murders, but she was not one to make assumptions.

"The wedding murders." The Wedding Murders. That was what the press had dubbed them.

"Can't you talk to me over the phone?"

"I'm at work. I've only got a few minutes free between clients. Can I come to your office after work?"

"What time?"

"I'm in Colne. I finish at five. Quarter past?"

"I'll be here."

"Thank you, Ms. Gallagher. I've got to go. See you later."

Having consulted Clematis immediately after putting the phone down, her secretary confirmed that Tez Garrity had never been to the office before, but clearly she knew where the office was, unless she had inadvertently forgotten to ask, and that Gallagher was party to the investigation.

Gallagher was standing at the window of the main office, coiling a few locks of hair between her fingers and pondering the shafts of light that pierced the clouds and descended to the ground, somewhere beyond the trees on the far side of the canal. Clematis had gone home and she was alone. It was somewhere between five fifteen and five twenty when the door opened. She knew that because she had glanced at her watch a couple of minutes prior to the sound of the door interrupting her thoughts. She turned round and heaved herself away from the windowsill. The slim woman, with long, straight, strawberry blonde hair, styled with a playful fringe, wearing a contour-hugging pink top, brown, velvet miniskirt and pink, leopard-print ankle boots approached tentatively. The lack of office bustle appeared to unnerve her. Gallagher greeted her, in the centre of the room,

126

with a formal handshake.

"Come through to my office." She could have conducted the conversation in the outer office, but she felt more comfortable doing so in her own space. She led the way and Ms. Garrity followed. "Please, sit down." Gallagher indicated the client chair with a perfunctory wave of her hand, while walking around the desk to her own seat.

"Thank you." She seemed to eye the chair suspiciously before accepting the invitation.

"You wanted to talk to me about the killing of Casey Hardacre, Carmine Seacroft and Crispin Molyneaux."

"Yes."

"How did you get my name?"

"I'm a friend of Madge – Magenta Seacroft. Molyneaux." She flushed, embarrassed by her error. "She gave me your name and I Googled you." She smiled. Gallagher nodded.

"Do you have some information that might be relevant to the case?"

"Maybe. I think so. I'm not sure."

"Why haven't you gone to the police?" Again, woman's face reddened slightly.

"I'd prefer not to. They know I was the woman that met Casey on the night he was murdered, but… I don't want to risk my boyfriend finding out. I thought there'd be less risk if… if I came to you. Also…" She continued hurriedly, but then stopped abruptly.

"Also?"

"Also, I don't know if it is relevant. I only thought of it afterwards, like. It doesn't seem like much, but it's been playing on my mind. I thought you could decide."

"OK." Gallagher drew a notepad towards her, flipped it over to a fresh page and hunted around for a pen, eventually finding one lodged under the desk phone. "How do you spell your name?"

"It's Theresa, but everyone calls me Tez. Garrity." She proceeded to spell out her surname and Gallagher wrote it at the top of her sheet in block capitals, underlining each name separately, then added the date to one side.

"Talk to me, then, Tez." She kept hold of the pen, but leaned back in her chair and gave an almost imperceptible side to side swivel.

"It was about the time that Casey asked me to meet him behind the stables. Before he came over to me, I noticed him talking to Rupert – Rupert Molyneaux; Crispin's brother. Rupert was doing most of the talking and he didn't, like, look very happy. Casey put his arm around his shoulders, but Rupert shrugged him off. I know Rupert has difficulty in social situations and I suppose a wedding would be a nightmare situation for him. I just put it down to him feeling overwhelmed, like." Gallagher leaned forward again and made a couple of notes, more to reassure Tez that she was paying attention than out of necessity.

"Go on."

"When Casey came over to me, Rupert just stood there, watching him. After we'd arranged our…"

"Tryst?"

"Yes." She blushed again. "Sorry. Casey wandered off, casual as you like, and I saw that Rupert had moved to the side of the room, near the door, but he was still staring at Casey."

"Anything else?"

"No. I turned away. I was turned on by the prospect of a furtive fuck behind the stables with this feller, but didn't want to give the game away by… you know, looking at him. I didn't think anything of it at the time. I just put it down to Rupert's social awkwardness, but afterwards I, like, wondered if there was more to it." Gallagher contemplated the notes she had made before looking back at Tez.

"At what time did all this happen?"

"Between about quarter to nine and nine o'clock, I suppose. Casey asked me to give him ten minutes and then I followed him out at about nine."

"Was Rupert still by the door when you went out?"

"I didn't notice." She shrugged and smiled. "I had other things on my mind."

* * * * *

128

There were only two cars in the small car park to the side of The Coachman, but then, Molyneaux reasoned to himself, it was a Tuesday night. He reversed his blue, MG3 into a corner, switched off the engine and took a long, studious look at his watch. Ten to seven. Wherever he went, he liked to be early. He peered through the windscreen. There were still more grey clouds than there was blue sky, but it was a pleasant enough evening. He got out, locked the car, wandered around to the front and took a moment to admire it. He was proud of his little MG. He took a deep breath, composed himself and then strode, purposefully, around to the front of the pub and on to the corner, from which vantage point he would be able to see Magenta walking up the hill. He could see the best part of half a mile down the road, almost to her parents' house which was secreted just around the bend. He glanced at his watch again: six fifty-two. When he looked up, he saw her walking towards him. She was too far away to properly identify her, but he was sure it was her. He followed her progress up the hill. Halfway up she must have recognised him, for she gave him a flamboyant wave. He responded with a brief, hesitant wave of his own.

"Am I late?" She instinctively gave him a peck on the cheek, as she had done many times before.

"Not at all." From a couple more glances at his watch he knew she was five minutes late.

"Yes I am. Sorry." He smiled, sheepishly. He could not deny it, but he did not want to confirm it. She was wearing a loose-fitting, short-sleeved top in grey, with a curve of pink roses extending from her left shoulder to her right hip. The square neckline revealed a hint of cleavage. Her dusky pink trousers were elegant without being inappropriate in the circumstances. Over her head he could see a police car making its way, at a leisurely pace, up the road.

"Shall we go in?"

"Why not." They turned back towards the entrance. She looped her arm, in sisterly fashion, through the crook of his, formed as a result of him having his hands firmly thrust into his jeans pockets for want of knowing what else to do with them.

"I'm glad you suggested this. It is good to get out of the house for a while."

"It's good for me, too." As they reached the doorway, the police car turned the corner and parked up, on the opposite side of the road, ten yards or so beyond the pub.

Once inside, Molyneaux ushered his sister-in-law towards a circular table against a wall, surrounded, somewhat arbitrarily, by three wooden chairs with loose padded seats. Magenta sat in the chair facing the window and with her back to the bar, wedged her handbag between the table leg and the wall and looked up at him, expectantly.

"What would you like?" He became conscious of the nervous feeling in the pit of his stomach, resulting from the realisation that this was probably the first time he had been alone with her in a public place.

"A glass of red wine, please." He gave a brief nod, turned and departed for the bar.

The only other occupants of the pub were an elderly couple, sat on a bench underneath the window on the other side of the doorway, a couple of men standing next to the bar, midway along it, engaged in earnest conversation, and an archetypal old-timer, who looked as if he had been one of the original features of the pub when it had been built, however many years ago, hunched in the farthest corner of the bar with a half-drunk, half pint of dark beer in front of him. The bartender finished wiping down a section of the bar, adjusted the bar cloth and ambled towards his new customer. Molyneaux placed his order, with the minimum of fuss, and waited for it to be fulfilled. He paid for the drinks with a card, carried them back to the table, whereat he found that Magenta had rearranged the two beermats: one in front of herself and one directly opposite where, he supposed, he was expected to sit.

"One glass of The Coachman's finest house red." He set the glass in front of her. She looked up and smiled.

"Thank you." He placed his beer on the other mat and took up his designated seat. A sup of beer helped to mask the awkward silence.

"How are you coping?" She sighed, looked wistfully over his shoulder, then re-focused her attention on his face.

"One day at a time. It's OK when I'm busy at work, but the evenings are long. You?" He shrugged.

"About the same. Work helps, but going back to the flat afterwards... I'm used to being on my own and used to being alone with my thoughts, but when the same grisly thoughts are continually intruding... It's not easy, but, as you say, one day at a time." She patted his wrist.

"I hope they catch who's done this soon."

"So do I. It must be terrible for you. Knowing that... Knowing that you... That the police think you could be next." She took a sip of her wine.

"I try not to think about that."

"No, I'm sorry, Madge. I didn't mean to..."

"It's fine. I feel quite safe. Living here and with the police on guard twenty-four seven. I just want to know why as much as anything. Why Cris? Why Carmine? What did she ever do to hurt anyone? Why Casey?"

"I don't know. I want answers as much as you. They will catch them, though."

"Do you think so? There doesn't seem much likelihood of that at the moment."

"They will, Madge." He clasped her free hand and gave it a gentle squeeze. He felt her fingers respond momentarily before he withdrew. "They probably know more than they're letting on."

"You think?"

"They probably have a suspect in mind. They're probably, quietly, building a case." She smiled, indulgently, and took another sip. She wanted to believe him.

"I can't get it out of my head. Carmine's last moments. Under that bridge; by the canal. Did she know her attacker? Did she try to scream? Was it quick? Did she suffer?" She looked, imploringly, at the man across the table; her brother-in-law; united in grief. "And Cris. He must have been terrified in the boot of his car. Did he struggle? Did he know his attacker? Did they

131

speak?" He took her hand again; she clung to it. He forced a smile.

"It'll be OK, Madge. We'll be OK. They'll find the killer and we'll get through this."

XII

DISCREPANCIES

"Good morning, Beth. What can I do for you this morning?"

"Morning, Danny. Do you know if Rupert Molyneaux has a car?"

"Not off hand, but he probably does. Most people do. Why?"

"Could you pull the details for me?"

"I could if there was a good reason. What are you up to?"

"I'm going over to the museum to check out the CCTV."

"Their CCTV doesn't cover the wedding venue, Beth."

"No, but the museum CCTV probably covers the car park and it'll almost certainly cover the road between the museum and the wedding venue."

"What are you thinking?"

"It may be something; it may be nothing. If it turns out to be something, I'll let you know. Can you get me those vehicle details?"

"It'll take me five minutes. I'll text them to you."

"I appreciate it, Danny. Thanks."

Gallagher had called Wainwright at an opportune moment. He was waiting for his team to assemble and settle themselves in the briefing room and, consequently, had a few minutes to spare. To his dismay, the whiteboard behind him had changed little over the last forty-eight hours. All he was in a position to do was to inform the gathering of the progress in interviewing the wedding attendees. The problem, he conceded, was that, at weddings, people were focused on the happy couple and on having a good time, preferably at someone else's expense. The only development that he had to impart was that the fibres that John

Oldfield had found beneath Crispin Molyneaux's fingernails had been analysed by forensics and found, as surmised, to be the type of polyester commonly used to make the shell of padded jackets. The colour had been identified as navy, which accorded with the clothing of the attacker captured by CCTV at the tennis club. A lack of epithelial or connective tissue (which Oldfield had translated as skin or blood), suggested that the killer's clothing had done its job of preventing any possible transfer of DNA during the course of a struggle.

"Are you still with us, D.S. Bowden?" Wainwright had noticed that Bowden had lapsed into an uncharacteristic state of pensiveness.

"Yes, sir." He looked up, a little startled. "I've been thinking, sir."

"Thinking's always good."

"Yes, sir." He paused to collect his thoughts. "Casey Hardacre was killed on a Saturday."

"Correct."

"Carmine Seacroft was killed three days later on a Tuesday." Unsure of where his detective sergeant was going, Wainwright allowed him to continue, uninterrupted. "Crispin Molyneaux was killed, we believe, on the Friday, three days after that. Coincidence?"

"Our murderer kills their victims at three-day intervals. Why?"

"I don't know, sir, but killers are often creatures of habit; routine. It could be significant."

"But if they were planning to strike again, they would have done so on..." Wainwright paused to make his calculation "...Monday. Two days ago. So what can we infer from that?" Bowden looked blank.

"Maybe, sir," Kershaw had also been applying her mind to the matter, "he had intended to kill again on Monday."

"But?"

"If, as we hypothesised, Magenta Molyneaux is next in his sights, then giving her police protection, may have denied him the opportunity. Maybe they're biding their time; waiting for us to slip up or, possibly, waiting for us to conclude that she's no longer in danger and withdraw protection."

"In which case, we need to be extra vigilant. Get on to the protection team, Kate, and impress on them that they're not to let Magenta out of their sight whenever she's out of the house; not for a second."

"Sir."

When she had entered her office, Gallagher had not even bothered to sit down before calling Wainwright on her mobile. She had not been planning on staying. Immediately after ending the call, she collected her black shoulder bag from where she had temporarily dumped it on the client chair and breezed back out into the main office.

"I'm going over to the witches' museum, Clemmy. I shouldn't be too long. I just need to check on something."

"Don't you want coffee? I've just made it." Clematis, standing by the kettle and coffee mugs, sounded distinctly put out.

"Drink it for me." Before Clematis could respond, her boss had disappeared through the door, closing it, noisily, behind her.

By the time she reached the car park opposite Sycamore Mill she heard a message ping into her phone. She unlocked the Peugeot, climbed in and, with her bag in her lap rooted around for her phone. The text was from the detective inspector. She smiled to herself. If Wainwright had been there, the smile would have been directed at him. He could easily have left calling up the details of Molyneaux's car until he had a few moments to spare but, instead, he had done it immediately. There was no greeting, explanation, or sign off; just the message: MG3. Blue. MR64QVD. She exited the message, replaced the phone in the bag and placed the bag in the passenger footwell.

Within fifteen minutes Gallagher was standing at the reception desk of the Pendle Museum of Witches, awaiting Linda Whitehorn, who had been summoned from her office upstairs. She was not kept waiting long. Mrs. Whitehorn approached, an affable smile on her face and an arm extended in greeting.

"I wasn't expecting to see you again." The two women shook hands. "Is there something I can help you with?"

"I hope so. You don't have CCTV cameras around the wedding venue, do you?" She knew the answer, but thought there was no harm in confirming it.

"No. I feel a wedding…"

"That's OK. I was just checking. But you do have CCTV around the museum."

"Yes."

"Does that cover the road outside this building and, maybe, the venue car park."

"It covers the road outside and the museum car park. It might just catch the wedding venue car park, but it's not specifically designed to do that."

"That's OK. It'd be a bonus if it did. As long as it covers the road. I presume you still have the footage of the day of the Molyneaux wedding."

"We should have. Do you want to see them?"

"Just the one covering the road – and, maybe, the car park."

"They'll be upstairs. Do you want to come up?"

"Thank you." Mrs. Whitehorn turned and led the way back to her office and Gallagher followed, obediently.

It became clear that Linda Whitehorn was very efficient and knew what she was doing. Within minutes of sitting Gallagher down in front of a computer screen – and subsequently pulling up a chair beside her and sitting down herself – she had located the required video and was ready to play it.

"Where do you want to start?" Gallagher gave the question due consideration.

"Let's start at around seven forty-five that evening."

"No problem." Another few clicks of the mouse and Mrs. Whitehorn had moved the video on to the requested time. "Ready?"

"Let's go and let's see what we can see."

"Are you looking for anything specific?"

"Yes." The answered was delivered in a manner that brooked no further discussion. Gallagher took a few seconds to get her bearings. As the manager had indicated, the camera was trained predominantly on the road outside the museum. The arched, wrought iron gate leading to the ornamental garden could clearly be seen. In the bottom, left hand corner of the screen the entrance to the museum car was just visible, while in the top, left hand corner the wedding venue car park could be discerned. "Can you fast forward, please?"

"Of course." Gallagher kept her eyes fixed on the screen, noting the time as it passed. "Tell me when to stop."

"Can you pause there, please." Mrs. Whitehorn did as asked. Gallagher unconsciously grasped a lock of hair and began coiling it around her fingers. The video had stopped at eight seventeen, but no blue car matching the description of Molyneaux's had exited the venue car park or passed by the museum. "Fast forward again, please." Mrs. Whitehorn clicked the mouse. The time moved on to nine o'clock. That was shortly after Theresa Garrity had claimed to have seen Rupert by the door of the stables. The video continued to roll. A couple of cars left the party, but neither was Molyneaux's. "Stop there, please, Linda." The screen froze. A blue car had come out of the car park and had made its way towards them. "Can you go back a little please?"

"No problem." She reversed the video.

"Stop!" Mrs. Whitehorn obeyed. Gallagher leaned in towards the screen. "Can you zoom in on the car, please." Again, she patiently complied. It was not possible to positively identify the driver, but the badge on the front of the car appeared to indicate that it was an MG and while the camera angle precluded being able to read the full registration plate, MR64 was clearly visible. Gallagher sat back. The timestamp was frozen at twenty-one thirty-two.

"Have you got what you want?"

"I think so, Linda. Thank you. Could you forward this video to me?"

"Of course." Gallagher continued to look at the screen, trying, in the moment, to process and rationalise what she had witnessed.

* * * * *

137

What a difference a day makes. After her visit to Pendlehurst, Gallagher had returned to her office, checked her inbox and discovered that Linda Whitehorn had been as good as her word and had forwarded the CCTV footage which she had recently viewed, and had spent the next twenty minutes in her office, with Clematis, watching the pertinent sections again. Having satisfied herself about the import of the video she had called Wainwright and asked him to meet her, which he had agreed to do a couple of hours later. The weather, the previous morning, had been cool and drizzly. This morning, she could almost persuade herself that summer had arrived. She ordered coffee from the counter at Café Cleo on the, so she reckoned, safe assumption that Wainwright would be on time. She considered the purchase of a cinnamon bun for herself, but decided against it. As she carried the tray outside, she caught a glimpse of the detective inspector scurrying down the pedestrianised way as she searched around for a vacant table. There was just one, but, she reasoned, they only needed one. By the time she had reached it, arranged the coffees – and the three packets of sugar to accompany the Americano – on the table, dispensed with the tray and sat down, Wainwright had arrived, clad in the same navy blue suit as yesterday, but augmented, today, by a cream shirt and the tie, horizontally striped in three shades of yellow and orange, that Gallagher thought Mrs. Wainwright might, by now, have surreptitiously donated to a charity shop. He sat down opposite her, effusively thanked her for the coffee, wasted no time in emptying the sugar into it and gave it a brisk stir.

"What have you got for me, Beth, that couldn't wait?"

"I went over to Pendlehurst this morning. By the way, thank you for getting those registration details to me so promptly." Wainwright took a slurp of coffee.

"You're welcome. Were they of any use?" Gallagher sipped her latte.

"Maybe. I'll let you be the judge."

"Go on."

"The CCTV at the museum covers the road between the museum and the wedding venue – and also just catches the venue car park." Wainwright waited for her to continue.

"When I spoke with Rupert Molyneaux he said he'd left the wedding at about eight. He said it'd got all too much for him and he'd had to walk away, which would be very plausible for someone suffering with anxiety, as he evidently does. However, Theresa Garrity came to see me yesterday afternoon."

"Oh?" Wainwright, his cup betwixt saucer and mouth, suddenly looked interested.

"In the light of her assignation with Casey, she was reluctant to come to you and have you stir the pot unnecessarily, especially if what she had to say didn't amount to anything."

"And what did she have to say?" He sounded a little piqued at the implication of police insensitivity.

"She said she'd seen Rupert talking to Casey, immediately before Casey came over to her with his proposition of a bit of illicit sex, and that Rupert didn't look happy. She got the impression that Rupert was upset about something, but, at the time, she put it down to Rupert's difficulty with coping in social situations."

"So that would have been about…"

"Nine."

"An hour after he said he'd left."

"I checked the CCTV from before eight. Rupert clearly didn't leave at that time. The only time his car's seen leaving the venue is just after nine thirty."

"After we think Casey was killed."

"I had the manager send the footage on to me. I'll send it on to you and you can verify it for yourself."

"Thank you, Beth. Interesting."

Dinner was over and the washing up done. The Otis Rush album that Nick had discovered in the vinyl record shop in Nelson was on the turntable, playing it's opening track. He, himself was sprawled in the corner of the sofa, a glass of Old Speckled Hen in one hand and his other arm around Gallagher. Her head was resting on his shoulder and her, as yet, untouched glass of merlot was on the coffee table. He was struggling to find something constructive to say that might offer some insight.

"Maybe he just lost track of time." He did not sound convinced and she was even less convinced.

"An hour and a half?"

"It's a wedding celebration; the booze is flowing. It's not unheard of."

"If he and Casey were arguing about something…"

"No one said they were arguing."

"No, you're right, but if Casey had done or said something to upset him, what could it have possibly been to make him want to kill him?"

"Presumably something that happened at the wedding; unless he'd been harbouring a grudge about something and it all came out after a few drinks."

"Maybe, but he was driving – and I don't see Rupert as a man prone to drinking and driving." She paused, stretched an arm out to retrieve her glass, took a sip of wine and kept hold of it. "What does the best man do at a wedding?" Nick was not sure if the question was intended rhetorically or whether he was expected to give an answer.

"Make sure the groom gets to the church on time; provide the rings at the appropriate time; deliver a speech; make sure everything runs smoothly." He gave her a little squeeze, careful to avoid spilling her drink. "Organise the photographer."

"Well, Crispin seems to have got to the venue on time; there weren't any miscues with the rings, as far as I'm aware, and the photographer was properly organised."

"Something he said in his speech?"

"Casey was chosen because he was a safe pair of hands; guaranteed not to say anything embarrassing."

"Maybe he had a little dig at Rupert and he took it the wrong way."

"So much so that he wanted to kill him? And assuming that was the case, unlikely as it seems, where does that leave Carmine and his brother? What possible reason could he have for killing them?" Whether or not he was expected to provide an answer to that question, Nick did not know, but either way, he did not have one.

XIII

THE PLAYERS

Considering it is little more than a mile from the centre of Burnley, Campion Lake is a relatively secluded spot. The only vehicular access is from the south-west side of it, along Campion Lane. From Brunview Road there is only the obligatory brown sign, directing visitors to the picnic site and car park along the lane, to hint at its presence. The few houses along the lane quickly give way to parkland on the right-hand side, within which lies the lake, and farmland on the left. The farmland is guarded by sheep netting, while low, drystone walling cordons off the parkland, albeit eventually petering out to leave open access. The car park is situated on the left of the lane and about a quarter of a mile along it. The car park itself is of an irregular shape, having been constructed using the natural spaces between the trees, creating a series of parking bays off the main parking area. The once neat, tarmacked surface is now in an advanced state of decay.

When she arrived, there were just a couple of other cars there. It did not surprise her; in fact, she had anticipated as much. There were no young people in sight, though the lake did attract its fair share of truants, and fishermen would often shun the car park and continue down the lane, parking wherever they could, to be as near to the water's edge as possible. The only reason that she was there was because she had arranged to go into school late, given that, on that particular morning, her only class was during the hour immediately before lunch. She reversed the Focus into one of the bays, opened the door to check that she would not be stepping into any residual puddles, then switched the engine off, got out, thought about whether or not she needed to lock the car and decided to err on the side of caution. It was warm enough to be wearing a sleeveless, V-necked top over her jeans and trainers.

She ambled across the car park towards the tattered and fluttering remnants of police tape. The police had concluded their investigation of the site. She stopped at the point at which Crispin's car had been parked and peered down at the ground. What she expected to see, she did not know. A few traces of blood, perhaps? A vital clue, overlooked by the crime scene investigation team? As it was, she saw nothing and continued on, beating a path through the undergrowth, to where Crispin's body had been found. It had not taken long for nature to reclaim the territory. Her eyes flitted, intently, about the area, searching. She squatted down, pushed aside a few straggly shrubs and brambles; parted the coarse grass with her fingers. For what was she looking? Something the police had missed? Something Bethany Gallagher had disregarded? She paused, looked up through the trees, heaved herself to her feet, retraced her steps back to the car park, stopped, turned around with a defiantly inscrutable expression and gazed upon the innocuous site. She wondered if the other people that had passed by there that morning had realised they were tramping over a murder scene.

Rather than returning to her car, she walked out of the car park, followed the lane a little further down the hill and turned into the official entrance to Rowley Lake. While she knew the lake was no more than fifty yards away, it was obscured by the early summer verdancy of the trees. She followed the track until it met the path that circumscribed the lake. The path was raised above the surface of the water, such that, when she looked down upon it, through a gap in the trees, it seemed strangely distant. She could not help but marvel at the efficiency with which the police had recovered the knife that had killed her brother from its depths.

Considering that universities and other such institutes of higher learning are people intensive environments – students being both the main input and output of them, though it may be argued that adolescents are inputted and adults outputted – it often surprises the casual visitor at how few people one sees when passing through their glass-plated doors. It never failed to strike

Rupert Molyneaux just how few people he encountered on his way from the university car park to his purpose-built office at the back of the building. Had it had any eye-level windows, it would have had a view of the car park, but it had been constructed with narrow windows at just below ceiling level (admitting enough light such that the occupant could tell if it was day or night, sunny or overcast) so as to minimize the potential damage to important and valuable books and documents from natural light. The artificial light in the room was meticulously controlled to meet the needs of both paper and people. This morning he met just three fellow members of staff and one student, each of whom he greeted perfunctorily, but cordially. It was not his inclination to stop and exchange a few words about work or weekends, social or professional activities. He scurried along to his archive room where he felt secure and comfortable. Today he would continue to sift through the two boxes of documents, letters, photographs, plans and sundry other items relating to a prominent Victorian building and its inhabitants, demolished half a century previously (the site of which is now occupied by a retail park), which had been donated to the university six weeks earlier. He was in sole command of his domain and spent most of his time working alone, which suited him very well. He always took his own lunch with him and would retire to a corner of the room to eat it, possibly with a newspaper, or a book, or to play a few games of solitaire on his laptop. Sometimes, in summer, he would go and sit in his car to enjoy the natural warmth and sunshine. Virtually his only interaction with other people was when colleagues or students came into the archive room for the purpose of research, but his talk was confined to what was essential to facilitate the requests and requirements of those people. Nevertheless, it had not gone unnoticed by many denizens of the university's corridors, that, since the murder of his brother, he had become yet more brusque and reclusive. They attempted to sympathise, console and support, but were not offended when their efforts were politely rebuffed; they were all aware of the difficulties he experienced in the company of people and occasionally remarked among themselves that he had found the ideal job to be compatible with his temperament. While the women on the campus vied to afford him maternal concern, the men tended to leave him to his own thoughts. Whether those thoughts, on this, or any other morning this week, were of the dead or the living, only he knew.

A construction site is a busy place and, for the managing director of a construction company, if he takes a hands-on approach, there is little time to relax. There are men – and the occasional woman, which David Molyneaux was very happy to employ – machinery and supplies to organise, without unduly encroaching upon his site foreman's territory. This morning, however, he was not on site; he was prowling around his offices, engaging with the secretarial staff and the financial and human resources departments. Several of his conversations were unnecessary and some of the personnel involved found they had to curb their irritation at his superfluous intrusions. However, this was a man whose son had, recently, been brutally murdered and, hence, their willingness to exercise forbearance. It can only be surmised as to the cause of his restlessness. To the casual observer it might have been attributed to the grief occasioned by the loss of his son, but it could also have been, in no small measure, the result of the discomposure felt at the, potentially hazardous, disruption to his hitherto blithe and unsuspected relationship with Mrs. Seacroft.

For Laura Seacroft, Mr. Molyneaux was rapidly becoming a distraction she could well do without. She was more focused on trying to balance the, frequently conflicting, demands of her current household. Mr. Seacroft was becoming increasingly moody with the passing of days. His work absorbed him during the day – he was fastidious in his attention to detail when working on a restoration – but during working hours he was at his workshop. However, when he was at home, the shock, horror and anger at the murder of, first, his daughter and then his son-in-law was ever present and palpable, exacerbated by his frustration at, what he perceived to be, the incompetence of the police in having failed to apprehend the perpetrator. Mrs. Seacroft attempted to alleviate his frustrations with reason and rationality, but to little avail. Concurrently, she was attempting to offer succour and solace to Magenta who, patently, felt the loss of her sister keenly, as well as trying to reassure her in respect of her own safety. Being the rock to which her husband and daughter anchored themselves, as well as the compulsion to maintain her business interests was enervating. She sometimes felt that she had little energy remaining with which to grieve Carmine, although, as she and Warwick agreed, grieving could not properly take place until the murderer of their daughter had been arrested, charged, convicted and duly sentenced. In addition, there was the small matter of how to proceed, or otherwise, with her illicit liaison with David Molyneaux, which had been so unceremoniously impinged upon. It is, however, to be presumed that Mr. Seacroft had no notion of his wife's infidelity with the father of his son-in-law. What can be said, with a high degree of certainty, is that Laura was beginning to experience a sense of disquiet, precipitated by Rupert Molyneaux having visited Magenta twice in the space of two days.

When Richard Fenmore, son of the late founder of Cyril Fenmore Fine Art, had ambled into the workroom, in search of a newly framed watercolour, which was due to be collected by its proud owner that afternoon, he spied Magenta Molyneaux through the permanently open connecting door, sitting on the chair upon which she habitually sat to eat her lunch. Of late, he had found it difficult to talk to her; he did not know what to say. What could he say? Within the space of a week her sister and husband had been killed; murdered. He could not conceive what emotional turmoil must, he assumed, be playing out in her heart and mind. She had only given glimpses of her thoughts and feelings in fleeting, unguarded, teary moments. Words, of a paternal nature, frequently presented themselves, but they invariably sounded, trite, banal, clichéd. Occasionally, he wished she would not come into work, but understood that occupying herself at work was better for her that sitting at home brooding and, as she was as diligent as always, he said nothing on that score. Today, as he caught sight of her, she appeared particularly pensive, chewing mechanically on a sandwich, the uneaten half of which was held in the hand that, absent-mindedly, rested on her knee. He presumed her mind was brimming with thoughts of Carmine and Crispin, but he had no way of knowing. She could, equally, have been musing on her parents or meditating on Rupert Molyneaux. He heard her phone ring and, not wishing to pry, he turned away and continued with his quest to recover the watercolour.

Lewis Appleby had been negotiating a deal with a new supplier for a line of ladies' autumn casualwear. He was now alone in his office, examining the samples the sales representative had left, variously draped over two of the chairs and shrouding one of the clothes rails. He was not a Molyneaux nor a Seacroft; he was an unequivocal in-law. He offered unreserved support to his wife over the murder of her brother, but the death of Carmine Seacroft was probably a little too remote for him to have strong feelings, which would possibly explain a somewhat dispassionate response to it. As for Casey Hardacre, one can only guess at his sentiments. Since the debacle of his investments, there had been no love lost between the two men. He had made no secret of his perception that Vanessa had been prepared to give Hardacre the benefit of the doubt, arguing that any investment was always a risk, rather than criticizing him for his costly ineptitude. Had her attitude fuelled a suspicion that there had been, perhaps, something more between her and Hardacre than simply business? He had never exhibited any petty jealousy, but one never knows what mental machinations are going on just beneath the surface. As he stroked the fabrics and scrutinized the workmanship of the garments, only he was privy to his thoughts.

A hospice is a place of comfort, providing palliative care to those afflicted with a terminal illness. The end, whenever it may come, is inevitable, yet the emphasis is invariably on the positive, offering support, contentment and joy during the last weeks, months or years of a person's life. Vanessa Molyneaux's office was divorced from the hospice itself and, thus, she had little direct contact with the patients. Her job was to balance the books; to keep the hospice running; to make sure the nursing staff had everything they needed to do their jobs effectively. This morning, though, she felt conflicted; torn between the dying in the building beyond and the deceased. The dying, at least, knew why they would be passing on; the dead, in the form of Crispin, Carmine and Casey, would not have had the consolation of knowing. Was it better to know or not to know? She stared out of the window, contemplating the question. It did not take her long to conclude, that it was the wrong question; that she was indulging herself in a conceit. The choice between a peaceful death and a violent one, did not require discussion. She turned away from the window and returned to her desk, the expression on her face, had anyone been in the room to see it, still betraying an internal conflict.

XIV

THE BEST MAN'S SPEECH

The phone call that Richard Fenmore had diplomatically avoided eavesdropping on had been from Bethany Gallagher. Her conversation with Nick, the previous evening, had given her food for thought and she had wanted to try and resolve what was niggling her. Both Casey Hardacre and Crispin Molyneaux being dead, the most likely person to be able to do that was Magenta Molyneaux.

"Magenta? It's Bethany Gallagher." She had only half expected Mrs. Molyneaux to answer, not being familiar with her work schedule.

"Oh, hello."

"I haven't rung at a bad time, have I? I wasn't sure…"

"No, not at all. I'm just on my lunch break."

"Good. I'll not keep you too long. I just have one question that you may be able to answer for me."

"Ask away."

"Presumably Casey Hardacre gave a best man's speech at your wedding."

"Of course. It's traditional. Some aspects of the wedding might have been a little unconventional, but Cris wanted to keep a few traditions."

"And that would have been read from a prepared script."

"Yes. It wasn't terribly long; only a couple of sides of A4, but he had it all written down."

"What happened to the speech afterwards?"

"What happened to it?"

"Did he put it back in his pocket? Did he leave it on the table? Did Crispin, or someone else, pick it up?"

"I don't know."

"Think back, Magenta. It could be important."

"Why?"

"There may be a clue as to why he was murdered in that speech."

"What sort of a clue? He didn't say anything to upset anyone. That's why Cris chose him to be his best man."

"Maybe not, but please think back. Try and remember what happened to it." There was a substantial pause while Magenta gathered her thoughts and tried to visualise what had happened that afternoon.

"Casey stood up, took his speech out of his inside pocket and read it. He was the centre of attention. All eyes were on him. When he finished, he put the speech down, picked up his glass and raised a toast to Crispin and me." She paused, but Gallagher did not interject. "Toast over, he sat down and… yes! The papers were covering his coaster – we had coasters specially made to celebrate the occasion; something guests could take away with them if they wanted. He had to pick them up in order to put his glass down and he automatically folded them and put them back in his pocket."

"The inside pocket of his jacket."

"Yes."

"Thank you. That could be a vital piece of information."

"Could it? How?"

"To be honest, Magenta, I'm not sure at this point in time, but I have a gut feeling that it could be significant."

"Oh." She sounded perplexed.

"Anyway, how are you coping?" Gallagher not wanting to abruptly end the call was, nevertheless, keen to change the subject. She sensed a shrug.

"One day at a time."

"The protection team not being too intrusive?"

"No. They're very good. Most of the time I don't notice they're there."

"Good. And it's good you're with your parents."

"Yes." She did not sound convinced of the assertion.

"But?"

149

"We're all trying to cope with our grief in different ways and sometimes…" She let the sentence hang.

"I understand."

"But Rupert has come round on a couple of occasions and that helps."

"Rupert?"

"Yes. He came round for an hour on Sunday and we sat outside and talked things over. We went out for a drink together on Tuesday – only to the local pub – and it was good to get out of the house for an hour or so. We're the same age and, I suppose, we see things in a similar way. Conversations aren't as intense as with my parents. He's been very kind."

"Beth." It was the sort of tone that suggested that 80% of Wainwright's mind was engaged elsewhere and only 20% was paying attention to the caller.

"Have you got a moment?"

"Not really, but go on."

"Casey Hardacre's jacket."

"What about it?"

"Presumably, after you'd found it, you went through it."

"Naturally." She estimated that she now had 50% of his consciousness. "Which is to say, it would've gone straight to the pathology lab and John Oldfield would've gone through it. Why?"

"But you would know what he'd found."

"He'd have put everything in an evidence box, told me if he'd found anything that he considered significant, but otherwise just sent me an inventory of the contents of its pockets. Why are you interested?"

"Was his best man's speech among the items?"

"Not that I'm aware of. I suppose you want me to check."

"If you don't mind, Danny."

"Bear with me." There was a pause and then she heard the clicking of a keyboard. "Keys, mobile phone, pen, comb. His wallet and cash were found in his trouser pockets. No speech. You still haven't told me why you're interested in it."

"I think it could hold the key to his murder. I think he did or said something at the wedding that provoked someone into killing him. He doesn't appear to have done anything to upset anyone – and as far as we know Theresa Garrity's boyfriend didn't know of their liaison – and he doesn't appear to have said anything to upset anyone, so I'm thinking it must have been something in his speech."

"Grasping at straws a bit there, aren't you?"

"Maybe, but straws seem to be all we have at the moment." Wainwright did not contradict her. "However, I spoke to Magenta again this morning and she's certain that, after Casey had made his speech and done the toast, he put the speech back in his inside pocket."

"Well, we didn't find it."

"Which suggests that someone took it; took it because of what was in it. That's why I think it might hold the key."

"So, we need to find that speech."

"I think so, Danny." There was a brief lull before Gallagher changed the subject. "Did you follow up on the CCTV from Pendlehurst?"

"We spoke to Rupert Molyneaux again, but he insists he must have lost track of time. The occasion, the drink... You know the story."

"Do you buy that?"

"No, but there's nothing to suggest he's lying."

Clematis had become irritated by her boss's restless coming and going between the two offices during the course of the afternoon and, consequently, Gallagher's announcement that she was going to meet Vivienne Appleby was met with a large measure of relief. She had phoned Mrs. Appleby and, discovering that she was still at work, arranged to meet her at the bus stop outside the school, rather than trek all the way over to Hinton. Following their last meeting, it was with considerable reluctance that Vivienne had agreed to do so.

Gallagher had parked in a side street, crossed the main road, dodging the dribble of students belatedly emerging from the school gates and waited. It did not surprise her that Mrs. Appleby was late for the appointment; she concluded that it might have been deliberate, a view substantiated by the fact that, when the woman did appear, she was clearly in no hurry.

"Sorry I'm late. Paperwork." She did not sound apologetic.

"No problem. Shall we sit?" The seat at the bus stop was vacant. Mrs. Appleby shrugged and sat herself down. "I'll not keep you long." She took up a position next to her.

"I'm in no hurry." The intonation suggested that she would prefer it if Gallagher kept the meeting as brief as possible.

"Crispin and Rupert and Magenta and Carmine often met up together, I believe."

"I believe so."

"And it was Carmine's machinations that brought Crispin and Magenta together."

"How do you mean?"

"Magenta told me that Carmine thought Crispin had a crush on her and, at every opportunity, Carmine would drag Rupert away and leave Crispin and Magenta on their own."

"It may have contributed." Vivienne permitted herself a wistful smile.

"So when Crispin and Magenta were left alone together, Rupert and Carmine would have been alone together."

"What are you getting at?"

"Only that it might have been quite natural for Rupert and Carmine to hook up together. It happens: a pair of brothers marry a pair of sisters."

"I can't imagine that Rupe would have initiated such a thing and come on to her – and if she'd come on to him, either he wouldn't have recognised it, or he wouldn't have known how to respond. I think you're aware that Rupe's socially a bit awkward and when it comes to women… He's a lovely lad and he'd be a great catch for anyone, but he just finds it so difficult. I think just the idea of dating is traumatic for him."

"I can understand that. But do you think he fancied her?" Mrs. Appleby shrugged.

"If he did, he never said anything – and Rupert's mind is

pretty much a closed shop."

"And I don't suppose you'd know if Carmine fancied him. Presumably she'd have been in a position to see past his anxiety."

"I wouldn't know."

"Dean!" While Gallagher had been irritating her secretary – and having finished the task to which he had been applying himself when the private investigator's phone call had interrupted him – Wainwright had been mulling over her theory.

"Sir?" From halfway across the room, Bowden peered around the edge of his computer screen to find his superior rocking back and forth in his chair, his pen pressed, pensively, to his lips.

"Do we have Casey Hardacre's computer, or whatever device it was he used at home?"

"Not as far as I know sir. I don't think we brought anything in when we looked round his place. Why?"

"But we have keys."

"They'll be in the box with his other things. Do you need it?" Bowden sensed, with a modicum of optimism that there might be an opportunity to get out of the office.

"Not the device itself, but maybe you could pop round there and take a look at it."

"Sir." He was already on his feet. "What am I looking for?"

"His best man's speech. He's bound to have typed it up and it shouldn't be too difficult to find. He'd probably still have been tweaking it up to the Friday before the wedding."

"And when I find it?"

"Just make a copy and bring it in."

"Yes, sir." He loaded his jacket with phone, notepad, pen, a flash drive retrieved from his desk drawer and was on his way.

"Why do we need the best man's speech, sir?" When she had heard Bowden's name called, Kershaw had ceased what she was doing and had listened in to the exchange.

"There may be something in it to explain why Casey was killed."

"What makes you think so?" Wainwright thought about the

question before answering.

"Casey put his speech back in his jacket pocket after he'd finished, but when we went through his jacket, it wasn't there. Someone must have removed it. And they must have had reason for doing so."

"How… I see. OK." She was about to ask how he knew that Hardacre had put his speech back in his pocket and that it had subsequently been taken, but then recalled hearing Gallagher's name mentioned in the context of an earlier phone call and put two and two together.

Bowden had not been gone more than an hour before he breezed back into the office that doubled as the incident room, Hardacre's house in Trevithick Avenue being little more than five minutes' drive from the police station. The wind was somewhat taken out of his sails by the fact that no one appeared to notice his return. He sat down at his desk, plugged the flash drive into his computer, fetched up the required document and glanced through it again. He had read it through at the house, but, to him, there seemed to be nothing in it that could cause offence, let alone provide a motive for murder.

"Sir." Wainwright looked up from his desk.

"You're back, Dean."

"Yes, sir."

"Did you find it?"

"Yes, sir. It's here."

"Good. Well done." He pushed his chair back and stood up. "Let's see what it tells us, then." He threaded his way towards Bowden and, not wishing to be left out, Kershaw summarily dropped what she was doing and made her way towards Bowden from the other side of the room. They converged on the detective sergeant's desk at much the same time.

"I can't see much in it, sir." Wainwright scrolled through the speech and the three of them read it in silence.

"I can't see anything in it, either." Wainwright straightened himself, albeit still staring at the screen. "Just the usual stuff you'd expect: eulogising the groom with a few, innocuous, humorous asides thrown in. Kate?" He looked across to his detective constable. She shook her head.

"I can't see anything there, sir." Wainwright exhaled a heavy, disappointed sigh. Whatever it was Gallagher was expecting to find in the speech, it patently was not there. Yet, he had the nagging feeling that, if she had been right and someone had deliberately taken it, there must have been a reason and he must be missing it. "Send it across to me please, Dean."

"Yes, sir." By the time he had got back to his own desk, the document was in his inbox. He read it over again, scrutinizing every sentence for anything that could have been construed negatively. Conceding defeat, he composed a brief email, attached the speech and sent it to Gallagher.

It had not been especially late in the day, but Wainwright had, nevertheless been possessed of the forethought to send his email to both Gallagher's office and her personal address. It did, indeed, prove prescient as, having spoken with Vivienne Appleby, Gallagher had gone straight home, rather than return to the office. One consequence of her doing so was that she had got in before Nick, which afforded her a little time to open her laptop and, amongst other things check her emails. Wainwright's mail had been prefaced by a reference to his comment that she might have been grasping at straws if she thought Hardacre's speech would disclose anything useful, let alone a motive for murder. As she read the speech through, her heart sank. She had not anticipated that the speech would solve the case, but she had hoped that it would reveal some key element that might set her on the right track.

When she heard the front door open, it was with some relief that she closed the laptop; she was otherwise sending herself round in circles. She heard Nick deposit his equipment in the hall, as he always did, then, rather than bound up the stairs, as was his habit, he poked his head around the lounge door, spotted her on the sofa and came in.

"I thought I saw your car outside."

"I went to see Vivienne Appleby this afternoon and came

155

straight home afterwards." He leaned over the back of the sofa and, when she tilted her head upwards, gave her a lingering kiss on the mouth. "How's your day been?"

"Good. I'll just go and freshen up and then you can tell me all about Mrs. Appleby." He gave her another peck on the top of the head, turned away again and headed back towards the hall.

"I'll cook tonight." He heard her, but he was already out of the room.

Cooking involved placing a couple of baking potatoes in the oven, eventually served with cream cheese, bacon bits, sprinkled with paprika, and rustling up a salad with whatever she could find in the fridge and the cupboard. Accompanied by a glass of pinotage, it proved to be quite acceptable. Over the meal (on Gallagher's insistence) Nick recounted his day's activities, which had been exclusively studio bound, though not without its incidents. She enjoyed listening to his humorous observations, of which there was invariably at least one; they provided a little levity to counterbalance the relative gravity of her days. She had discovered half of a blackcurrant cheesecake in the fridge, which she thought would be suitable for a dessert, and only realised, when it was too late, that it probably made the meal somewhat cream cheese heavy, but Nick was too tactful to mention it.

"What did you talk to Vivienne about?" He poured a generous quantity of cream over his wedge of cheesecake. Gallagher sipped at her wine.

"Before I went to see her, I called Magenta to ask if she knew what had happened to Casey Hardacre's best man's speech. It was something you said last night; it got me thinking. Anyway, she was sure that he'd put it back in his jacket pocket after the wedding toast. So, I then called Wainwright to see if it had been found." Nick was in the midst of savouring his dessert, but the pause suggested that he was expected to prompt her to continue.

"And?"

"It hadn't."

"Maybe Magenta had been mistaken. What he'd done with his speech would hardly have been at the forefront of her mind."

"True, but she seemed quite sure."

"So where is it?"

"I reckoned someone must have taken it out of his jacket for some reason; because of something that he'd said. Anyway, Wainwright followed it up. He checked Casey's computer, found the speech and forwarded it to me."

"And what did you find?"

"Nothing. Absolutely nothing. I'll show it to you afterwards, but it's just a catalogue of Crispin's virtues, with a few, harmless, light-hearted anecdotes thrown in. Absolutely nothing that could upset anyone."

"So where does that leave you?"

"I don't know, Nick. If someone took it, which seems the most likely explanation for the police not finding it, it must have been for a reason. I can't help thinking I must be missing something." Without having read the speech for himself, Nick was unable to comment.

"And all this, presumably, before you went to see Mrs. Appleby." Gallagher smiled. Speaking with Vivienne Appleby was all that she had let on about her day earlier on. She had, thus far, only eaten one spoonful of cheesecake and chose to remedy that situation before continuing.

"I wanted to ask her about Carmine and Rupert."

"Carmine and Rupert?"

"It was Carmine that brought Crispin and Magenta together, partly through carrying Rupert off at every opportune moment when the four of them were together. I just thought that, two sisters, two brothers, Rupert might have shown an interest in Carmine."

"And did he?"

"Apparently not."

"Hmm."

"What? That was a very pregnant 'hmm'."

"I was just thinking back to that photograph."

XV

HYPOTHESIS

"Good morning, Clemmy." Clematis looked over her shoulder. She had heard the door opened and assumed it was her boss that had entered.

"Morning, Ms. Gallagher." She turned her attention back to the serious business of making her first mug of coffee of the morning. "Coffee?"

"Please." She wandered over to her secretary's desk and rested her bag on it. "Did anything come in yesterday while I was out?"

"Not a lot." She prepared Gallagher's mug, retrieved the carton of milk from the mini fridge under the counter, checked the 'use by' date, sniffed it and poured some into both mugs before topping them up with the freshly boiled water. Gallagher waited, patiently. 'Not a lot' was not the same as 'Nothing', which implied there had been something. Clematis carried the mugs over to the desk, set them down in whatever space was available and then made herself comfortable in her chair. "There were a mail from D.I Wainwright. 'E sent a copy of Casey 'Ardacre's best man's speech." Gallagher nodded.

"Have you read it?"

"I took that liberty, seeing as you weren't 'ere and it might 'ave been important."

"What did you make of it?" She picked up her mug and took a sip.

"Make of it?"

"Did you find anything that might provide a motive for murder?" Clematis gained the impression that her boss had already seen and read the speech in anticipation of finding a clue, but had singularly failed.

"It just seems to be a pretty standard – and rather boring, if I may so – speech. Unless you're the oversensitive type."

"How do you mean?"

"Well, 'aving to listen to 'ow wonderful Crispin was and what an ideal 'usband 'e'd make, might piss some people off." She had a mischievous grin on her face. The observation was clearly meant as a humorous aside and not to be taken in earnest, but Gallagher considered it otherwise.

"How so?"

"Think about it, Ms. Gallagher." Clematis was attempting to do precisely that. She had not expected to be asked to explicate further. "If you were with a friend or relative and someone else kept banging on about 'ow brilliant that person were, and you were oversensitive, you might take it as a reflection on you. You might interpret it to mean that you were not all those wonderful things and that might piss you off."

"You might have a point, Clemmy. Someone else getting all the plaudits and all the attention and you being ignored."

"Something like that."

"Thank you, Clemmy." Still clutching her mug, she picked up her bag and made her way, thoughtfully, to her own office.

How quickly Gallagher got to see Wainwright depended on who was on duty at the front desk. Sometimes she was greeted with a smile, her credentials checked as a matter of protocol and, after the detective inspector's whereabouts had been ascertained, waved through on the assumption that she was capable of finding her own way. On other occasions, she was treated with suspicion, her credentials pored over and, after reluctantly ascertaining Wainwright's whereabouts, she was escorted to wherever he was. Today was one of the latter occasions and the officer escorting her was particularly sullen. She had learned, though, not to take it personally, simply smiled sweetly, obeyed instructions and said nothing that might antagonize. When she reached the incident room, her chaperone called Wainwright over and handed her over. Sometimes it felt like a prisoner exchange, but without the reciprocation. He led her back to his desk, found her a chair and sat her down.

"Did you manage to glean some small nugget from Casey's speech?" She allowed him to settle himself back into his chair before she answered, knowing that he was expecting a negative response and, therefore, probably not giving her his full attention.

"Possibly."

"Possibly? Does this 'possibly' explain why you've trekked all the way over here?" Whether he had been expecting a negative response or not, his interest had been piqued by her turning up, unannounced, at the office. Normally, if she had some information – or, as was more likely, she wanted some information – she would phone him or try and seduce him with a cup of coffee at Café Cleo. She smiled.

"I've spent the morning putting a few nuggets together and, together, they've suggested a theory."

"Go on."

"One of the problems has been trying to find a connection between the three murders."

"And you think you've found one." He sounded sceptical.

"The speech is full of praise for Crispin; telling the world how awesome he is, outlining all his achievements, explaining how he will make a wonderful husband, et cetera. Any rival listening to it would most likely have been pretty pissed off by it. A particularly sensitive rival might even have taken it as a deprecation of themselves, focusing attention on all the reasons why they weren't good enough."

"Presupposing Crispin had a rival."

"Maybe he had a secret rival. A rival whose love went unrequited because, firstly, they had been thwarted and, secondly because, even if they had had the opportunity, they'd have been unable to express it."

"You obviously have someone in mind."

"Carmine Seacroft was instrumental in bringing her sister and Crispin together. When she, Magenta, Crispin and Rupert were together, Carmine would find some pretext for steering Rupert away, leaving Magenta and Crispin alone. It would have been an ideal opportunity for Carmine and Rupert to get together

160

as well as Magenta and Crispin. Two sisters for two brothers; the potential for a double wedding. However, when I spoke to Vivienne Appleby about that, on the basis that she would know Rupert as well as anyone, she said Rupert had never given any indication that he was attracted to Carmine."

"I'm not sure where you're going with this, but carry on."

"Supposing Rupert fancied Magenta himself and resented Carmine for taking him away from her whenever he might have had the opportunity to woo her, notwithstanding his social ineptness, something which would only have added to his frustration. This might explain why, in the wedding photo, Rupert's gaze was fixed on Magenta – if we assume it wasn't just her cleavage he was attracted by – when Carmine was stood next to him."

"All quite feasible, if a little fanciful, if you don't mind me saying, Beth. Assuming the picture you've painted to be true, though, I don't see it leading to a triple murder."

"Supposing Rupert is besotted with Magenta. He might have resigned himself to her marrying his brother, but he's likely to have hated having to attend the wedding, which he could hardly avoid. He's already suffering with emotional overload, unable to cope with that kind of situation and then he has to sit through Casey's speech, with no means of escape. Sitting there believing it should have been him. When it all boils over, he vows to kill the messenger. He'd have become familiar with the venue and would've noticed the collection of artefacts in the smithy. He may have slipped into the smithy and purloined a couple of useful implements when no one was looking."

"He couldn't have known that Casey would come out for a bit of hanky-panky behind the stables, though."

"True – and maybe he only acted to relieve the turmoil he was feeling inside. As Vivienne said, his mind is pretty much a closed shop; who knows what's going on inside it? However, there he is, outside, probably not really sure what he's intending to do, when Casey comes out, quickly followed by Theresa Garrity. Theresa returns to the stables, Casey is left there on his own and Rupert seizes his opportunity, having grabbed the hammer and punch from the smithy in the meantime."

"It's a very nice theory, Beth…"

"Having killed Casey, the dam has been breached. Why not alleviate the resentment he feels towards Carmine. As you well know, Danny, killing is always much easier the second time round."

"And having killed Carmine, why not go on and kill Crispin?"

"Leaving the way open to pursue Magenta."

"I have to concede, it's a plausible hypothesis. But what about the missing speech?"

"We don't know when Casey took his jacket off. Maybe Rupert – or whoever the killer proves to be – took the speech beforehand, read it over and that's what tipped him over the edge, or he took it afterwards."

"A trophy. It's possible." There was a silence while both considered the theory.

"There's something else you should know."

"Go on."

"Magenta, herself, told me that Rupert's been to visit her twice this week. Once on Sunday and again on Tuesday. You've given her police protection, but the killer may well be freely coming and going right under their noses."

"Oh, fuck. If you're right…" He did not need to complete the sentence.

Gallagher's hypothesis had generated a good deal of consternation in the incident room, not least because it was better that anything Wainwright and his team had come up with over the last fortnight.

"We know Rupert lied about the time he left the wedding…" Bowden was not prepared to mince his words in the circumstances.

"We believe he was lying." Wainwright felt duty bound to correct him. "The losing-track-of-time excuse, especially at a wedding reception, is hard to refute. We know he did leave later than he stated, but we don't know he deliberately lied about it. As for the rest of Gallagher's theory, it's just that: theory. Based on pretty flimsy, circumstantial evidence.

"But it's plausible. We've got to take it seriously, sir."

"Don't worry, Dean, I am doing."

"What about Rupert's visits to Magenta?" Gallagher had elaborated on her conversation with Mrs. Molyneaux and, hence, Wainwright was familiar with the nature of Rupert and Magenta's interactions.

"Magenta Molyneaux's safety is my main priority at the moment."

"Do you think he intends to harm her?" Bowden did his best not to sound alarmist.

"I don't know, but we have to assume the worst-case scenario. He visited her at her parents' house on Sunday, then took her for a drink at the local pub on Tuesday. What does that suggest?"

"That he's gradually trying to lure her away from the house?" As was not uncommon, Kershaw, from her place at the side of the room, was quicker on the uptake than Bowden.

"If we run with Gallagher's theory, it's a possibility, but for what purpose? What's his intention? He's given no indication that he's going to act precipitously. Our protection may be an inconvenience, but he's prepared to bide his time."

"Can we search his house?" Bowden sought some practical action.

"On what basis, Dean? With what we've got, we'll never get a search warrant."

"If we could find someone who saw him take Casey's speech from his jacket…"

"If." Wainwright cut his sergeant short. "And if we do, what does that prove? We can make Rupert Molyneaux our prime suspect and we can make that our main line of inquiry, but we also have to keep all other options open."

A text message pinged into Magenta's phone:
'Hi Madge. Would u like to do lunch tomorrow?'
Shortly afterwards, a response was relayed to Rupert's

phone:

'Thanks for asking, but doesn't seem right.'

'Nothing seems right atm. What time u finish work?'

It took Magenta a good fifteen minutes to reply, as she wrestled with the propriety of meeting her brother-in-law again, but then simply texted:

'1.00'

'1.15 Jacquard's? Can't hurt.'

'OK'

Mrs. Seacroft was feeling conflicted. She was trying to reconcile very differing emotions. The previous weekend the Molyneauxs had hosted dinner at their place and Laura eventually concluded, given that circumstances had not materially changed over the last seven days, that it would be right and proper if she reciprocated. Thus, she called Vanessa Molyneaux and proposed that the two families get together for lunch on Sunday. It would, she reckoned, be difficult to accommodate such a relatively large gathering – plus it would have required a considerable amount of last-minute meal planning and shopping – so she suggested meeting at The Black Cat in Copfield, strategically chosen as it was appreciably more convenient for the Molyneauxs than it was for her, thereby making the invitation more difficult to decline, had that been in Vanessa's thoughts. She asked Mrs. Molyneaux if she would invite Rupert and the Applebys on her behalf.

'Hi Rupe. Mum's arranged Sunday lunch for all family.'

'I know.'

'Best we don't meet tomorrow. Sorry.'

'OK. CU Sunday.'

XVI

SCAVENGING

Gallagher was standing at the counter judiciously selecting red grapes from a bunch in a raffia basket to drop in her breakfast bowl. A little way away from her, Nick was making a bet with himself as to which would finish first: the toaster toasting or the kettle boiling. Neither felt the necessity to convey their thoughts to the other. The toaster, unceremoniously, ejected two slices of well-browned toast. Gallagher paused, cocked her head to one side and decided that another couple were required. Nick placed his toast on the bread board, picked up the knife he had to hand and lathered both pieces with butter. He was about to dip into his favourite, thick-cut marmalade when the kettle boiled. He hesitated before relinquishing the knife and prioritising the making of his tea and her coffee. Meanwhile, Gallagher peeled back the already opened foil cover of the yoghurt pot and spooned a lavish amount of its contents onto her grapes. She glanced across at Nick.

"Good timing."

"We make a good team, sweetheart." She smiled, picked up her bowl and spoon and carried it to the dining table. Nick let the teabag in his mug brew while he slathered the marmalade on his toast. He needed to make two trips to the table; one to transport the toast, that had been transferred to a plate and the second to carry the tea and coffee. "What are you thinking?" He sat down next to her, the more easily to see the map she had spread out on the table. The map was actually two pages from her A-Z that she had copied, enlarged and, somewhat crudely, taped together.

"There's only two ways back from Campion Lake. The killer would either have had to return along Campion Lane and back down Highlands Avenue," she traced the route with the forefinger of her left hand while scooping up a spoonful of grape and yoghurt with her right, "or gone back via Riverside Lane and out onto Eastway." Again, she delineated the route with her finger. Nick swallowed a mouthful of toast and found time to purse his lips before picking up his mug of very dark tea.

"Instead of going back down Highlands, he could have gone the other way."

"I doubt it."

"Why?"

"If our killer is Rupert Molyneaux, it's likely he would have gone straight back home to Sutcliffe Road." She pointed to it on the map. "He does only live a stone's throw from where Crispin was abducted at the tennis club, so he wouldn't have needed to drive there." She shifted her finger so that it obliterated the location of the club. "However, if they had needed to drive there, they would, presumably, have parked relatively close to the tennis club – and there's plenty of places they could have parked out of reach of any CCTV – so they'd have needed to get back to their car." Nick took another bite of toast.

"That makes sense."

"Consequently, I reckon they went back down Highlands Avenue. I can't see any point in making a detour all the way around Riverside Lane." She took a sip of coffee and followed it up with another spoon of yoghurt-coated grape.

"So where does that get you?"

"I'm thinking that, other than the weapons used to kill Casey Hardacre, they wouldn't have chanced disposing of anything else at the wedding venue. After killing Carmine and disposing of the screwdriver in the canal – and, given that nothing else was found in the canal – there's virtually nowhere else they could have got rid of anything else, other than litter bins – and the police went through all those in the vicinity. However, they'd have had plenty of opportunity to discard anything on the way back from Campion Lake."

"Unless they threw whatever it was they wanted to get rid of into the lake with the knife."

"The divers would have found it, unless they'd deliberately

gone to another spot to throw it in, which seems unlikely. The blacksmiths' tools and the screwdriver had been found so they could have anticipated the knife being found, so why go to a lot of trouble to try and conceal something else?" Nick conceded the logic of her argument, but could not fathom the point of it.

"So what do you plan to do now?"

"It might be worth going back over the killer's route from the lake back down towards the tennis club to see what I can find." Nick delayed another bite of toast to give her a distinctly sceptical expression. "If the killer considered their work to be done and the murder of Crispin Molyneaux was the final act of their killing spree, they may have wanted to ditch the hat, or gloves, or any other incriminating evidence." The unconvinced tone of her voice suggested that even she knew she was clutching at straws.

"That's going to be like looking for a needle in a haystack." She glanced across at him with an air of unintended resignation.

"Needles and haystacks seem to be all we've got at the moment." They lapsed into silence, each focusing on their respective breakfasts. In the absence of a better suggestion, Nick thought it best not to try and dissuade her. "Could you follow me up to the tennis club? I'll find somewhere to park near there and then perhaps you could take me up to the lake? If we leave ten minutes earlier than your normal time, you won't be late to the studio."

"No problem. I can do that."

It was relatively early in the day and Gallagher had found little difficulty in finding somewhere to park her Peugeot – quite coincidentally, approximately halfway between Rupert Molyneaux's flat and the tennis club from which his brother had been abducted a week previously. Nick had been able to wait, without causing an obstruction, while she gathered her things, locked her car and joined him. He had driven her up to Campion Lake and dropped her off at the car park, which was already graced by three other vehicles, whereat they went their separate ways, but not before Gallagher had expressed the fervent wish that his afternoon's wedding assignment would prove less eventful than the one of a fortnight before; a sentiment with which Nick had, only half-heartedly, concurred, provoking a look of mock admonishment from his partner. She watched him drive off, leaving her alone standing in the dappled early summer sunshine. She adjusted the tan bag slung over her shoulder. Dressed in jeans, a lightweight black jumper and black and grey canvas loafers, she could have passed for any casual, morning walker, taking advantage of the weekend weather and the serenity of the lake. She looked about herself, then mechanically wandered in the direction of the spot where Crispin Molyneaux's body had been discovered, questioning, in her mind, the wisdom of the jaunt. A week on from the event, no other observer would have had the slightest inclination of the brutal events that had taken place there a week prior, save perhaps for a few telltale scraps of police tape hanging, limply, from a couple of branches. She gave the site a cursory inspection before making her way back onto Campion Lane. Despite what she had told Nick, she had no real idea for what she was looking or for what she hoped to find. A man with a pair of spaniels on leads greeted her, cheerily, to which she responded with muted enthusiasm. She began to make her way back up the lane, glancing from side to side, hoping to spot something, or, at least, a place, a gap, where something may have been discarded by someone wishing to covertly offload incriminating evidence; something, anything, that the police might have missed. By the time she reached the top of the lane, she was as empty-handed as she had been when she embarked upon the enterprise. Only a couple of cars heading towards the lake had caused her to deviate from her path.

She looked from left to right and then started out right, along Brunview Road, following, what she was certain, must have been the exact route taken by Molyneaux's killer. There would have been, she reasoned, no cause for them to take any other route. The footpath took her past three or four houses before the road curved left and Highlands Avenue forked right. Logic dictated that the killer would have taken Highlands Avenue, that being the shortest and quickest way back to Sutcliffe Road and the environs of the tennis club where, either the killer lived, or they had left their vehicle. Within a few yards Gallagher was walking along the residue of woodland that formed the south-western boundary of the Campion Lake parkland area. A path looped through the woodland. She halted at the gap in the wooden fencing where the path began and asked herself whether it was likely that they would make that detour. She concluded that, if they were going to depart from their route home to dispose of any evidence, they would have done so at the outset. The kidnap and murder had been carefully planned; the killer knew what they were doing; it was unlikely, she reckoned, that they would incorporate that kind of diversion – one that would prolong their journey - in their planning. She continued along the road. The woodland, she estimated, only extended for about 200 metres. Near the end of the woodland, another gap in the fencing marked the end of the loop. Almost immediately afterwards, a short lay-by, cut into the woodland, preceded the start of a row of terraced houses. The end property of the terrace was an archetypal corner shop. At the end of the lay-by, closest to the shop, set back from the road and marking the corner of the woodland, stood a council issue litter bin. Gallagher again paused. The bin was overflowing. Clearly it had not been emptied for some time. While the killer may not have embraced a detour in their route to jettison any inconvenient items, they may, she considered, have taken advantage of the opportunity to do so *en route*.

She stood, looking at the bin. The very thought of sifting through its contents was patently absurd, but the straws at which she was clutching seemed to be becoming ever thinner. Closer scrutiny revealed that the door, which should have been locked, had been left ajar, either through carelessness or because the lock was broken. Either way, it invited her – maybe, even, dared her – to investigate. Gallagher coaxed her bag around to where she could open it and searched inside for the latex gloves that she always carried in the event of needing to handle potential evidence in a case. She glanced around, furtively, then made her way towards the bin, donning the gloves as she did so. She deposited her bag next to the fence, opened the door wider and paused. She felt ridiculous, but in the absence of other options, she slid the container out onto the grass and, before giving herself time to reconsider, tipped the contents out onto the lay-by. She sifted through them, spreading them out in a fan. Fortunately, there appeared to be nothing too repugnant or potentially noxious; just the customary collection of paper and plastic, bottles and cans and inevitable waste food. Towards the bottom of the jumble, the bin surrendered, first one and then a second, black glove which it had been sheltering. She dragged them out and laid them side by side. The two were indisputably a pair. Before examining them carefully, she glanced up and over her shoulder, towards the road. A thirty-something woman, with two young children, was standing on the pavement, gawping contemptuously at her. Gallagher, met their stares and raised a challenging eyebrow. The woman gathered her offspring about her, turned them around and walked on, though not without a brief, disdainful backward glance. Gallagher returned her attention to the task in hand. She picked up each glove individually, turned them over and examined them. The left hand appeared to be marked only by its contact with the enveloping refuse. The right hand one, however, appeared stained on the fingers and the palms. Dark stains on a dark fabric were impossible to identify by visual inspection, but she had a hunch that forensic analysis would reveal them to be blood. She returned to her bag, peeled off one of her gloves and rifled through it until she found a plastic bag, of the sort she used for collecting evidence.

Having stuffed the black gloves into bag she set about tidying the mess she had created, returning every last scrap of refuse – and probably a few additional items – into the bin liner. Somehow, she managed to manhandle the bin back into its receptacle without dirtying her jeans and swung the door back to its previous ajar position. The latex gloves she had used for the operation she pushed, with a slight sense of irony, into the top of the bin, then collected her shoulder bag, picked up the evidence bag, from where she had placed it on top of the bin, turned and resumed her perambulation down Highlands Avenue.

* * * * *

"Let me get this right: you're calling to tell me you've found a pair of gloves at the bottom of a rubbish bin."

"I've got to do something."

"And you think we're not?"

"I didn't say that, Danny."

"We're working around the clock, using all the resources at our disposal to try and crack this case, Beth."

"I know that."

"I appreciate that you like to keep busy, but you don't you have anything better to do on a Saturday morning than rummaging through garbage bins?" The reaction to her find was pretty much exactly as she had anticipated. When she had returned home, she had laid a sheet of plastic out on a section of the kitchen counter and placed the gloves upon it. When she had looked at them afresh, they exuded all the fascination of an old pair of gloves chucked into a rubbish bin. The apparent staining on the palms could, she conceded to herself, have been anything and, without forensic analysis, there was no telling what that 'anything' was. Nevertheless, she had found them, brought them home and, here they were, languishing on her kitchen counter. There was nothing she could do with them and, hence, she had phoned Wainwright with the news of her discovery.

"I wish I had, Danny. I know it was a long shot, but I think they may be material."

"What makes you think so?"

"The litter bin was the first such bin on the route the killer must have taken to return to the tennis club." She outlined the rationale she had related to Nick over breakfast. "If they had hoped to discard the gloves with little danger of them being found, that would have been the first opportunity. Secondly, they were found near the bottom of the bin. If the council empties the bins once a week," she heard a doubtful grunt at the other end of the line, "then the gloves would've been thrown in it about a week ago; about the time Crispin was killed." She added the addendum to ensure Wainwright got her point. "I admit that the stains could be anything, but they've got to be worth sending for analysis in case they are blood. And, if they are blood and it is a match for

171

Crispin's blood, then it ought to be possible to extract DNA from the inside of them." There was a prolonged silence which suggested to Gallagher that, at least, Wainwright was giving some credence to her theory.

"OK. I guess it can't do any harm. Bring them into the station on Monday. There's nothing I can do over the weekend. Forensics are strictly nine to five."

"Thanks, Danny."

XVII

SUNDAY LUNCH

When Laura Seacroft drew into the car park of The Black Cat, at the front of the building, it being set well back from the road, there was comfortable parking space, suggesting that the pub would be congenial, but not full. After much discussion it had been agreed that Mrs. Seacroft would drive. There had been an ulterior motive to her subtle insistence: she did not want to risk one too many glasses of wine drawing her into a compromising situation with David Molyneaux. As the three of them – Laura, Warwick and Magenta – extricated themselves from the confines of the purple beetle, Magenta could not help but notice that day's protection pairing pull up at the side of the road opposite. She was inclined to give them a wave, but as she had already acknowledged them that morning, she refrained.

The Black Cat is a four-square, stone-built inn of unblemished symmetry. The central door leads into the open-plan bar area that extends into the right-hand wing, while an impressive archway to the left affords ingress to the dining area. Warwick and Magenta headed towards the bar, with a request from Laura to buy her a glass of non-alcoholic white wine. Meanwhile, Mrs. Seacroft introduced herself to the *maître d'* and asked to inspect the table they had been allocated. The table – actually two tables - had been arranged along the back of the dining room, underneath the window that overlooked a patio, surrounded by borders of mature shrubs and trees. Three tables, each with a sunshade bearing a black cat motif, were grouped in an equilateral triangle formation. One of them was occupied by four adults and another by a family of five, of which three were children. Laura Seacroft beheld her table to be perfectly amenable.

When Laura returned to her husband and daughter, she found them chatting with Rupert Molyneaux. Rupert abhorred being late anywhere, whether it be for work or for a social occasion. In fact, being on time stressed him. He invariably preferred being early, but not so early as to be the first one there. On this occasion he was able to congratulate himself on his timing; the Seacrofts had arrived, as he had anticipated, Laura having arranged the shindig, early, but none of his family were yet present. If he was the first to arrive anywhere, he felt conspicuous and self-conscious, which raised his anxiety levels, but to walk into a crowd, even if the crowd comprised family and friends, was considerably more nerve-racking. Either no one noticed his entrance, which was embarrassing, as he then had to make his presence felt, or everyone turned towards him, causing him the discomposure of being the centre of attention. He could manage to cope, though, with a reception party of two. Mrs Seacroft greeted him with a temperate kiss on both cheeks, a gesture to which he was only able to respond with a large degree of gaucheness.

Mr. and Mrs. Molyneaux arrived at five minutes before the appointed time. They paused immediately inside the door and both scanned the room, expecting the Seacrofts to have got there before them. Having spotted them and their son at the bar, they made their way towards the quartet at an appropriately sedate pace. Laura greeted David with a kiss on both cheeks in identical manner to that in which she had greeted Rupert. Warwick kissed Vanessa on the right cheek. Swapping partners, Laura, very consciously, kissed Vanessa on both cheeks while the men shook hands. Warwick offered to buy each of the Molyneauxs a drink, which was gratefully accepted. Laura initiated the requisite exchange of enquires as to how the others were coping, expressing, at the same time, disappointment at the apparent lack of progress in the police's investigation. Vanessa was halfway through an apology for Vivienne and Lewis's belatedness when she spotted the pair in question walk in. She raised a discreet hand to attract their attention and the Appleby's threaded there way towards them. Three-quarters of the way there, Vivienne launched into a profuse apology of her own accompanied by the imperative justifications. There followed a repeat performance of welcomes and hospitality. Once the preliminaries had been successfully navigated, Laura suggested they go through to the dining room, if only to avoid the perfunctory conversation descending into awkward silence at the bar.

Having reconnoitred the room earlier, Laura was able to lead the party to their table with poised confidence. The table was set with four places on each side of it, allowing space for the waiter to negotiate both ends. Sufficient space had similarly been left between the table and window to allow the waiter easy access behind it. Mrs. Seacroft, wine in hand, steered her way to one of the two middle seats with their backs to the window, that position creating the least obstruction for her fellow diners. Not wishing to appear too eager, David Molyneaux hovered behind the chair opposite her, thus precluding anyone else from stealing it, while not actually claiming it. Magenta ambled around the opposite end of the table to which her mother had taken and seated herself to the right of Laura. Vanessa Molyneaux chivvied David to sit and she took up the seat to the right of her husband. Vivienne Appleby appropriated the seat to the left of her father and opposite Magenta. Meanwhile, Lewis Appleby, perhaps with improper haste, grabbed the chair next to Magenta. Warwick Seacroft simply took the nearest of the two remaining seats, that being the one to the left of Vivienne and opposite Lewis, relieving Rupert Molyneaux of having to make a decision as to where he should sit. He ended up to the left of Mrs. Seacroft and opposite his mother.

No sooner had they settled than the waiter, dutifully, brought them each a menu, for which each, in their own way, was grateful. It meant no one felt obliged to initiate conversation. Even Laura Seacroft, who had convened the lunch, had begun to doubt the wisdom of the gathering; everything that could be said had been said at the previous Saturday's dinner at the Molyneauxs – and, since then, nothing had changed; at least in respect of the investigation into the murders of Casey Hardacre, Carmine Seacroft and Crispin Molyneaux. They each deliberated the fare on offer with whomsoever should be sitting next to or opposite them, until all had decided upon what they would order and, one by one, they laid the menus in front of them, the cue for the waiter to return.

Comments, observations and perceptions of the venue, menu and ambience rapidly petered out, appreciative though they all were and it was left to Vivienne to broach the subject that united them. Her opinions of the police's efforts to catch the killer were unflattering, with which they all, generally, concurred (though Vanessa Molyneaux proffered some lukewarm mitigation), but when her husband tossed in the element of 'that meddling private detective', the conversation became less inhibited and more animated. When the food arrived, the company was feeling appreciably more at ease – and ready for a second round of drinks. Laura stuck with her non-alcoholic wine. The other drivers were similarly circumspect: David Molyneaux ordering another bottle of mineral water, Lewis Appleby switching from his usual lager to a low alcohol substitute and Rupert Molyneaux changing from ale to Coca-Cola. Vivienne and Magenta replenished their glasses with the house red wine, Warwick Seacroft ordered another pint of Moorhouse's Blonde Witch and Vanessa Molyneaux continued with her sauvignon blanc.

The circumstances of the lunch had necessitated Laura searching her wardrobe for something suitable to wear. She had opted for a plain, lilac, short-sleeved Queen Anne top. Her hair, as normal, draped her shoulders with an affectation of careless disorder. Occasionally her large, hooped earrings would peek through. The pentacle on the thong around her neck was a permanent fixture. Whether she regarded the pale mauve lipstick and corresponding eyeshadow to be restrained, only she would know. Whatever the intention, the overall effect made an impression on the man sitting opposite her. He had not failed to notice, from the moment he had walked up to her, that the neckline of her top revealed a suggestion of the upper contours of her breasts and a tantalising suspicion of cleavage.

Mrs. Seacroft aware of Mr. Mr. Molyneaux's unashamed attention attempted, with admirable dexterity, to include Mrs.

Molyneaux in their discourse, along with Rupert, on her left. Vanessa, while very amenable to engaging with Laura, also, consciously involved her son, knowing that if he was not included, he would quickly drift into the periphery of any conversation. However, it did not escape her notice that her husband was very much focused on Laura Seacroft. She persuaded herself that his attention was simply a consequence of the two sitting opposite one another; that she could not expect her husband to be constantly turning to her. As for their son, he appeared to be invisible to him and it appeared to surprise him on the occasions when Rupert did contribute a thought or observation of his own volition. Rupert, himself, was conscious of his mother doing her best to keep him present, knowing that, otherwise, he would simply concentrate on his chilli con carne, using it as an excuse to be a non-participant. More than his mother's endeavours, though, the one thing that kept his attention was Laura Seacroft's perfume, which he found inexplicably bewitching. He had never, before, been in such close proximity to her, for such a prolonged period of time, but now that he was, he could not ignore her delicate scent. Furthermore, while he might not have appeared to be paying a great deal of attention to proceedings, he, like his mother, was cognizant of his father's seeming fixation with Mrs. Seacroft.

At the other end of the table (for the party had neatly divided itself into two groups of four) Vivienne Appleby discovered herself to be much captivated by Warwick Seacroft's anecdotes, of which he appeared to have an inexhaustible supply. He was, she inferred, proud of his skills in the fields of woodcarving and furniture restoration, yet self-effacing in his achievements, with a seductive line in self-deprecating humour. Unlike the others at the table, including herself, his dress was unapologetically casual: jeans and a loose-fitting biscuit-brown smock. Despite his reciprocal interest in her career, she felt distinctly inadequate beside him. Across the table, Magenta and Lewis Appleby had not, initially, found a natural commonality and Vivienne and Warwick had felt obliged to make conspicuous efforts to include them in their conversation. Vivienne knew what it was like to lose a sibling in traumatic circumstances and could empathise with Magenta on that score, though she was not prone to overt displays of emotion, but could not imagine what it must be like to lose a sister and a husband to acts of violence in quick succession. Similarly, Warwick shared in Magenta's grief over the murder of Carmine, but found it difficult to relate to the death of Crispin on top of that. Vivienne could not help but be fascinated by the young woman sat opposite her. Tragedy often takes its toll on those left behind, making them look older than their years, but in Magenta's case, she looked younger. Her blonde hair was tied in a ponytail, held in place by a black, velvet scrunchy. Her face was devoid of make-up, other than a discreet application of pale lipstick. She wore a Prussian blue, halter-neck, keyhole top that, inadvertently or otherwise (which was part of the fascination for Vivienne), accentuated her bust. The only jewellery she wore was her gold wedding band and diamond and sapphire engagement ring. Gradually, as the meal progressed, Magenta and Lewis became more at ease with each other and pursued their own course of chat. Vivienne also noted that, increasingly, Lewis took every opportunity to lean in towards her in an attitude of confidentiality, occasionally touching her wrist or forearm in a gesture of solace.

Meanwhile, whenever Rupert gave himself cause to lean forward to listen to his mother, he would glance down the table towards Magenta and Lewis. He could not hear what they were saying to one another and he could not see their physical interactions, but his interpretation of their body language riled him; he wondered how he had managed to allow himself to be sat just about as far away from Magenta Molyneaux as it was possible to get.

Once the main course had been completed and the plates and sundry other items cleared from the table, they were each presented with the dessert menu. The men pored over it with an unbecoming gusto, David and Lewis taking the opportunity to discuss it, in conspicuous detail, with Laura and Magenta respectively. For Rupert, it afforded the chance to enjoy some respite from the conversation. Warwick, out of politeness, shared his thoughts with Vivienne, though he was, essentially, indifferent to it. With the exception of Laura, who shared in David's enthusiasm, the women were more circumspect. For Vanessa, Vivienne and Magenta, to a greater or lesser degree, dessert felt inappropriately frivolous. Nevertheless, each reservedly undertook to order something relatively modest. Whether they were attracted to it or not, everyone avoided the knickerbocker glory.

The desserts, in a way that main courses do not, had made the table look gay – almost festive; joyous - resulting in each partaking of his or her own with something ranging from a twinge to a pang of guilt. In the seclusion of their own homes, they would not have thought twice about it, but knowing the emotions everyone else was experiencing, dessert felt discourteous, even offensive. Whether he wished to wash the sweetness from his mouth - or whether he misjudged the mood - when their bowls, plates and glasses, depending upon the dessert they had chosen, had been scraped clean, Warwick expressed a desire for coffee. Magenta responded with a slightly disapproving shake of the head and a low 'not for me, dad', while Vivienne's declining of the suggestion sounded more like a rebuke, which was either ignored or undetected. Lewis glanced at Magenta and then across at his wife before concurring that coffee sounded like a good idea. When the proposal reached the other end of the table, Laura and David were both happy to have an excuse to prolong the occasion. Vanessa voiced indifference, but took the 'if everyone else is going to have coffee…' approach. Rupert, having all but exhausted his supply of sociability, resigned himself to the inevitable extension of proceedings. When the five coffees arrived, they were sipped and slurped with a measure of discomfort, except for Warwick, who appeared quite at ease, while the conversation descended into awkward small talk.

"If you'll excuse us, I think it's time we were getting back." Lewis had hardly had time to replace his cup in its saucer when Vivienne made her announcement to no one in particular.

"I'm glad you and Lewis could come, Vivienne." Laura looked at her with genuine warmth.

"Thank you for arranging it." Vivienne's tone softened, perhaps regretting her erstwhile abruptness. "It was good for the two families to get together again." She edged her chair back, twisted around and unhooked her bag. "How are we going to pay?"

"If everyone gives me what they owe, I'll settle up on a card." Laura seemed unperturbed by the fact that, in all likelihood, no one would be able to remember, precisely, how much their meals had cost.

"Maybe," Vanessa chimed in, looking past her husband to her daughter, "round it up and then there'll be enough for a tip." Laura nodded her agreement of the idea.

"I've got it." Lewis dragged his wallet from his trousers pocket before his wife could initiate a search for her purse. "How much was yours?" Vivienne made a quick, mental calculation and told him. Meanwhile, Warwick had shoved his chair back, stood up and moved the chair out of the way, allowing Vivienne to extricate herself from the table with ease.

The financial transaction having been made, Vivienne circumnavigated the table, kissing everyone goodbye. Lewis, somewhat sheepishly (he not being a big hugger and kisser) followed her example, leaning over Magenta's shoulder to kiss her on the cheek – using it as a pretext to gently clasp and affectionately stroke her upper arms – shaking the men's hands and giving both his mother and mother-in-law a familial peck on the cheek. When they had departed, Vanessa gave her husband a meaningful look while, with Lewis' exit, Rupert felt his cordial spirit a little revived. Having consulted his wife, David counted out the notes required to cover their bill and handed them to Laura. Rupert totted up his own bill and did the same.

"Shall we adjourn to the bar?" David Molyneaux was already on his feet. The question appeared, to the others, to have been addressed to Laura.

"I'll have to go to the bar, anyway, to settle up." Mrs. Seacroft's reply was delivered while, exaggeratedly, rifling through her bag for her credit card case, thereby avoiding eye contact. Warwick, having already been on his feet, had begun to amble back through the restaurant. Vanessa fussed and dithered until David had no option but to accompany her out. Rupert made his way to the front of the table and paused to allow Laura, who had followed him, to go before him. Having noted that Magenta had gone the other way around the table, the contrivance rewarded him with the satisfaction of being able to bring up the rear at the shoulder of the younger Mrs. Molyneaux.

"Does anyone want another drink?" The five of them had been hovering near the bar while Laura discharged their account. Warwick looked enthusiastic. Vanessa frowned. Rupert looked towards Magenta, who looked unenthusiastic.

"Not for me, thank you, David." Laura was the only one who actually verbalised an answer. "But I will need to visit the ladies' room before we go." She took a sweeping look around the group, her gaze coming to rest on David and Vanessa. "You don't have to wait."

"That's alright, Laura." Mrs. Molyneaux smiled. She disliked the moral blackmail of being challenged to do something of which the opposite was perceived to be expected. "We don't have to be anywhere."

"In that case," David tried to not sound too eager, "I think I'll go to the gents." Laura was already on her way to the toilets and he, as casually as he could, followed her. Warwick looked at Vanessa and smiled, self-consciously. Vanessa murmured a few appropriately consolatory remarks, to which he felt relieved to be able to reciprocate. Rupert plucked up the courage to direct a vacuous comment about the meal towards Magenta, to which she responded somewhat dolefully.

"I don't know what you women do when you go to the bathroom. Laura always takes and age." They had depleted their supply of mutual solace and Warwick had glanced at his watch with a hint of impatience. It was another two or three minutes before his wife reappeared. Rupert was aware that, in his experience, women took appreciably longer to use the toilet than men, so it was with some perplexity that he noted his father's reappearance half a minute or so after Mrs. Seacroft's, considering that they had left the bar at the same time. Vanessa Molyneaux further noted that her husband seemed a little flustered when he made his excuses for keeping them waiting.

"I think that went well." Laura turned her beetle left, towards Burnley.

"Not too depressing, at any rate."

"You seemed to be getting along well with Vivienne."

"She's a nice woman. They both are. Don't you think, Magenta?" Warwick half turned towards the back of the car.

"Yes." The subdued monosyllable was all she had to say on the matter.

"I'd never really talked to them before." He turned his attention back to the road ahead.

"That seemed to go well." David turned his Mercedes right, towards Padiham."

"You think?"

"Don't you? It was good of Laura to arrange it."

"You spent all lunch ogling her fucking cleavage."

"Ness!"

"Even Rupe was embarrassed."

XVIII

MATERIAL EVIDENCE

The gloves, in their plastic pouch, lying on Wainwright's desk had attracted a range of responses. The detective inspector's scepticism had only permitted indulgence on the basis that he had no other material evidence to present. As her story unfolded, Gallagher had noticed Bowden's level of amused derision increase exponentially. Kershaw had tried to look sympathetically appreciative. Nevertheless, Wainwright had promised to send them to forensics immediately and have them prioritise their processing, if only, Gallagher inferred, so that he could dispense with an unnecessary distraction. The more she had mulled over her find, during the course of the weekend, the less convinced she had become of its import. As she had left the incident room, she sensed the sneers and sniggers following her. If – or, probably, when – the gloves came back with the stains having proved not to be blood, Wainwright would never let her forget it – and Bowden would never forgive her for wasting their time – but it had been a risk worth taking.

Back at her own office, Clematis was already hard at work. She felt obliged to explain her lateness, especially as it gave her the opportunity to relate the events of the weekend and, she hoped, garner a little moral support for her efforts. As she gave her account, from the comfort of the tub chair in the corner, her secretary made her a particularly welcome mug of coffee. By the time Gallagher had completed her narrative, which, she conceded to herself, sounded even more iffy every time she told it, Clematis was ensconced, once more, in her own chair, peering across the desk at her, with a mildly bemused expression, while turning the bi-metal braided ring around the middle finger of her left hand. The inconclusive end to the tale caught her unawares and it was a little unsettling to see Gallagher staring at her with a look of expectation, though what she was expecting, Clematis was unable to fathom.

"With all due respect, Ms. Gallagher…"

"Don't give me that 'with all due respect' *kak.*"

"Sorry, Ms. Gallagher." She had the decency to appear appropriately chastised. "I can understand why the police might be sceptical." Gallagher offered a faint acknowledgement of her secretary's opinion, stood up and made her way to her own office, leaving the half-drunk mug of coffee on the table beside the chair.

"So can I."

D.I. Wainwright was beginning to think that he was barking up the wrong tree. Despite the evidence to support the theory that a member of the immediate families must be the murderer, not least being that the first killing had taken place at a wedding at which there were only invited guests and, as far as they had been able to ascertain, no gate-crashers, he was asking himself whether they should be casting their net wider. From the guest list on the screen in front of him, there appeared to be no other obvious suspects. He pushed his chair back, swung round and was about to get up when an email pinged into his inbox. He swivelled back round, changed screens and saw the mail was from the forensic laboratory. With a click of his mouse, he opened it.

"Well, well. Whaddya know?"

"Sir?" Wainwright had not intended for his expression of surprise to be overheard, but Bowden was ever alert to his superior's changes of mood or body language. Had he hoped for immediate elucidation, however, he was disappointed. Having drawn it closer to his desk to read the mail, Wainwright shoved his chair back again, spun around, got up, threaded his way across the room towards his whiteboard, clapping his hands as he did do in order to gain the attention of his officers.

"We've had the report back from forensics about the glove Gallagher brought in this morning." Bowden feared the worst; Kershaw, despite her lukewarm support for the private investigator, was prepared for the best. As it turned out, both were justified in their perspectives. "The blood on the gloves is that of Crispin Molyneaux." A murmur of anticipation circulated the room. "It would suggest that these were the gloves worn by Crispin's killer. It's not a lot, but it's the first substantive evidence we've got."

"Anything else?" That Gallagher should have been vindicated was galling enough for Bowden, but, while they were desperate for an indication as to the identity of the killer, it would be doubly irksome if she had found it and not them.

"They managed to get DNA samples from the insides of the gloves. Clearly those of the wearer and, we can assume, of our murderer. They don't match anything we have on record, though."

"If it's one of the family, they wouldn't be." Kershaw was well aware that none of those thus far interviewed had crossed swords with the police at any time previously.

"Precisely."

"What do we do now?" Bowden knew very well what their immediate course of action should be, but what he really meant was how Wainwright planned to go about it.

"We've had no reason to request, let alone compel, DNA samples from the family, but now we have. We need to get this sorted a.s.a.p. Today."

"If they don't want to cooperate?" Bowden was keen to cover all bases.

"Threaten to arrest them on suspicion." If any of their suspects refused to provide a voluntary sample, they could be arrested on suspicion of involvement in a crime, if not actual murder, which would give the police the power to compel a sample. "They're all working and there's no need to intimidate them unnecessarily, so we'll orchestrate it for this evening."

"What do we tell them?" Kershaw assumed the operation would need to be coordinated as it was more than likely that they would each contact one another, after the fact, to cross-reference experiences.

"The usual: we've found an item of clothing – no need to specify what; keep them guessing – with Crispin's blood on it.

185

Other, as yet unidentified, DNA traces and we just need to be able to eliminate them from our enquiries."

"Are you going to tell Gallagher?" Bowden was fairly sure what the answer would be, but he wanted to hear it from Wainwright. The detective inspector pursed his lips.

"Can't really not do. We owe it to her." He was under no obligation to tell her that she had been right, but it would be a matter of courtesy and it was always good to have her onside. He did not want her becoming a loose cannon, which, from past experience, she was wont to do. Nevertheless, he was anticipating her becoming insufferable at having got one over on the police, though it would probably only last a few days.

Wainwright organised his available officers, including himself, into four pairs, one pair for each of the family households: the Molyneauxs, the Seacrofts (including Magenta), the Applebys and Rupert Molyneaux. He reckoned that everyone should be home by seven that evening and that was the time it was agreed that each pairing should knock on the door of their assigned property. If one of the family was the perpetrator of the crimes, he did not want to risk family loyalty kicking in and the killer being alerted before the police had time to get to them. Bowden and Kershaw were delegated to the Appleby household. If anyone was going to be difficult about providing a sample, Wainwright figured it would be Vivienne and/or Lewis Appleby and, consequently, he thought it advisable to send the detectives that were most familiar with them. He did not anticipate the Molyneauxs or the Seacrofts raising any objections, even if one of them was the killer. While he did not question his superior's wisdom, it was clear that Bowden took umbrage at Wainwright's decision to take Gallagher along to tackle Rupert Molyneaux. There being no further discussion necessary, the detective inspector returned to his desk and called Gallagher. Rather than gloat, she sounded relieved that her efforts had been vindicated and, as she pointed out to him, the fact that there had been blood on the gloves and that it had been Crispin's blood, was of little use if the DNA samples from inside the gloves could not be matched. Having asked him how he intended to proceed, it caught her off-guard when he asked her to accompany him to collect a swab from Rupert. Nevertheless, it was an invitation that she was not going to refuse.

"Hello, Viv"

"Hi, mum. Don't tell me: the police have been round."

"Have they been to you as well?"

"I think they're going to everyone."

"Did they want a DNA sample?"

"Yes. What time did they come to you?"

"About seven. You?"

"About seven." There was a brief pause while both mother and daughter weighed up the implications of the concurrent timing. "They said they wanted to eliminate us from their enquiries."

"That's what they told your dad and me."

"But I still think we're suspects."

"Do you think so?"

"I bet they've gone to all of us at the same time. Have you spoken to Rupe?"

"Not yet."

"They think one of us killed Cris – and Casey and Carmine – and the rest of us know who it was and they're scared one of us would tip them off."

"That's being a bit melodramatic, Viv."

"You think so? That's the way the police think."

"Did they tell you why they've waited 'til now, to ask for our DNA? Ten days after Crispin's…" Mrs. Molyneaux could not bring herself to finish the sentence.

"Said they'd found an item of clothing with Cris's blood on it, together with someone else's DNA."

"But they didn't say what."

"No."

"Didn't tell us, either."

"Hello, Rupe."

"Hi, mum."

"Have the police been to see you tonight."

"Yes. Well, the inspector and that private detective."

"They've been here as well. And to your sister's."

"They wanted a DNA sample."

"Yes. Said they'd found something with Crispin's blood on it."

"Clothing, but didn't say what. And some other DNA."

"At least they'll be able to eliminate us from their enquiries."

"Yes."

"I can't believe they really thought one of us might have done it."

"No."

"Are you OK, Rupe?"

"Fine, mum."

"Good. I worry about you having to deal with this on your own."

"I'm fine. Really. How's dad?"

"He didn't like doing the swab, but he did it."

"Good."

"Hello, Laura. It's Vanessa."

"Hi, Vanessa."

"We've had the police round again this evening."

"Same here."

"About seven?"

"Must have been."

"Did they want your DNA?"

"Yes. Even from Magenta. Can you believe it, Vanessa? As if she isn't going through enough as it is. How could they think she might have killed her sister and her husband?"

"Hi, sweetheart." She had kissed him on the top of the head, rounded the sofa, tossed her bag into one of the slightly shabby, mid-century, brutalist corduroy armchairs and snuggled up beside him on the sofa. "You're back earlier than I expected."

"Wainwright only wanted a DNA sample and Rupert didn't make a fuss about it. It was very perfunctory. In and out."

"You sound disappointed."

"A little. I'd hoped to have an opportunity to snoop around. Or, at least, have a bit more time to gauge his reaction."

"You thought he might refuse." She considered the assertion for a few moments.

"Not really. He was hardly in a position to. If he refused it would make him look guilty. In any case, Wainwright was prepared to threaten him with arrest if he didn't provide a swab voluntarily, in which case he could've compelled him to, although he wouldn't have known that." Gallagher had met Wainwright outside Sutcliffe Place and he had explained his plan of action on their way up to Molyneaux's flat.

"But you thought he might give something away."

"He displayed his usual level of anxiety, but, in the short time we were there, nothing more than expected. Had we spent more time there, he might have done."

"But Wainwright wanted in and out."

"He wanted to make it as matter-of-fact as possible, but he told him that they had a DNA sample from an item of clothing that also had his brother's blood on it – he had to tell him that to justify the request - and, if he is the killer, he must have known forensics would be able to match it."

"So not a very productive evening, then." She hesitated, eased herself away from his shoulder and hoisted herself to her feet.

"Not really. I'm going to open a bottle of wine. Do you want anything?" Nick had not been wholly convinced by her avowed disappointment and, to him, her sudden desire for a glass of wine smacked of deflection. He had become accustomed to her not always being able to share aspects of her work with him, especially where there was an issue of confidentiality, but she would normally be upfront and tell him if that was the case. In this instance, though, he had a sense that she was withholding something.

XIX

TRACING AND TRACKING

When Wainwright had requested that the eight DNA samples be analysed as a matter of urgency, he knew he was liable to exhaust his supply of goodwill credit. Nevertheless, the head of the forensics laboratory had reluctantly agreed to expedite the job at the expense of other work. However, he had made it clear, in no uncertain terms, that to analyse and process the samples would still take twenty-four hours and that the detective inspector could not expect the results before the following morning. Wainwright, though, had not been too disappointed by the hiatus imposed upon the investigation; he had enough work to keep him and his team occupied, not least going over the statements of his eight possible suspects with a fine-tooth comb to try and identify any flaws or inconsistencies. Furthermore, he had reckoned, the thirty-six hours between the gathering of the samples and the time by which the results had been promised, would give one of those eight suspects an opportunity to make an ill-advised, revelatory move. The brief, preliminary report, landed in his inbox mid-morning on Wednesday. The samples had been analysed and a match had been found for the DNA extracted from the inner lining of the gloves.

"And?" Bowden did not approve of his superior's increasing tendency to keep his team on tenterhooks at such moments.

"We need to get down to the university. Now." Bowden looked across at Kershaw and the pair exchanged a brief nod, before the latter shovelled her things into her bag and the former collected his jacket.

Having ascertained, precisely, where Rupert Molyneaux worked, Wainwright, Bowden and Kershaw proceeded, with casual haste, towards his office.

"The archive room?" Bowden, going ahead, paused to ask a passing student to confirm that he was going in the right direction.

"End of the corridor, round the corner, first door on the right." The young woman barely broke step, let alone found the time to give the detectives a second glance.

Wainwright knocked on the door then, without waiting for a response, pressed the handle. The door did not move. He knocked again.

"It's not open." All three of them turned to see a middle-aged woman standing, facing them, in the middle of the corridor some ten or fifteen yards away. "Can I help?"

"D.I. Wainwright. I'm looking for Rupert Molyneaux."

"He hasn't come in this morning."

"Are you sure?"

"As you've discovered, the door's locked." The woman was strolling towards them. "I wanted to ask him about something, but he's not here."

"Did he say he wouldn't be in?"

"I wouldn't know, inspector, but not to me. Rupert's always in work; never misses a day. Never comes in late; never goes home early. I'd have thought he'd have told me, though, if he wasn't going to be in. We work closely together." She sounded put out.

"Perhaps he's sick." Bowden made the obvious suggestion.

"Maybe." The woman had stopped a couple of yards short of them. "He seemed perfectly alright yesterday, though. But he could have gone down with something overnight." She gave a little chuckle. "I've never known him be off sick, though."

"So, he was here yesterday." Wainwright sought reaffirmation of her statement.

"All day."

"And he was perfectly OK then?" Kershaw further solicited verification of Molyneaux's health.

"As far as I could tell. What's this about? The murder of his brother? Terrible that." Wainwright declined to confirm or deny the nature of his enquiry.

When they pulled into the entrance to the car park at Sutcliffe Place, a police car and van were already stationed outside. Wainwright had called ahead to arrange for uniformed officers to be there on the assumption that Molyneaux was attempting to evade them and extra officers might be needed.

"Is Rupert Molyneaux's car here?" The four uniformed officers had congregated at the main entrance to the flats on seeing Wainwright arrive. They looked from one to the other in a display of blank disinterest. "Check the car park, Dean."

"Sir." Bowden scampered back along the street, from where they had lately come, swooped around the stone pillar at the end of the wall and continued on into the car park at the rear of the building.

"You two wait here." He pointed to two of the uniformed officers at random. "You two with us." He indicated the other two. Again, they looked from one to other before rearranging themselves into the pairs in which they had arrived and, ignoring Wainwright's arbitrary selection, the two that had arrived in the car followed the detective inspector and Kershaw into the building, while the other pair ambled back towards their van.

The quartet ascended the stairs, strode along the corridor, checking each flat number as they went, until they reached Molyneaux's apartment. Wainwright rang the bell. On receiving no response he knocked, as loudly as his knuckles permitted, on the door.

"Mr. Molyneaux? It's the police. If you're in there, I need you to open the door." They waited, listening. No sound was detected from within. "We need to speak with you, Rupert."

"His car's not there, sir." Bowden had come running, surprisingly light-footedly, Kershaw thought, towards them. Wainwright sighed, wearily, then turned to the uniformed sergeant.

"Go and get the big red key."

"Yes, sir." The sergeant turned, with renewed vigour at the prospect of seeing some proper action, and cantered back down the corridor.

"Flown the coop."

"Looks like it, Kate."

"But he was at work yesterday." Bowden reminded them of what they had been told at the university.

"He's not the sort of person to act on impulse and he probably reckoned it would take us at least twenty-four hours to process the DNA."

"Nevertheless, not hanging about longer than necessary."

"No. Though we don't know for certain that he's not in there." Bowden shrugged.

"True."

The sergeant, accompanied by the two other officers returned, carrying the enforcer. Wainwright stepped back from the door, with the others following suit, and authorised the door to be broken down. It took several attempts before the door eventually gave away. When it did, the constable tasked with the job stood back, satisfied with his work. Wainwright stepped across the threshold.

"Police! If you're in here, Rupert, show yourself." There was no response. He indicated to his fellow detectives that they should check all the rooms in the flat. Given its open plan nature, the other rooms to which he had alluded comprised the bedroom and the bathroom.

"He's not here, sir." Bowden confirmed what they already suspected.

"OK. Let's search the place. See what we can find." Wainwright surveyed the room for a moment, noting its neatness, with everything in its allotted place, before crossing to the side table, donning latex gloves and opening the two drawers. One contained table linen, neatly folded and looking as if it had never been used, and the other, sundry items of stationary. He rifled through both of them, but to no avail.

"Sir." He turned around to see Kershaw standing in the doorway to the bedroom, holding up a sheet of paper enclosed in an evidence bag.

"What've you got?"

"I'm guessing it's Casey Hardacre's best man's speech."

"Good work, Kate." He closed the drawers and hurried across to her to inspect her find for himself. "I think you're right." He paused, a slight frown crumpling his forehead. "Did you find a passport."

"No, sir."

"Nor me."

"Maybe he doesn't have one."

"Maybe."

"Sir!" The call came from the kitchen. Wainwright spun around.

"Yes, Dean."

"I think I've got something." The inspector crossed the room to the kitchen area, where Bowden was stood at one of the counters, Kershaw following.

"Good. I'd hate for you to be outdone by Kate." Bowden looked up with a mixture of puzzlement and irritation clouding his face. "What is it you've found?" The detective sergeant waited until Wainwright was at his side, before indicating, with a wave of his hand, a set of screwdrivers."

"They were in one of the kitchen cupboards. Phillips screwdrivers. Just like the one used to kill Carmine. And the largest one is missing."

"Well done, Dean. Bag them up." He sauntered over to the sink, peered out over Bellevue Park, turned around and leaned against it with a look of satisfaction, tempered by consternation. "So, we have DNA linking Rupert Molyneaux to the murder of Crispin Molyneaux, the best man's speech linking him to the murder of Casey Hardacre and a set of screwdrivers linking him to the murder of Carmine Seacroft." He turned his attention back to D.C. Kershaw. "Did you go through his wardrobe, Kate?"

"Yes, sir, but difficult to say if anything's missing."

"Did you find a padded jacket and baseball cap, like those our killer was wearing at the tennis club?"

"No, sir, but if he's done a runner, he could easily be wearing them."

"True. What about his wedding gear? He certainly wouldn't

194

be wearing that."

"From what I remember – and anything that flamboyant would stick out like a sore thumb – no sign of it."

"Probably disposed of it."

"Or, maybe, it was hired." Bowden was beginning to feel left out of the discussion.

"Possibly. Either way our priority now has to be to find Mr. Molyneaux."

Outside the flat a crowd of two had gathered near the top of the stairs, attracted by the commotion and huddled together in conjectural confabulation. Kershaw approached them to enquire as to whether either of them had seen Rupert Molyneaux during the last twenty-four hours while Wainwright gave instructions to arrange for the flat to be appropriately secured, stationing one of the uniformed officers outside the door pending that happening. Having assured them that there was no more to see, Kershaw sent the spectators on their way and waited for her superiors and the other officers to join her, greeting Wainwright with the news that neither of them had seen Molyneaux for several days.

Standing on the pavement outside Sutcliffe Place, Wainwright gave instructions for the police constable – whose partner had remained inside - to drive Bowden and Kershaw back to the station.

"Get the usual checks organised, Dean: CCTV," he looked about him, but did not spot any cameras in the immediate vicinity, "- there must be a camera at the fire station at the top of the road and there must be cameras at the other end, in town – mobile phone use, credit card activity, social media."

"Where are you going?" Bowden bridled at the ignominy of having to travel in a marked police vehicle.

"To see if I can find his mother. She's the one most likely to have known where he might have gone." Though, he realised, she was the one least likely to disclose her son's possible whereabouts. "And," he added as an afterthought, "she might know if he has a passport."

Mrs. Molyneaux's office was housed in a modern building,

detached from the main hospice complex, but within its grounds, on the edge of town. It was with some trepidation that she admitted him to the office, less than two days after she – and the rest of her family – had been required to provide DNA samples. One half of her was persuaded that the detective inspector was calling to give her, as the matriarch of the family, the news that the samples had exonerated all of them and that they no longer formed part of their investigation. The other half feared the worst: that they had made a match and that one of them was a prime suspect.

"What can I do for you, inspector?" She had seated him in a surprisingly comfortable tubular steel chair with generously padded fabric seats and armrests.

"I'm trying to trace Rupert."

"Rupert?" She sounded alarmed.

"He hasn't been in to work today and he isn't at home. Do you know where I might find him?"

"If he's not at work, no."

"Did he have any appointments anywhere?"

"Not that I know of."

"Something to do with work, perhaps?"

"Possibly." The suggestion clearly came as some relief to her. "He does often have to go out to pick up stuff; historical material that's turned up in someone's attic, or basement, or… wherever."

"But he didn't mention that he was going anywhere today."

"No. Usually, if Rupe's going somewhere or doing something, I find out after the event." She gave a little, indulgent smile, common to mothers who are feeling redundant as their children forge their own lives.

"Maybe he's taken some leave and gone somewhere. Anywhere he particularly likes to go?" She pursed her lips and shrugged.

"Nowhere in particular. Anywhere away from people. He tends to avoid people. Doesn't like crowds." Wainwright had the sense that she was being honest rather than evasive; that she was not obfuscating in an attempt to protect him. "Why do you need to find him?"

"I just need to clarify one or two things." He adopted his best, disarming smile and started to get up from the chair. "Thank you for your time." He straightened his jacket. "By the way," he paused, theatrically, "does Rupert have a passport?"

"A passport?" He hoped she would not press him on his reason for asking.

"I'm not sure. I think so. Why?"

"Has he been abroad recently?"

"Not recently. The last time he went abroad was before Brexit." Wainwright did not want to get involved in discussion lest he became obliged to provide explanations for his questioning, but he inferred, from the mention of Brexit, that he had probably gone somewhere in Europe, in which case, he reasoned, her son would not have needed a passport.

"Thank you, again, Mrs. Molyneaux." He was on his way to the door before she was able to pursue the matter further.

During the twenty-four hours since she had accompanied D.I. Wainwright to Rupert Molyneaux's flat in Sutcliffe Place, Gallagher's focus had been somewhat different to that of the detective inspector and, on the Wednesday morning, she was to be found sat at her desk in her office, with her laptop open. Wainwright had afforded her the courtesy of calling her to let her know that she had been right about the gloves and that DNA traces found on the inside of them had been matched to that of Molyneaux. On asking about how he intended to proceed, he had told Gallagher that he was on his way to Molyneaux's place of work at UCLAN to pick him up. As he was clearly on the move - and in a hurry – at the time of his phone call, she did not detain him for longer than necessary. However, had she been so inclined, she could have told him that he was embarking on a wild goose chase. Similarly, had she known that he and his colleagues would subsequently return to Sutcliffe Place, she could have told him that expecting to find Molyneaux there would prove equally fruitless, notwithstanding the evidence that they discovered at the flat.

When Gallagher and Wainwright had visited Rupert

Molyneaux on Monday evening, they had obtained a DNA swab from him in as routine a manner as possible. The inspector had thanked him for his cooperation and they had departed without further ado. Both had parked their cars in the road, opposite Sutcliffe Place, albeit some distance from one another. Gallagher had thanked him for inviting her along and they had returned to their respective vehicles. Having noted where he had parked, Gallagher had watched him drive off and had then got out of her Peugeot again. Slinging her bag over her shoulder she had crossed the road, made her way around to the back of the block of flats and had located Molyneaux's MG. Still convinced that he was the most likely killer, she had taken a tracking device, with which she had purposefully armed herself, from her bag and attached it to the underside of the front, nearside wheel arch.

During the course of Tuesday, Molyneaux had, from the intelligence she had gathered, driven to Nelson in the morning, remained there all day, then driven home again in the afternoon, stopping only at a convenience store on the way. On Wednesday morning he had, again, driven to Nelson. After Wainwright had called her with confirmation of the DNA analysis, she relaxed back in her chair, with a slightly smug smile on her face, gave a little swivel, caught a loose strand of hair between her fingers and entwined it around them, continuing to keep an eye on the small, green dot on the map on her laptop, and contemplated how she would proceed.

XX

ONE STEP AHEAD

Clematis Davenport entered Gallagher's office, bearing the requested mug of coffee, to find her boss still playing with her hair and, patently, deep in thought. She cleared a space on the desk and set the mug down.

"Trouble at mill, Ms. Gallagher?" Gallagher's expression indicated something was, indeed, troubling her, the smug smile having dissipated as she pondered the stationary green dot.

"What's he doing in Nelson?" Her eyes were boring into the desk. "He was there all day yesterday and he's there again today." She looked up at her secretary with, it seemed, an expectation of elucidation. Clemmy pursed her lips and gave a little shrug.

"Collecting material for 'is archives?" It appeared, to Clematis, to be the obvious explanation.

"All day yesterday? And again, this morning?"

"Maybe 'e's ferreting around in someone's attic."

"I don't think so. Do you know what this area is here?" She rolled her chair back to make way for her secretary to join her. Clematis, always eager to be of assistance in her boss's investigations, nimbly skipped around her desk, stood by Gallagher's side and peered at the screen. "This little area between the canal and the motorway." She assumed that the green dot would be sufficient to indicate the area to which she was referring.

"I think it's a little business park, or something like that. I'm not certain, but I think it is."

"Do you know what sort of businesses are there?"

"Sorry, Ms. Gallagher, I don't. I think there's, maybe, a large tool shop, 'ardware, that sort of thing down there. I think Gabe's been there a few times for various bits and pieces." The allusion to her boyfriend did not, noticeably, impress Gallagher, who had sunk back into thought.

"Maybe I need to check it out." Clematis permitted herself a wry smile. Her boss did not like being desk-bound and she invariably looked for an excuse to escape the office.

As she drove the relatively short distance from her office to Forest Business Park, Gallagher attempted to reconcile the work of an archivist with what possible gems of historical value a business park could have to offer. Furthermore, as she negotiated the intersection with the M65, she became aware that the site was a mere stone's throw from Pendlehurst, the location of Crispin and Magenta's wedding. Could that, she asked herself, be of significance?

As she turned into the entrance to the business park, she glanced at the laptop that was open on the passenger seat of her car. The green dot remained resolutely immobile. She passed a carpet warehouse, a car parts store, a joinery, a tool store (which, she assumed, was the one that Gabriel frequented), before reaching a supplier of kitchen units, at which point, her position was almost directly on top of the green dot. She pulled up in one of the vacant parking spaces outside the unprepossessing concrete and glass building.

Once outside of her car, she looked about herself. According to her tracker, she should have been a matter of feet from Rupert Molyneaux's car, but there were no blue cars to be seen, let alone a blue MG3. She followed the signal, which enabled her to pinpoint the vehicle being tracked, and found herself standing next to a white Dacia Sandero. Bewildered, she looked at her laptop and then at the car. She glanced around, somewhat furtively before ambling to the front of the vehicle and, as discreetly as she could, ran her hand around the front wheel arch. She moved along to the side, bent down felt along the underside of the sill. Her fingers touched something that felt familiar. She pulled it away from the chassis, stood up, opened her hand and stared at the object nestled in her palm.

"Shit!" It was, undoubtedly, one of her vehicle tracking devices – and, specifically, the one she had attached to Molyneaux's MG.

Being required to provide a DNA swab had triggered Rupert Molyneaux's anxiety, though it is unlikely anyone would have perceived it as years of practice had made him adept at disguising it. Despite sitting down to recompose himself, after Wainwright and Gallagher had departed, he had felt the need to go into the kitchen and get himself a calming beer. As he had entered the kitchen and glanced through the window, he had glimpsed Gallagher standing by his car. His instinct had been to shrink back, out of sight, not wishing to be caught staring at her if she chanced to look up. As it happened, Gallagher, exercising due diligence, had looked up to ensure that she was not being observed, but, not discerning him, had continued with her mission. Having convinced himself that he was fully entitled to look out of his own window, Molyneaux had done just that, only to discover Gallagher squatting down near the front of his car. She had only spent a few seconds there, but clearly there had been a purpose to her action and, intrigued by what he had witnessed, he waited a sufficient length of time for her to leave and had then gone down to the car park. Taking up a similar position to that of Gallagher he had made an examination of the front bumper and wheel arch of his car and duly discovered an object that he knew should not have been there. It had been held in place by a strong magnet, but he had managed to remove it. He had not been sure what it was, but, being a fan of crime drama, he imagined that it may have been some form of tracking device. His first thought had been to simply dispose of it, but then considered it might be a lot more fun if he attached it to another car. Consequently, he had pivoted on his haunches, and attached the offending article to the underside of the sill of the adjacent Dacia.

"How are we doing with CCTV?" Wainwright was in his customary position in front of the whiteboard, addressing his officers.

"The fire station's sending their tapes over." Bowden was sat at his desk, flicking through his notes. "We've located a couple of cameras in town, but without a time frame it's not easy to pin anything down."

"Hm. Credit cards?"

"We've had more success with that." The detective sergeant sounded considerably more perky. "Molyneaux withdrew two hundred and fifty pounds from the ATM at Sainsbury's at twenty thirty-seven on Monday evening."

"Shortly after I'd left him."

"Yes, sir. It's probably the nearest ATM to where he lives." Wainwright nodded. "He withdrew another two hundred and fifty from the petrol station on Waterloo Road at thirteen nineteen on Tuesday."

"That's close to the university. Probably during his lunch hour."

"And we know that he was in work on Tuesday. He also bought petrol on his card there at the same time."

"Planning a journey, by the sound of it."

"There was another withdrawal of two hundred and fifty pounds from the Sainsbury's ATM at seven forty-six this morning."

"Two fifty is probably his maximum daily withdrawal allowance, but he's still amassed seven hundred and fifty pounds. He could get quite a long way on that."

"He could. Perhaps it would be worth checking to see if he drove to the ATM this morning. All supermarkets have CCTV these days. If he did, it could mean that he made a run for it this morning."

"Hm." Bowden's rationale clearly did not please Wainwright, especially given that it was perfectly valid. "But if you're right, we ought to be able to pick him up on CCTV at some time after a quarter to eight, which is, at least, something. Get on to it, Dean."

"Sir."

"Phone records?" He scanned the room.

"Nothing unusual until yesterday lunchtime." Kershaw was

leaning against her desk, waiting for her superior to afford her an opportunity to make a contribution. "At thirteen fifty-one, probably after he came back from the petrol station, he called Magenta Molyneaux."

"Really?" Wainwright's interest had been piqued.

"The call only lasted about six minutes."

"I wonder what he wanted."

"Perhaps we should go and ask her, sir."

"Perhaps you should, Kate." He, pointedly, changed the pronoun.

"Sir."

"Anything else?"

"Nothing after that."

"Try calling him, but don't be surprised if his phone's off."

"Yes, sir."

"Social media?"

"Not a lot yet, sir." Kershaw took a certain delight in demonstrating how industrious she had been. "He doesn't seem to use Facebook a lot – the usual memes, comments about work, music, the occasional petition about environmental issues, *et cetera*. No red flags. I'm still following up on Instagram, TikTok and whatever else he might be on."

"OK. Keep at it."

For the remainder of the afternoon, Bowden was chasing up CCTV footage from wherever he could find it. Kershaw tried to phone Rupert Molyneaux, but, as Wainwright had supposed, his phone was switched off. Following that, she made her way to Cyril Fenmore Fine Art, whereat she found Magenta Molyneaux in the process of reconstructing a gold gilt picture frame.

"I believe Rupert Molyneaux phoned you yesterday lunchtime." Magenta had stopped what she was doing, it not being a task that could countenance distraction, and perched herself on a stool.

"Yes. He did." She sounded surprised that the detective sergeant should be aware of the fact.

"What did he want to speak to you about?"

"Not a lot, really. He just asked me if I'd like to meet him for a drink after work." She pushed a wayward lock of hair back over her shoulder.

"And what did you say?"

"There's a lot going on at the moment. It didn't seem quite appropriate. Anyway, I wanted to be with my parents. It quite upset them; having to give DNA samples." Kershaw nodded.

"How did Rupert react?"

"He made a rather tame attempt to persuade me – he's not exactly the most silver-tongued person in the world. I don't mean that disparagingly. His occasional gaucheness is part of his charm."

"But you resisted."

"As I say, I wanted to get back to my parents."

"And then what?"

"That was it. We chatted for a minute or two and then he said he had to get back to work."

"And you haven't heard from him again?"

"No. Why are you asking, anyway?" Kershaw thought, for moment, about how to respond.

"He seems to have gone missing. I thought he might have said where he was going."

It was evident to Mrs. Seacroft that something was troubling her daughter. It was equally clear that she was reluctant to discuss whatever the problem was. Rather than press Magenta against her will, she let the matter fall into abeyance, but then felt obliged to raise it again over the dinner table.

"I had a visit from the police again this afternoon. At work."

"Oh?" Warwick sounded surprised and suddenly interested.

"Oh." Laura sounded perturbed, borne of the feeling that such a development did not augur well.

"It seems Rupert's gone AWOL."

"What do you mean, Rupert's gone AWOL?" She rested her knife and fork against her plate in order to give her daughter her full attention.

"I don't really know." Magenta suddenly realised that she

could not elaborate; all Kershaw had told her was that Rupert had, apparently, gone missing. She had not been given any details as to why the police thought that. Laura was not sure if her daughter was being deliberately obtuse. "They just said they believed he'd gone missing and wondered if I knew where he might have gone."

"Why did they think you might know where he's gone – if, indeed, he's gone anywhere?" Warwick Seacroft took a more analytical line that his wife might have been disposed to do. Magenta glanced across at her father, somewhat sheepishly.

"Rupert called me at work, yesterday."

"You didn't mention it." As with many mothers, Laura tended to expect that her daughter would confide everything to her.

"There was nothing to mention." She responded more sharply that she had intended. "He just asked me if I wanted to go for a drink with him after work." Laura considered the implications of that for a moment.

"I take it you said 'no'." It appeared to be a reasonable conclusion given that Magenta had been home at her usual time the previous afternoon.

"It didn't seem appropriate. And, anyway, I didn't really want to. Rupert's been very kind since… Over the last week or so, but he's not the easiest of people to get along with." Both parents nodded.

"But now the police think he's gone missing." Warwick voiced his considered opinion. "Why would he do that? Have they found something that makes him a prime suspect?"

"Warwick! Surely not." Laura could only express disbelief at the suggestion. "I'm sure there's a very simple explanation. Maybe he's taken a couple of days leave and decided to get away for a while."

"Without telling anyone?"

"You know what Rupert's like. He likes his own company. He doesn't like getting involved in explanations."

"Possibly. But it's very ill-advised. From a police perspective, it's bound to make him look guilty."

* * * * *

"Who was it?" When David Molyneaux's phone had gone off, he and his wife had been sat out on the patio, enjoying the evening sunshine. He had left his phone in the kitchen and, on answering it, rather than return to the patio, he had gone and sat himself in the conservatory to conduct the conversation. When Vanessa had followed him inside, a few minutes later, having concluded that he would probably remain inside, he was just ending the call. He placed the phone on the glass-topped, wicker table and leaned back on the matching wicker sofa, decked with oatmeal, fabric cushions, a look of consternation on his face.

"Laura. She said that Rupert's gone missing."

"Laura? Why did she call you?"

"Why not? Anyway, the point is…"

"I'd have thought she'd have called me."

"Maybe because D comes before V so mine was the first name she'd have come to." He was alluding to the initials of their respective given names and the fact that his name would appear above hers in a list of contacts. If he had been paying attention, he would have seen that she did not look convinced by the explanation. She sat down in one of the wicker chairs that had identical cushions.

"What did she mean, Rupe's gone missing?" David recounted to his wife everything that Magenta had latterly related to her parents.

"For fuck's sake, David. You don't seriously think, for a moment, that Rupe could have killed Cris?"

"No, of course I don't, but you know what the police…"

"I'm going to call him. See where he is." Mrs. Molyneaux was out of her seat before she had finished speaking, through the French doors and into the lounge, in search of her mobile, before her husband had any time in which to respond.

Nick drained the remains of the Pinotage into Gallagher's glass. He had rarely seen her quite so agitated.

"I didn't see him. I looked. But he must have seen me. Figured out what I was doing, came down, found it and

206

transferred it to the nearest vehicle at random."

"So, he could be anywhere by now."

"Correct." She took an unusually large draught of the wine. "Shit!"

XXI

TEXTS, CALLS AND CONVERSATIONS

The pace and intensity of the investigation had increased and the industrious hum in the incident room had been amplified. Wainwright had rearranged his whiteboard such that the annotated photo of Rupert Molyneaux was in prime position at the top and centre.

A more exhaustive search of Molyneaux's flat had unearthed, wrapped in a plastic bag under his bed, a navy blue, padded jacket, which had been sent for prompt forensic analysis. The examination had revealed that a crude attempt at cleaning it had been made, but that it had been insufficient to disguise evidence of blood stains which proved to be a match for that of Crispin Molyneaux. Furthermore, a slight tear on one shoulder of the jacket had been discovered and testing of the fibres showed the fibres to be compatible with those found underneath Crispin's fingernails. Molyneaux's wedding attire, however, had not been unearthed, confirming Wainwright's previous supposition that it had been disposed of.

"Anything from his computer?" Wainwright addressed Kershaw directly.

"Not yet, sir." The detective constable had been combing Molyneaux's files with her trademark meticulousness, but had discovered nothing out of the ordinary. "The family photos are just that: run-of-the-mill snaps of family gatherings and individuals, but nothing to suggest an obsession with Crispin, Carmine or Magenta."

"Social media?"

"Doesn't appear to have much of a digital footprint. Facebook seems to be about all he uses. In the absence of his phone I've had to go through all the social media companies.

From what I can find he doesn't use TikTok or WhatsApp. He has an Instagram account, but doesn't seem to use it much. Nothing recently."

"OK. Good work, Kate." He turned to Bowden. "How are you doing with CCTV, Dean?"

"He was picked up on Sainsbury's cameras yesterday morning. Went straight to the ATM, took out some cash, went back to his car and drove off. That just confirms what we already know. Knowing the time he left there made it easier to track him. He headed north, towards Nelson, but he was clocked turning off onto Briar Lane at seven fifty-eight, heading towards Highridge. After that, we've lost him. I'm still trying to collect footage from Padiham and Barrowford, but I'm not holding my breath." Wainwright scanned the map he had attached to a second whiteboard he had commandeered for the purpose.

"If he'd been going west, through Padiham, he wouldn't have gone that way, unless it was a clumsy attempt to throw us off the scent, but I don't think he'd have wasted his time doing that. If he was heading north, why not just go up the motorway? Keep looking, Dean," he did not want to discourage his sergeant unnecessarily, "but he was probably looking for the quickest way to slip under the radar by heading for the hills."

David Molyneaux was on site, discussing the late delivery of a quantity of bricks - and how it would impact upon the project – with his foreman, when a message pinged into his phone. He took the phone out of his hi-viz jacket pocket and glanced at the screen without faltering in the conversation. The message sender was not identified and he did not recognise the number. Concluding that it was not urgent, he put the phone away and continued to plan how to proceed with the work in hand. When he had reached a satisfactory compromise, the foreman about turned and went on his way, while he ambled back to his car and leaned against the boot. He took out the phone again, opened his message box and stared at the unfamiliar number. It was rare for him to receive a message from someone he did not know. He opened it up.

'I know all about it dad. What the hell do u think u doing?'

Dad? His first thought centred on which of his children could have sent such a message. His second was to question the meaning of such a message. Belatedly, his third thought was that it was possibly a scam. He was aware that it was not uncommon for scammers to steal the identity of a child to con the parents out of money. He considered what he should do, before deciding to confront the texter head on. Rather than pressing 'Reply', he keyed in the number. The phone was switched off. It had not been so long ago that the message had come through. Why, he asked himself, would someone send a message and then immediately switch off their phone? He could, simply, have ignored it, with the presumption that the sender would call or message again, but the use of the word 'dad' had the desired effect and he eventually opted to send a text back.

'Who is this? What do you know about?'

He pressed 'Send', returned the phone to his pocket, then made his way across the site to where three contractors were poring over a plan, one with a bottle of water in his hand, another with a cigarette between his lips and the third simultaneously consulting his phone. Molyneaux reckoned that, if the sender of his message had deliberately turned their phone off, it would probably be a while before they turned it back on again and received his message. Even then, there was no guarantee, he reasoned, that they would respond. It was only when he was satisfied that all was well – or as well as could be expected – on site and he was returning to his car, ready to make his way back to the office, that another message pinged into his phone. He fished it out of his pocket without breaking step.

'Saw the 2 of u at the wedding. Started to suspect at our dinner with the Seacrofts. Became certain at lunch last Sunday. U were hardly discreet.'

The message stopped him in his tracks. It was clear what the sender was talking about. It was also clear that, if the sender was one of his children, it was most likely to be the one that had gone missing – and who was using an anonymous phone. He walked on to his car, got in and sat behind the wheel. Recent experience dictated that he did not even consider calling the number from which the text had been sent, assuming that he would only discover it had been switched off again.

'Is that you Rupert? Where are you? What are you talking about?'

He slotted the phone into the holder attached to the dashboard, turned the key in the ignition, shifted the gear stick into 'Drive' and was about to move off when the phone pinged again. He paused, shifted the gear back into neutral and, again, opened his messages.

'How long u been shagging Laura? Does mum know?'

Shaken by the calculated brusqueness, he removed the phone from its holder.

'It's not what you think Rupert.'

It was only after he had sent the message that he realised that, rather than issuing an emphatic denial, what he had sent was a *de facto* confession.

'Its exactly what I think. Want u to do something for me.'

The situation snapped into crystal clear focus. In an instant, his day had become a nightmare. Rupert was in trouble. He needed his father to extricate him and, having somehow figured out what was going on between his father and Laura, was trying to use that to blackmail his father into helping him.

'Are you in trouble Rupe? What do you want me to do.'

He continued to sit, staring through the windscreen. The Mercedes continued to idle. He knew he would receive another message shortly.

'I want to see Magenta.'

It was not the message he had been an anticipating, though what he had been anticipating, he could not have said.

'Magenta? Why? What's this about? I don't have any sway with Magenta.'

He was becoming overcome by confusion and was merely typing the first thing that came into his head.

'Maybe but Laura does and u have sway over your lover.'

Lover? He instinctively rose to the accusation, in the way one does when confronted by an unpalatable truth, but kept his emotions in check. The word had been intended to provoke.

"Rupert knows." The first words he uttered after she had answered her phone were unnecessarily, but deliberately, melodramatic in an attempt to grab her full attention.

"Rupert knows what?" In reality, her attention was focused on struggling to create a positive spin on what was proving to be a particularly negative Scorpio natal chart. However, as David recounted his text exchange with his son, Laura's astrological conundrum was edged further and further towards the back of her mind. "Why is Rupert so keen to see Madge?"

"I've no idea."

"Do you have any idea where he is?"

"None."

"You ought to call the police, David." Laura waited for a response to the suggestion, but none was forthcoming. "They're able to trace a mobile phone, so, when he calls again, they'll be able to find out where he is. More or less. Not precisely but a rough location."

"I can't."

"Why not?" Maybe her mind had still, partially, been on her troublesome Scorpio, or maybe she had not been giving Molyneaux's narrative her absolute attention and had not appreciated the implication.

"If…" He hesitated, swallowed hard and recomposed himself. "If Rupe is involved in the death," he could not bring himself to directly attribute the murders to his son, "of Cris, Carmine and Casey – and I can't believe that he is – he maybe feels he has nothing left to lose if he thinks the police have found evidence against him. If he realises he's destroyed his own life… He wants me to help him; he wants us to help him. The suggestion is, if we don't find a way of persuading Magenta to see him, he'll spill the beans on us. He'll destroy us. Not just you and me, but Vanessa, Warwick, Magenta. As if she hasn't been through enough. If we put the police onto him…"

"But he doesn't have any proof, David. He can't have." She tried to sound rational, but the rising note in her voice hinted at her rising fear.

"Wake up, Laura! He doesn't need proof. He only needs to insinuate; to start a rumour. That's enough to get people thinking; questioning anything they may have noticed at the wedding, or dinner, or lunch. Maybe he's bluffing, but if he noticed, then maybe others did. You know what people are like; you sow a seed like that and things they considered innocuous at the time are given a whole new meaning; they persuade themselves there's no smoke without fire. We can't go to the police."

Since moving in with her parents, Magenta Molyneaux had not been back to her house in Brindley Leas, a fact of which her mother was well aware. Hence, Laura Seacroft had called her daughter to suggest that it might be a good idea to check on it after Magenta finished work. Magenta had met the idea with undisguised indifference, not considering it necessary, but her mother had been insistent, which had aroused her suspicions of an ulterior motive. Laura had eventually conceded that there was a reason for wanting to meet her, but was not prepared to divulge what that reason was. In her turn, Magenta had acknowledged, for the sake of the charade, that maybe, checking up on her house was not such a bad idea, if only to discover what new scheme her mother may have been hatching. It was not unusual for Laura to devise, often hairbrained and impractical, plans for her own amusement. Hence, the arrangement was sealed. Laura called her husband to apprise him of her intentions and mother and daughter met at the latter's home at around 5.30 that afternoon.

"So, what's the real reason you wanted to meet here?" Magenta set two mugs of tea down on the coffee table in the lounge. Her mother was sat, a little uneasily, she thought, in a corner of the chesterfield. She opted for one of the armchairs. Despite the time of year, the house seemed cold; empty; strange. She was glad her mother was there. "Mum?" Laura had not shown any inclination to reply to her initial question.

"We've got a bit of a situation, Madge."

"What do mean 'a situation'?" Mrs Seacroft took a sip of her tea.

"You know you said Rupert called you, on Tuesday I think it was?"

"Yes. He wanted me to go for a drink with him and I said 'no'. What about it?"

"He called again today. Well, actually, he texted."

"He texted you?" She could not contain her astonishment. "Why would he do that?" Then she had an afterthought. "Do you know where he is?"

"No, he didn't say." She was glad to have the subsidiary question to answer before deciding how to respond to the main question. She had not, comprehensively, thought through her approach to the rendezvous that she, herself, had initiated. "He didn't actually message me; he texted David."

"David Molyneaux?" Her mother remained silent. "I don't understand, mum. You're talking in riddles." She picked up her own mug of tea and held it between her palms, as if to warm them.

"He reiterated his desire to see you. He wanted David to facilitate it and David called me."

"Why? I told him I didn't think it was appropriate to see him again at the moment. Not that I particularly want to. He's a very nice lad and he's been very kind, but his company can be a bit heavy."

"He seems very insistent."

"Didn't you tell David that I'd said 'no'?"

"Not in so many words, I don't think."

"Well, just tell him to tell Rupert that the answer's still no. Anyway," her mind had gone off on a tangent, "if Rupert is texting his dad, it ought to be possible to trace where he's calling from. You – or David – ought to tell the police."

"I can't. We can't."

"Can't what?" Magenta was beginning to become exasperated with her mother's apparent obtuseness.

"I can't tell David to tell Rupert that you refuse and we can't go to the police." Magenta put her mug down again, lest she spill it, but before she could remonstrate, her mother blurted out what she had been gearing herself up to say. "You're going to have to see him."

214

"Why? What the hell's going on, mum?" Her mother took another sip of tea, set the mug down again, adjusted her position, took a deep breath and composed herself.

"You remember the wedding." She suddenly flushed in embarrassment. "Yes, of course you do. It was your wedding." Magenta could not remember ever having seen her mother quite as flustered as she was now. "Well, it was a wedding and, at weddings, people have a few drinks."

"Mum, get to the point. What's this got to do with Rupert wanting to see me?"

"We'd had a few drinks and... well... David and I had a moment."

"You had a moment?" Magenta was not sure whether she should laugh or cry. "You mean he tried to snog you?"

"It wasn't even that, but Rupert must have seen us together and imagined there was something going on."

"I still don't understand."

"Rupert obviously thought, we'd had a bit of a thing at the wedding." She held her hand up to forestall an interjection. "Do you remember when we went over to the Molyneauxs for dinner a couple of Saturdays ago?"

"Yes."

"I went out into the kitchen to help David with the washing up." Rupert's got a fertile imagination and he put two and two together and made five. And then, last Sunday, when we had lunch together, Rupert got it into his head that we'd sneaked off together, after the meal for... well... who knows what goes on in his head."

"That's ridiculous." She chuckled, dismissively, then had another afterthought. "You're not – you and David – having…"

"Magenta! Of course not." She forced a laugh. "Don't be silly."

"Then what's the problem?" Laura gave her answer due consideration.

"The police think that Rupert is involved in the murder of Crispin and Carmine. And Casey. David is being forced to countenance the possibility that may be so. If we go to the police,

215

we'll have to cooperate with them in tracking his phone. That's another thing: he's not using his usual phone; he's got another one. Why would he bother to do that? Whether he's scared of being caught or whether he just wants to see you, for whatever reason, I don't know, but if he doesn't get to see you, he's threatening to go public with what he believes he knows about David and me."

"But if there's no truth in it…"

"Madge, don't be naïve. People are always willing to believe the worst. He'll make the most of what he's put together in his own mind and people will always say there's no smoke without fire. You know what the rumour mill's like. It'll hurt your dad and it'll hurt Vanessa. And you won't escape either. Even after everything's died down and Rupert's shown to have been out for some kind of vengeance – though for what, I don't know. I don't know what anyone's ever done to hurt him. – there'll always be the whiff of suspicion." She paused to catch her breath. "No one wants any of this, especially not on top of what's already happened. If David can arrange something that you're comfortable with – and your protection officers will never be far away, so you'll be perfectly safe – will you meet with Rupert?"

XXII

CAT AND MOUSE GAMES

Magenta Molyneaux had sounded agitated on the phone and that impression had been endorsed by her demeanour as she perched upon the chair on the opposite side of the desk. Normally, as a client unburdened themselves of their problem, they became more relaxed, but in this instance the woman had become increasingly anxious as her story had unfolded. When that happened, it was Gallagher's experience that it was because they were withholding a key element that they were trying hard not to divulge. All she had said was that Rupert Molyneaux had contacted his father and tried to persuade him to persuade Laura Seacroft to persuade her daughter to meet him, but that she was worried about doing so.

"I'm not sure why you've come to me, Magenta, or what it is you're expecting me to do. You really need to go to the police. You are aware that the police are looking for Rupert."

"I can't go to the police. We can't go to the police. That's why I've come to you." Gallagher leaned forward, conspiratorially, and raised a quizzical eyebrow. Mrs. Molyneaux glanced towards the window, but when she looked back, Gallagher was still peering at her, expectantly. She stared back for a few moments, but at a disadvantage: she was a mere amateur at this game; the private investigator was a professional. "Rupert's got it into his head that my mother is having an affair with David Molyneaux." She went on to unload herself of all the details as she had been given them by her mother, concluding by emphasising the fact that, in their opinion (she seemed keen to leave Gallagher in no doubt that they were at one in this belief) going to the police was not an option. "Mum pointed out that there's nothing to worry about because my bodyguards are always with me. They're outside now. But, I was thinking about that afterwards, and that's what's worrying me as much as anything." Gallagher had reclined back in her chair and was now twirling a few strands of hair between her fingers. As Magenta's narrative had tumbled out, it had occurred to her that one element of the story was not adding up and she was of the mind that Mrs. Molyneaux had, in her retrospection realised this as well. However, she wanted to hear it from the woman herself.

"Go on."

"Rupert doesn't want the police involved because he knows they'll be able to trace his whereabouts through his phone, yet he knows that I have police protection and they follow me everywhere. If I meet him, I'll lead the police straight to him. I'm worried about what he's planning to avoid that." Gallagher had gleaned everything she needed to know about the state play. She sat up in her chair again; a fully attentive and reassuring figure.

"So what is it you want me to do?"

"I want you to be there when I meet him." Gallagher nodded and proceeded to bring the interview to a conclusion. They exchanged parting formalities and she checked to ensure that Magenta had her mobile number.

"As soon as you know something – Rupert's unlikely to contact you directly, I think – call me."

When Magenta Molyneaux had left the office, Gallagher ambled through to her secretary, preoccupied, not so much with Magenta, but with Laura Seacroft and David Molyneaux.

"You look as if you need another coffee fix, Ms. Gallagher."

"I think I probably do, Clemmy."

"Everything alright?" Patently it was not.

"No." That was a cue to put the kettle on and make coffee, while her boss ensconced herself in the tub chair in the corner.

"Do you want to talk about it?" Clematis felt she was on safe ground in making the suggestion; her boss would not have come into her office unless she did want to discuss whatever was troubling her. While she fiddled about, making the coffee, Gallagher gave her a brief synopsis of what had passed between her and Magenta.

"Whether or not Rupert has any evidence to support his claim that his father and Laura Seacroft are having an affair, he knows his dad. And he probably knows Laura, too. He knows that people like that will go to any lengths to avoid any suspicion of marital infidelity, even if it doesn't exist. They'll go to any lengths to snuff out any hint of it. As Magenta implied: the default position of ninety percent of the population is, there's no smoke without fire. Her mother and father-in-law are prepared to put her in danger rather than risk damage to their reputations and marriages."

Having divested her mind of her thoughts on the perceived moral ambiguity of David Molyneaux and Laura Seacroft – and having gained her secretary's concurrence into the bargain – Gallagher retreated to her own enclave. There, she made herself comfortable, turned to her computer, opened the file of Nick Corvino's wedding photographs and selected the ones she wanted to re-examine. Yes, Rupert did appear fixated on Magenta; he seemed not to be able to keep his eyes off her. Could it be, she asked herself, that Rupert had been infatuated with Magenta Seacroft, as was, and fancied marrying her himself? Had he become so embittered when she had married his brother that he was driven to kill all those who had materially contributed to that espousal? What was he plotting now? Did he still think he could have her for himself, or was she the final piece in his macabre puzzle? If he could not have her, did he intend to kill her, too?

She opened one other photograph: that showing Mr. Molyneaux and Mrs. Seacroft, conspicuous by virtue of their singular wedding attire, engaged in an apparently intimate *tête-à-tête*. Maybe, she conjectured, Laura and David had sneaked out, like Casey Hardacre and Tez Garrity, for a quickie behind the barn and maybe Rupert had seen them. In the light of Rupert's allegations, which, Gallagher had inferred, were not without substance, was this photo evidence of an affair? Had Nick's pictures unwittingly revealed the guilt of their subjects? How would the remainder of this drama play out? Of one thing Gallagher was certain: just as the participants felt precluded from going to the police with their story, so, by extension, she was precluded from informing D.I. Wainwright of the information with which she had been entrusted.

"Could we take your car?" She threw the question into the conversation between sips of coffee and while Nick was changing the record. He slipped the John Lee Hooker back into its sleeve, replaced it in its proper place, ran a finger along his collection of vinyl albums and finally settled on one by Joe Bonamassa. He always found it a somewhat disquieting when she used that particular pronoun. Hitherto, 'we' had not entered into the strategy.

"Do you want me to come along?" It was a question to ascertain whether or not she wanted his company or the convenience of his car. She smiled behind his back.

"He probably knows my car. He's less likely to recognise yours." He placed the record on the turntable, lifted the tonearm, gently lowered the stylus onto the lead in and turned to return to the sofa. "Plus, I would like you there." He sat down beside her.

"You're not happy about this are you?"

"He's unpredictable. I don't know what he's planning. I don't know what outcome he's looking for. All I know is, there is a plan. He'll have thought it through. He knows what he wants to achieve even if no one else does."

"I still think you should tell Wainwright."

"So do I. But I don't feel I can. Magenta's in the middle of this and her safety is paramount."

"Do you think she's in danger?"

"I don't know Nick. I have no idea what's going through Molyneaux's head."

"And what about you?" She shrugged and took another sip of coffee. A shrug was, he considered in retrospect, probably the best answer to a question to which he did not really want to know the answer.

"I'll have you there to protect me." She tried to make light of the matter. Had she looked up she would have seen an expression that suggested that, while he appreciated her confidence, he was not convinced of the veracity of it.

Magenta Molyneaux's version of what had transpired over the twenty-four hours since her visit to Gallagher's office, had been a little incoherent, but the gist of it had been plain. Rupert Molyneaux had continued to contact his father through text messages. The messages had been relayed to Laura Seacroft, who had passed them on to her daughter. Rupert wanted to meet Magenta on Sunday. He had not, as yet, specified a time. He wanted to meet in Barrowford but, similarly, he had not specified a place. Why he had chosen Barrowford, David Molyneaux had been unable to elicit from his son. David had reminded Rupert, after Laura had reminded him, that Magenta had round the clock police protection. Rupert had taken that into consideration. He had pointed out that he was familiar with the layout of the front of the Seacroft's house and knew that the police were not parked exactly opposite the drive. He had given instructions that Magenta should be smuggled onto the back seat of Laura's Volkswagen and covered with a blanket. He would text her, direct, to tell her at what time to leave. Once they were out of sight of the police and Laura was sure they were not following, Magenta could emerge from hiding. Laura was then to drive to Barrowford. When they reached the village, she was to stop and text him to let him know they had arrived. Rupert would then give them further instructions. This was as much as Magenta knew of Rupert's plans. Gallagher asked her to send a message the moment she had any further details. She attempted to allay Magenta's anxieties with assurances that she would be right behind her, albeit at a discreet distance so as not to run the risk of arousing Rupert's suspicions.

"Have you got any idea at all what time they'll set off?" Nick had been asking variations on the same question ever since they had got up. Gallagher had tried to be patient. For her, hanging around all day, sitting in a car, waiting for something to happen, or someone to show up, was par for the course, but she understood that, for him, the nebulousness of it was an irritation. Without knowing where in Barrowford Molyneaux would arrange to meet Magenta – or what his plans were, subsequently – the latest she had dared to leave the house was nine that morning. If, she calculated, Magenta contacted her while they were on the road, either they would pass the purple Beetle while going up Wellgate Road, or, if Laura had elected to go over the top of the ridge (the only other way to get from Wellgate to Barrowford) they would not, she hoped, be too far behind them. As it was, they had reached the crossroads at Wellgate without any contact. She had instructed Nick to turn the Antara around and park more or less opposite The Coachman pub. From that vantage point they could not fail to see the Volkswagen and whether it turned left to go down Wellgate Road or continued straight on to go over the top. Having parked, she had asked Nick to walk down Todmorden Road and, discreetly, check on whether Laura's car was still there. He had got there and back and reported that it was. All they could do now was wait.

"Look on the bright side, Nick: in another three hours the pub'll be open and we can go and get lunch and sit outside and watch from there."

"Yes, sweetheart."

They had been idly chatting about their plans, relating to their annual visit to the Rhythm & Blues Festival in Colne later in the summer, when Gallagher's phone pinged.

'Just leaving. M'

It was, Gallagher reckoned, probably as much as she could type without attracting attention. Nick looked across at her, expectantly.

"We're on our way." Gallagher glanced at her watch. It was a shade after ten thirty. Nick started the engine. The wait seemed interminable, but it was probably less than five minutes before the Volkswagen appeared and turned down Wellgate Road. Nick shifted the car into gear and began to follow.

It had to be admitted that following a metallic purple Volkswagen Beetle, that could be detected a mile away, was not the most challenging pursuit she had been engaged upon, but Gallagher was grateful for that, given that it was not she who was driving. To ease the situation further, Laura took the route that she would have taken had she been making that journey: straight up Colne Road, onto the motorway at Junction 12 and off again at Junction 13. Once over the bridge that spanned Carr Brook, the Volkswagen turned right into the garden centre car park. Gallagher instructed Nick to turn left into the street opposite the entrance, thence to turn the car around and await further developments. She assumed Laura was stopping so that Magenta could text Molyneaux to tell him she had arrived in Barrowford.

"What now?" As was his wont, Nick was entering into the spirit of the task at hand and having difficulty curbing his growing enthusiasm for it. For him, it was a cloak and dagger adventure. Gallagher knew better, but she was not going to disabuse him at this stage.

"We wait. She's probably getting further instructions from Molyneaux." She took a quick look through each of the car windows to see if Molyneaux might be watching. It was only precautionary; she did not expect to see him since he would have had no way of knowing where Laura would stop.

"We're on the move again." Nick had kept the engine running. Laura turned right, out of the car park. Nick waited at the junction for a car and a light van to pass before he turned left to follow. Having a couple of vehicles between the Beetle and themselves was a fortuitous convenience. They were, however not on the move for long. Laura turned left. When they reached the spot, they found it to be the car park of the library. Without prompting, Nick took the first right past the library and found himself in a cul-de-sac. Gallagher kept an eye on the Beetle through the rear window. The cul-de-sac had private parking bays along one side, only one of which was occupied, affording ample space in which to turn around. To Gallagher, a library seemed a strange place to meet. "It won't even be open on a Sunday." She felt a little chagrined that Nick had grasped something that she had not.

"You're right. And she hasn't parked up. She looks like she's not expecting to stay." Nick had turned the Antara round, giving Gallagher a clear view of Laura and Magenta through the windscreen. "I wouldn't mind betting Rupert's somewhere about."

"Checking to make sure the police aren't tailing her?"

"More than likely. He's not going to trust anyone. He wants to make sure they're alone before he gives them the meeting place." Once again, they did not have to wait long. "This could be it." Nick edged forward. "Easy does it." He held back as much as he could while allowing her to see which way Laura turned coming out of the car park. They turned left. Gallagher ducked as low as she could, given the constraint of the seatbelt, lest Laura should glance in their direction and spot her."

"All clear."

"I should've anticipated that." Nick moved up to the junction, just in time to see the Beetle take the first left. Being a Sunday and there being little traffic, he had minimum difficulty getting out onto the main road. The road Laura had taken curved away to the left, leaving the Beetle out of view. "Hold it!" Nick, ever vigilant, checked the rear-view mirror before hitting the brakes. "Back up." Nick obeyed without question. "There they are." She pointed along the side street they had just passed. Nick reversed a little further and then made the left turn. The street took them behind the library. Gallagher pointed through the window again. "Rear access to the library. Rupert must have been observing them from here."

"Then his rendezvous place can't be far from here. He wouldn't have much time to get back to it once Magenta set off." The beetle turned right. Nick slowed down as they approached the turning and drew up at the curb opposite it. The speed at which Laura was driving suggested that she was looking for a parking spot. Eventually she found one and performed a neat piece of parallel parking.

Grant Street was a very pleasant road of recently sand-blasted terrace houses with compact frontages that allowed for a small rectangle of lawn, flower beds or two or three shrubs. From what Gallagher could see, most had new windows and doors. The residents, she concluded, took pride in their own houses and the street as a whole. It was a quiet neighbourhood.

"Why has he chosen to meet here?" Gallagher could not

quite make sense of the choice of venue.

"There's nothing along here except houses. Unless he owns a property here, which doesn't seem likely, he must have lured her to someone else's house."

"A friend?"

"Accomplice?"

"I'm not sure I like the way this is going, Nick." She saw Magenta's head appear above the roofs of the line of parked cars. She appeared to brace herself and then began to walk back along the pavement.

"I need you to check, as discreetly as possible, the number of the house she goes into. I'll move the car away from here." Nick got out of the car, crossed the road and waited at the corner, out of sight of Magenta, until she came to a halt, turned, opened a gate and walked up to a front door. Meanwhile, Gallagher clambered across into the driving seat and shifted the car a few yards past the end of Grant Street.

The front door appeared to open and a few words seemed to have been exchanged before Magenta disappeared inside the house. Nick, staying focused on the property, crossed the road and checked the numbers of the first two houses on that side. Having established whether they were odds or evens, and ascending or descending, he crossed back to the other side and ambled, as nonchalantly as he could, up the road, counting the houses as he went, until he was certain he had established the number of the house that Magenta had entered. Satisfied, he turned and retraced his footsteps. Gallagher was waiting for him at the corner.

"Number twenty nine."

"Which one is it?"

"The one next door to the one with the hedge." Nick pointed to the house. "On the other side of it."

"Thank you." Gallagher stared at the house, wondering what was transpiring inside and hoping Magenta was safe. Laura had remained in her car.

"Now what?"

"We wait. There's nothing more we can do. Except…"

"Except?"

"I have to call Wainwright. She's kept her part of the bargain. The police haven't followed her. Now I have to tell him where Rupert is." She reached into her bag, took out her phone and keyed Wainwright's number.

"Beth." He did not seem surprised that she should be calling, despite the fact that it was a Sunday.

"I know where Rupert Molyneaux is."

"You do?" He did not sound convinced.

"He's in Barrowford."

"Barrowford?"

"Grant Street."

"Beth, hold on. How do you know?"

"Number twenty nine."

"Beth, how do you know…"

"I'm there now."

"How did you…?"

"I'll explain later." Explanations were the one thing she was keen to avoid at the present time. "You need to get here."

"Hold on; let me write it down." There was a pause while, she supposed, he hunted for a pen and a scrap of paper. "Twenty nine, Grant Street…"

"No marked cars anywhere near; no flashing lights; no sirens."

"Beth…"

"It shouldn't take you much more than fifteen minutes." With that, she ended the call.

"Impressive." He had gleaned all he needed to know about the interaction from her tone of voice while he kept watch on the house.

"And now we wait for them to arrive."

"And if she comes out in the meantime?"

"There's nothing we can do about that. If he stays put, fine; if he moves on, at least they'll have a starting point." She returned her phone to her bag. "The only thing that's bothering me is that I can't see his car anywhere. He ought to have been able to park along here if he'd wanted."

"Maybe there wasn't space when he got here. Or maybe it was just easier to park in an adjoining street."

"Maybe. And there's still the question of whose house this is."

The minutes before Wainwright's arrival had passed slowly, as they always do in such situations. There had been no comings or goings to or from the house under surveillance. Nick had grown anxious. Gallagher had tried to reassure him with the suggestion that Molyneaux probably had a lot to explain to Magenta. When the detective inspector did arrive, it was discreetly. He had driven the same way as she had: along the road behind the library. He had parked his, now ageing, but favoured, blue Volvo, behind Nick's Antara, closely followed by a grey BMW in which Gallagher had discerned D.S. Bowden and D.C. Kershaw. Further down the road – and a good way away – a patrol car and a police van had pulled up.

"What's going on, Beth?" He was, as might have been expected, dressed casually: blue chinos and a sandy-coloured, short-sleeved shirt and no tie, but with his black, leather jacket draped over his shoulder.

"He's in twenty nine, Danny; the one next to the one with the hedge." She pointed it out just as Nick had done. "Magenta's with him."

"Magenta?"

"She's been in there the best part of half an hour." Given that he was most likely to have been at home, she had fully appreciated that it would take him considerably more than the fifteen minutes she had suggested on the phone to get there.

"Beth, I need some sort of explanation here. How…"

"That can wait, Danny. Laura's parked further up the street, beyond the house."

"Whose house is this?"

"I've no idea. I only know Magenta arranged to meet Rupert here and that they're inside that house." Wainwright was about to question her further, but thought better of it, knowing that doing so would be fruitless and, possibly, wasting precious time.

He had, he reckoned, to trust her. Instead, he signalled to Bowden and Kershaw, still waiting in their car, to join him. He put on his jacket, got out his phone and called his other officers, instructing them to bring their vehicles up behind the BMW.

"Sir?" Bowden sounded even more irritated at having his Sunday morning unceremoniously disrupted than Wainwright had done.

"Rupert Molyneaux and Magenta are in one of these houses. Twenty nine, to be precise. She, apparently, arranged to meet him here. She's been in there about half an hour. Laura Seacroft's waiting for her in her car further along."

"How do you know…?"

"I don't. I'm taking Ms. Gallagher's word for it."

"Whose house…?"

"I don't know, Dean. Let's just go and find out."

"Yes, sir."

"Beth." He turned, abruptly, towards Gallagher. "You stay here. Don't even think about following us." He then addressed Nick. "Make sure she does stay here." Straightening his jacket, he returned his attention to his team. "Right, you two, let's go." He led the way down the centre of the road. Bowden and Kershaw dutifully followed.

When they arrived opposite the house with the hedge, Wainwright paused to check the number. Confirming that it was twenty seven, he proceeded to the next house along, as Gallagher had indicated. Magenta had left the gate open. The three detectives walked up the short path in single file. Wainwright pressed the bell push. He heard it chime. Not getting a reply, he tried again, and then knocked on the door panel. Bowden peered through the window.

"There doesn't seem to be any sign of life, sir." Wainwright tried the handle. The door was unlocked. He, tentatively, pushed it open.

"Mr. Molyneaux?" The house exuded an almost eerie silence. "Rupert Molyneaux? It's D.I. Wainwright." He looked back to his colleagues and then stepped inside. "Magenta?"

The ground floor of the house had been renovated to create

a single, spacious, open-plan living area. What might have been supposed to be a lounge, dining room and kitchen had all been knocked into one. French doors led from the kitchen into a small garden, the high back wall of which could clearly be seen. The front of the room was dominated by two, maroon leather Chesterfields; a three-seater and a two-seater. A plush, dusky pink carpet extended as far as the kitchen area. The pale grey walls were hung with various prints in black and grey frames. The furniture was minimal and angular, with just a plant in a pot on a side table breaking up the horizontal and vertical lines. The re-modelled staircase ascended from some three yards inside the front door. Wainwright walked, warily, into the centre of the room, taking in as much as his eyes could accommodate. Bowden craned his neck to see as far as he could up the stairs. Kershaw advanced to the kitchen.

"Sir!" The urgency in her voice was unmistakable.

"What have you got?" Wainwright hurried towards her, Bowden on his heels. "Oh, fuck!" Kershaw did not need to show him; the blood on the floor and splattered on the cupboard and refrigerator doors, and the smashed and bloodied jug was plain to see. Wainwright attempted to assess the scene before taking out his phone and calling for his uniformed officers. "Wait until they arrive, then check upstairs, Dean."

"Yes, sir." Bowden's natural instinct would have been to rush up the stairs on his own, but he had, since promotion to detective sergeant, acquired a modicum of circumspection and thus he complied, albeit impatiently.

"I'll get forensics down here."

"Do you think it's Magenta's blood?" While waiting for Wainwright to organise the dispatch of a forensic team to the scene, Kershaw had squatted down to examine the blood, as if, by doing so, she would be able to identify whose it was.

"I don't know. Let's hope not, but we're looking at an act of violence, and there aren't many possibilities as to who the victim might be."

"What about Mrs. Seacroft?" Kershaw got back to her feet. Wainwright had already apprised his colleagues, during their walk to the house, of Laura Seacroft's presence.

"I suspect she doesn't know we're here, else she'd have come running. Let her be. We don't have anything to tell her at present." Wainwright's supposition was correct. Laura was sat in her car, facing away from the house, largely preoccupied with her mobile phone, and had not noticed the police activity at number twenty nine.

"Sir." Kershaw had moved away from the blood and shards of pottery. "The back door's ajar." She donned latex gloves, crooked her little finger round the handle, and opened it. Wainwright joined her and followed her into the garden. She walked down the short garden path towards the back gate. "It's unlocked." Both the top and bottom bolts were drawn. Again, with her little finger she lifted the latch, opened the gate and peered out. "It opens onto a ginnel."

"Oh, fuck." Wainwright was stood right behind her. "Of course it does. This is Lancashire. These are terraces. Of course there's a back alley. Why didn't Gallagher realise that? Too busy trying to be fucking clever." He spun around and returned to the house.

A constable was hovering, aimlessly, in the lounge when Wainwright entered. Wainwright glanced across at the stairs in time to see one leg disappear from view.

"How many of you are there?"

"Four, sir. Three 'ave gone upstairs with D.S. Bowden."

"Thank you." He moved across the room to mount the stairs himself, but no sooner had he placed one foot on the bottom tread than Bowden yelled down at him. He scampered to the top. Bowden was waiting outside an open bedroom door. "What is it?" In reply, his sergeant simply re-entered the bedroom from which he had latterly come. When Wainwright arrived, he discovered a man, hands and feet bound, sitting on the bed, looking confused and disorientated.

"He'd been gagged as well." Bowden pointed to a length of material hanging over the footboard. "He was lying on the bed when we found him."

"Well, get him untied."

"Go and get a knife, or something, from the kitchen." Bowden barked the order in the general direction of the two officers in the room with them. One of them headed to the door and relayed the injunction to the constable standing on the landing.

It had taken Wainwright only a matter of seconds to appraise the scene with which he was greeted when he entered the bedroom. The man, in his forties, he estimated, was bound with blue, nylon rope. A wound to the back of his head was clearly visible. There was blood on the duvet and pillow, where, he assumed, he had been lying. A blood-stained towel was crumpled on the far side of the bed. He assumed that Molyneaux had grabbed the towel from the kitchen to staunch the flow of blood and, considerately, prevent it ruining the carpet in the lounge and on the stairs.

"I'm D.I. Wainwright. We'll have you free in a jiffy."

"Thank you. I thought I were goin' t' be 'ere forever."

"What's your name?"

"Tim. Tim Bulstrade."

"Is this your house, Tim?"

"Yes."

"Who did this to you?"

"Molyneaux. Rupert Molyneaux." Wainwright nodded. He was biding his time until Bulstrade could be freed. He heard feet bounding up the stairs and, moments later, the constable appeared, brandishing a kitchen knife. The inspector and Bowden stepped aside, indicating that the constable should perform the operation. Nylon rope is not easy to cut with a kitchen knife and it was some minutes before both ropes had been loosed. Bulstrade exhaled a sigh of relief and rubbed his wrists and ankles. Wainwright bent down to cursorily examine the head wound and then turned to the uniformed sergeant in the room.

"Get a paramedic here, please, sergeant."

"It's OK; I'm fine." Bulstrade's protestation was somewhat half-hearted.

"You've sustained a nasty wound there, Tim. You need to have it checked out." Bulstrade acquiesced without further ado.

"Sergeant."

"Yes, sir." The sergeant turned and trotted out of the room. Wainwright pulled up a faded, green, Lloyd Loom chair, positioned it opposite Bulstrade, and sat down.

"Can you tell me what happened, Tim?"

"Rupert got 'ere about ten, maybe a bit after."

"Were you expecting him?"

"Yes."

"In your own time."

"'E wanted t' show me somethin'."

"Show you something?"

"Sorry. Yeah. We both belong to East Lancs 'Istorical Society. 'E called me last week. Said some woman 'ad offered 'im some artefacts. 'Er grandma 'ad worked in the mills during the First World War and 'ad kept a few things. I don't know the full story, but she said she thought Rupert might be interested in them, 'im bein' an archivist an' interested in 'istory an' all that."

"Go on."

"So, 'e comes in an' the first thing I do is offer 'im coffee, as you do. I went into the kitchen an' 'e came with me. I just put the kettle on an' then... well, 'e must've 'it me over the 'ead with somethin'. Next thing I know, I'm on the floor an' e's got me 'ands be'ind me back an' tyin' them up." Wainwright picked up a length of the rope and examined it.

"It looks new, sir." Bowden was standing at his shoulder, hands in his pockets.

"Is this your rope?"

"No. 'E must've brought it with 'im." Wainwright gave him a quizzical look. "'E 'ad a bag; a sorta sports bag. I supposed 'e 'ad the artefacts, or whatever, in it."

"Then what happened?"

"Not sure. I suppose I were shoutin' at 'im; askin' 'im what the 'ell 'e were playin' at. Anyway, 'e 'ad 'is knee in me back. Forced me 'ead back and tied a gag round me mouth. Then 'e drags me to me feet an' forces me upstairs an' shoves me on the bed."

"Did he say anything while all this was going on?"

"Not a lot."

"Then what happened?" Bulstrade shrugged.

"Nothin'. Not for about 'alf an hour. Maybe longer; maybe shorter; I don't know. Then the doorbell rang. I 'eard 'im answer it, as if 'e were expectin' someone. I 'eard a woman's voice. She came in. They talked for a while."

"Did you hear what they said?"

"No. I 'eard voices, but the door were closed."

"Were they just talking, or were they arguing?" He shrugged again.

"Didn't sound like they were shoutin' or anythin'. Just talkin'. Then they stopped. I think they went out back. I think I 'eard 'im unbolt the back gate, but it's 'ard to 'ear from 'ere. I did 'ear a car engine, though. 'E must've parked 'is car in the ginnel."

"Thank you, Tim. We'll need to take a formal statement from you later. Meanwhile, this is a crime scene. I'll have to leave a couple of my officers here until the paramedics arrive." Wainwright got to his feet. "A forensic team will be here shortly. They'll need to go over the house and they'll need to ask you for fingerprints and a DNA sample."

"DNA? Fingerprints? Why?"

"We need to match the blood we found in the kitchen with yours."

"'oose else would it be?" Wainwright thought for a moment before answering.

"We need to be certain. Fingerprints are just for elimination. We'd expect yours to be all over the house. We need to isolate those that are not yours." He concluded the interview with instructions to one of the constables to remain with Bulstrade until the paramedics arrived. He then, along with Bowden and the other officers, made his way downstairs, where they were met by Kershaw.

"So where do we start?" Bowden had clearly forgotten it was Sunday and was keen to get on to Molyneaux's trail.

"CCTV, ANPR. You know the drill. And see if we can get a trace on Magenta's phone."

"Sir."

"Kate."

"Sir?"

"Go and tell Ms. Gallagher and that boyfriend of hers to go home – and make sure she does. Tell her I'll speak to her later.

"Yes, sir. What are you going to do?" He took a deep breath.

"I'm going to have to go and have a talk with Laura Seacroft."

XXIII

A COTTAGE IN THE COUNTRY

D.C. Kershaw had conveyed Wainwright's instruction, together with his displeasure, in no uncertain terms. Gallagher had little cause to object. She still felt that she had done the right thing but, equally, felt chastened by her own folly. She should, she knew, have realised that there would be a ginnel running along the back of the houses and, when she had not spotted Molyneaux's car parked in the road, considered the possibility that he may have parked along it to facilitate an escape. She now felt responsible for Magenta's safety. When they had got back home, she only spent as much time in the house as it took to drink a mug of coffee. On the journey home she had been mulling over how to proceed. Having finished her coffee, she went back out to her own car and set off for Padiham. She had reasoned that, if anyone would know where Rupert Molyneaux was likely to have gone, it would be his parents. When she had arrived at the house, she had discovered the Molyneauxs in a state of high agitation. They had hastened her into the lounge and sat her in one of the armchairs, while they seated themselves on the sofa.

"Laura Seacroft phoned us this morning."

"Phoned you." Mrs. Molyneaux was keen to emphasise the distinction. Her husband ignored her.

"She said Rupert had abducted Magenta. What's going on? Where has he taken her? And why? What does he want?"

"We don't know for certain that he has abducted her." Gallagher attempted to allay some of their fears. "We only know that Magenta is with him. She could have gone with him voluntarily."

"Do you think that's likely?" Vanessa tried to temper her scepticism with hope.

235

"We have to keep an open mind. As for what he wants, I can't say, but I'm hoping you might be able to help with where he might have gone."

"We've no idea." Mr. Molyneaux's current, distressed state, did not permit him to think before speaking.

"I need you to think. Is there anywhere that you know of that me might have gone? A favourite place; somewhere he likes to go." They looked at one another then back at Gallagher.

"I can't think of anywhere." He turned, again, to his wife. "Can you?" She shook her head.

"Somewhere that's familiar; somewhere that he might feel safe." They lapsed into deep thought before Vanessa glanced at her husband, as if to gain permission to speak.

"What about the house?" David looked at her, apparently uncomprehending as to what she was alluding. "The house at Gissington."

"What about it? Why would he go there?"

"I don't know." She sounded irritated. "It's just a thought. It's the only place I can think of that he might possibly have gone. And you haven't come up with a suggestion."

"He doesn't have a key to it."

"A house in Gissington?" Gallagher was, temporarily, feeling completely out of the loop.

"David's bought a cottage in Gissington. He's renovating it."

"It's a personal project. Nothing to do with the company. I bought it on spec at an auction. It was a bit of a wreck, but I thought it would be fun to do it up and either sell it on or let it."

"Is it possible he could have gone there?"

"It's nowhere near finished." He sounded dismissive. "And, as I said, he doesn't have a key." Vanessa gave him a look suggesting he was not being perfectly honest in that respect."

"There is a key there, David. He could…"

"Rupert wouldn't know about it. He isn't interested. Crispin knew about it because he's an architect." He returned his attention to Gallagher. "Crispin took an interest from a design perspective. We don't work together professionally, but this is a personal project."

"Tell me about the key."

"It's kept hidden on the property." He afforded himself a wan smile. "An under-the-doormat sort of job. It's there so that when my contractors go up there – electricians and the like – they can access the property. Crispin knew where it was so that he could get in as and when he felt like it and, maybe come up with a few ideas as to how to develop it."

"And Rupert doesn't know where it is. You're sure?"

"We never talked about the place."

"Does Vivienne know about it?"

"Viv?" He seemed surprised that Gallagher should bring his daughter into the conversation. "Not as far as I know."

"Could Crispin have talked about it with Rupert?"

"I don't see why he would."

"But he could have done, David." Vanessa was, at least, attempting to be less obstructive.

"I suppose he *could* have done."

"You never know what brothers discuss when they're together." Mr. Molyneaux could only shrug his shoulders.

"So, it's a possibility Rupert could have known about the key. Presumably he does know about the cottage."

"Of course, he knew about the cottage and I suppose it's possible he could have found out where the key's kept." Molyneaux, eventually, had to concede the point.

"I'll need the address of this cottage."

During the drive home, Gallagher reflected on her conversation with the Molyneauxs. The cottage in Gissington was a long shot, but, at present, it was all she had. She also conjured up her mental map of east Lancashire. Gissington, she reckoned, must be a good twenty kilometres from Padiham. Surely, she asked herself, if Molyneaux wanted a development project, could he not have found somewhere nearer to home? Why seek out somewhere that distance away? Vanessa Molyneaux had not appeared particularly enamoured by the idea. The conclusion she came to was that twenty kilometres was near enough to be relatively easily accessible, yet far enough away such that no one would recognise him there. More pertinently, she mused, no one would recognise them there. Far from selling it on or renting it out, she wondered if David was intending it as a love nest for him and Laura Seacroft.

"So what do you intend to do now?" He chomped on a piece of baguette and cheese.

"There's only one thing I can do." Gallagher prodded, disconsolately, at her salad. "I have to check out that cottage. It's a long shot, but I don't have anything else." The answer did not surprise him.

"I'm coming with you. We can take my car." She was somewhat taken aback by Nick's uncharacteristic assertiveness.

"Have we got anything on Molyneaux's car?"

"Nothing yet, sir." Bowden sounded apologetic.

"If he met Magenta at Barrowford, it's likely he intends continuing north. There'd be no point in doubling back." Wainwright was tapping the relevant area of his map with the tip of a pen. "Get tech to focus their efforts there."

"It's a maze of country lanes. It's too easy to fly below the radar."

"Got a better suggestion?"

"No, sir."

"Kate, how we doing with Magenta's phone?"

"Not good, sir." She looked up from her desk. "The last time she used it was at Barrowford. She sent a couple of texts a few minutes apart. Since then it seems to have been switched off."

"Molyneaux's phone?"

"Magenta's texts went to a pay-as-you-go phone. Don't know if it was his, but assuming it was, that's the last time he used it. Again, it seems to have been switched off."

"He's ditched his usual phone and bought a cheap burner for the purpose. If he's had the wherewithal to do that and then to keep it turned off, he'll must likely have taken Magenta's phone to make sure she doesn't try and use it. Bugger!"

* * * * *

238

Having been given the address and precise directions to David Molyneaux's cottage at Gissington, Gallagher would have been able to demonstrate her navigational skills had Nick not insisted on using a satnav. At the turn-off to Crowhill Lane, just before they entered the village, he drew up to the verge to await instructions.

"It's quite a way up, so I think we're OK." Nick put the car into gear, checked his mirror, indicated and made the right turn. "But stop at the first opportunity." A little to her exasperation, that opportunity was the car park to the village hall, a mere hundred yards along the lane, but she could hardly complain – and it did give her the chance to assess the situation. Her first observation was that, as might have been expected, Crowhill Lane was narrow. Parking, it appeared, was confined to the road itself, the frontage of the properties, or, in a few cases, to the side of the houses. Molyneaux's cottage was detached, but nevertheless, there was, she reckoned, little possibility of hiding a car. "Let's keep going. I'll keep an eye out for his car." Nick obeyed. They drove in silence until Gallagher leant across, conspiratorially, towards him. "Can you find somewhere to turn round and then find somewhere to park up around here." Nick glanced across at her. She smiled. "I spotted his car four or five houses back."

"You sure it was his?"

"Positive." She sounded offended that he should doubt her powers of observation.

"After all the trouble he's gone to so far, isn't that a little bit careless to leave it parked in plain sight?"

"Not really. He wouldn't have expected anyone to track him to the house – and I wouldn't have been able to if Magenta had followed instructions to the letter – but, just in case, I imagine he came up here using the back lanes, out of sight of cameras."

"And you don't think he'd be worried by attracting the attention of the neighbours."

"The house is a personal project. David Molyneaux would probably only work on it in his spare time; which means, more often than not, weekends. Ditto, Crispin. He would probably only have come up at weekends as well. As for David's contractors, I reckon this was a bit of extra work for his mates, cash in hand. Again, probably working at weekends. The neighbours would probably be used to seeing various cars and vans parked near the house on Sunday." Nick nodded, then set off again, up the lane, until he was able to find somewhere to turn the car around.

"So what's the plan, sweetheart?"

"Plan?" Nick shot her a sideways glance.

"Yes, sweetheart, plan."

"I'll let you know when I've got one."

"Beth,…"

"Just focus on finding somewhere to park." An uneasy silence pervaded the car. "Maybe I'll just go and knock on the front door."

"Beth, be serious."

"I am being serious."

"Beth, you can't just walk up and knock on the front door of a serial killer who's holding his sister-in-law hostage."

"Why not?" As the sprinkling of houses had become sparser, so fields became interspersed with them. Nick found a gateway to a field, that he had noted on the way up the lane, that afforded just enough space in which to park such that he did not obstruct the lane. It was a useful diversion while he thought about how to respond. "What's he going to do? He'll almost certainly answer the door. He'll want to retain control of the situation. He won't want to risk people snooping around the place."

"And when he does? He's already killed three people…"

"He's not going to kill me."

"How do you know?"

"He's got Magenta in there."

"Exactly! Holding her hostage. You're putting her at risk by charging in like a bull in a china shop."

"If my theory is correct – and all his actions support my theory – he wants Magenta for himself. He's not going to harm her and he's not going to do anything that would create disfavour, like harming me in front of her."

"Apart from killing her husband, sister and kidnapping her."

"You're just going to have to trust me on this one, Nick."

"Well, I'm coming with you."

"No you're not. You're staying here."

"Beth…"

"If he poses the threat that you think he does, we're going to need someone on the outside." Had the statement not been delivered with an air of finality, her logic was, Nick conceded to himself, irrefutable.

Before getting out of the car, she took his hand and gave it a reassuring squeeze, though whether she was trying to reassure him or herself, might have been a matter of conjecture. He watched, through the windscreen, as she sauntered down the lane, jauntily adjusting her tan shoulder bag as she went. The sky was blue and dotted with small, pristine fair-weather cumulus, morphing, at higher altitude into cirrocumulus. She picked up the refrain of various birdsong. Further down the road, away to her left a lawnmower droned. Trees were in early summer leaf and the verges were sprinkled with flowers. Under other circumstances, she mused, her surroundings could have been described as bucolic. However, as she approached the Molyneaux cottage, she reminded herself of the far from idyllic, extant circumstances. As she passed it, she mentally checked the registration plate of the blue MG, to confirm that it was Rupert Molyneaux's. She took a deep breath and instinctively readjusted her bag. She knocked on the panel of, what was clearly, a new front door. It opened, with little delay, catching her unawares.

"Ms. Gallagher. What a surprise." If he was surprised, she reckoned, he effortlessly maintained a façade of equanimity.

"I thought I might find you here."

"Evidently." There followed a momentary stand-off, each challenging the other to speak.

"Aren't you going to invite me in?"

"The house isn't really fit for guests." She nodded, slightly, and forced a thin-lipped smile. She may not have had a plan of action, but she did want to avoid provoking him in any way.

"Do you have Magenta with you?" Molyneaux considered the question, then stepped back and opened the door wider to allow her unfettered ingress.

"Perhaps you had better come in."

"Thank you." She did not hesitate to accept the offer, lest he should change his mind. She found herself standing in a spacious, but bare, vestibule with a smooth, concrete floor. A door opened into a room on her left and another door into another room on her right, as might have been expected of a double-fronted cottage. On the left of the hall, a pine staircase ascended to the first floor. To the right, a passage extended to, Gallagher presumed, the kitchen.

"Do go in." With an extravagant gesture of his arm, he indicated the door on the left. She paused for a moment, then acceded to his offer.

The room, as denuded as the hall, would, she imagined become a lounge, stretching from the front to the back of the cottage. Underneath the front window, a sports bag had been dumped on the floor. Against the outside wall, towards the back of the room, on a folded piece of sacking, sat Magenta. Her wrists and ankles were bound with heavily studded, leather restraints. Gallagher surmised that they had been acquired from a, probably online, sex shop, which suggested to her a considerable measure of premeditation. The two women's eyes met. Magenta looked frightened, but calm. Molyneaux had not gagged her, but had, Gallagher speculated, scared her into silence.

While Gallagher had been engaging with Molyneaux, Nick Corvino had not been an entirely passive bystander. He had waited until she was halfway to her destination, then got out of the car and clambered up onto the gate, from which vantage point he had a clear view of Gallagher entering the cottage. At the time she and Magenta were assessing each other, the former thankful to see the latter unharmed and the latter relieved to see a friendly face, Nick was considering his options.

"Are you alright, Magenta?"

"Yes." She was scared, but she made an effort to keep her voice clear and steady.

"Has Rupert hurt you?"

"No." Gallagher expected Molyneaux to intervene, but he

remained silent, behind her.

"What happened in Barrowford?" Magenta shifted her gaze towards Molyneaux, but he clearly, Gallagher inferred, must have given his consent to her answering.

"He was very calm when I went in. Pleased to see me. He kissed me on the cheek. Held my hand. He told me he loved me; that he would look after me. He said we could be together now. I said that wasn't possible, but he insisted. He said it would be OK; said he'd got a plan for us to go away."

"Then what?"

"I think I asked him what he wanted; what he was going to do."

"And what did Rupert say?"

"He dragged me into the kitchen. There was a bag on the counter. That bag." She nodded towards the sports bag beneath the window. "He took something out of it. I didn't realise what it was at first, but it was these handcuffs." She raised her wrists slightly. "He told me not to be frightened. He said he loved me again and would never hurt me, but he didn't want to risk me spoiling things."

"In your own time, Magenta." She wondered why Molyneaux was allowing her to question his hostage and concluded that he was revelling in being the centre of attention; of having his exploits described in this way.

"He grabbed my wrists and I tried to struggle, but then I saw the blood on the floor and all over. It looked fresh. I asked him what he'd done. He said not to worry about it; that he would never hurt me. I was scared. I didn't know what had happened before I came in, or what he might do. I let him put the handcuffs on. They don't hurt. He said his car was in the ginnel and that he was going to take me somewhere safe. Then he marched me out the back. I wanted to scream, but I was scared about what he might do. The blood in the kitchen and knowing that he might have been responsible…" She looked up, drew breath, then let her head sink onto her chest.

"Are you satisfied now?" For a moment Gallagher had forgotten he was behind her. She spun around. He wore an earnest, troubled expression.

"What do you intend to do now, Rupert?"

"I think we need to talk about that, Ms. Gallagher." She raised a questioning eyebrow. "In the other room." He moved his head to indicate that she should go the room on the other side of the hall. For a few seconds she stood her ground.

"What about Magenta?"

"She's quite comfortable here."

"Aren't you worried she might…"

"Madge is a very sensible woman, Ms. Gallagher. She won't do anything that might put your life at risk," he looked across at her, "will you, Madge?" A faint, but distinct, hint of threat lay behind the question.

"No, Rupert." He turned back to Gallagher.

"After you." Gallagher complied, slowly, trying to figure out Molyneaux's intent and to formulate a plan that might, at least, delay whatever it was he had in mind. She reckoned that, whatever it was he had to say to her, he could have said it in front of Magenta, but he wanted an excuse to separate his two women.

The second room was just as inhospitable as the first, but smaller. Gallagher went across to the far wall, turned around and let her bag slip from her shoulder to the cold, grey, concrete floor. This was one instance when she felt safer with her back to the wall. Molyneaux had followed her, carrying his bag. He placed it, neatly, on the floor, beneath the window, just as it had been in the larger room, then stood, appraising her; maybe, she thought, evaluating his options.

"You want to talk about your intentions." She had not meant to speak first, but she did not want to grant him too much thinking time.

"You've complicated matters, Ms. Gallagher." He squatted down, parted the top of the unzipped bag, peered inside, withdrew a large carving knife and stood up again. "Now I'm going to have to uncomplicate them." He took a step towards her, jiggling the knife in his right hand.

"Don't make matters worse for yourself, Rupert." It was the first thing she could think of to say. "The police are on their way here." She was not sure that she had sounded convincing.

"I don't think so, Ms Gallagher." His demeanour and intonation indicated that he was wholly unperturbed. She shrugged, attempting to feign indifference.

"Please yourself, but when I saw your car, I..."

"You like to think you're clever; cleverer than the police. You like to think you can outwit them. That's why you put a tracking device on my car. That wasn't so clever, though, was it?" There followed a momentary impasse.

"Why did you kill Casey and Carmine and Crispin?" It was the first question that came into her head. She needed to buy herself some time and reckoned he might be arrogant, or egocentric, enough to happily talk about his deeds, especially if he was intent on killing her. He cocked his head slightly to one side, giving the impression of deep thought.

"It wasn't planned. Just circumstances." He composed himself, preparing to tell his story. "I've always been the runt of the litter. The last to be considered. Viv's forged a successful career for herself in teaching; happily married; nice house; couple of kids. But Cris, he's an architect. He designs things for all to see and gets showered with praise for them. Casey couldn't help banging on about his achievements. Viv got an honorary mention in his speech. But me, I just beaver away in some gloomy office, collating the area's history. No one ever sees the fruits of my labours and they go ignored. I was just a footnote. There he stood, telling everyone what a wonderful friend he was, son, brother, uncle; how everyone was proud of him; how lucky Magenta was to be marrying him – and how lucky he was to be marrying someone like Magenta. And there was the tennis. How popular he was at the tennis club and all the cups and trophies he's won." He snorted. "They're just bits of tinware, no bigger than an eggcup. What've I ever won? Nothing. And that's what I am to them: nothing. I could've killed him. Casey. It was just a thought; I hadn't any intention of doing so."

"So what happened on the night of the wedding?" He thought for a few seconds, glancing out of the window.

"I'd gone outside to get some air. It was starting to get all a bit much for me inside. I saw Casey come out. I saw him wander off behind the stables. I wasn't really watching him, but then I saw that other woman come out. I don't know who she was, but I'd seen her talking to Casey inside. She followed in his footsteps. It was obvious what going on. I remembered seeing my dad and Laura together. Seems everyone was having a bit on the side. I felt incensed. Betrayed." He paused. "I'd been in the smithy and seen all the tools in there. I went back in and grabbed the hammer and punch. The guard was outside, having a fag." He gave a short, ironic grunt. "I could've walked out with a bloody anvil and he wouldn't have noticed. I hid behind the barn. I don't know what I intended to do. I saw the woman emerge from behind the stables. They hadn't been at it long. A real quick, quickie. Then Casey came out and hung around by the statue. I crept up on him and… well, I don't really know what happened. I left him there, threw the tools in the river and went back inside."

"And took the speech from his jacket."

"I wanted to see it for myself. Hold it. Read it. Proof that I was justified." He took half a step towards her.

"What about Carmine?" He sighed.

"Poor Carmine. They say you shouldn't kill the messenger – and Casey was really only the messenger. Magenta only married Cris because of Carmine. It was really her fault and it seemed unfair to have killed Casey, but not kill Carmine. It seemed the least I could do was kill her as well."

"Why was she to blame?"

"She kept us apart. Whenever we met up, Carmine always had some excuse for dragging me away and leaving Cris and Madge together. If I could just have spent some time with Madge…" A hint of wistfulness swept across his face, but then it was gone and he resumed his focus. Gallagher reckoned that he would never have had the confidence to approach Magenta independently; he relied upon the gathering of the foursome to see her.

"So you ambushed her under the bridge by the canal."

"I knew she often walked that way to the park during her lunchtimes. I just had to take my lunch break at the same time and wait for her."

"And what about Crispin; your brother?"

"Casey and Carmine were dead, but Cris was still married to Madge. It felt like there was unfinished business. I had to finish the job. I did try to explain to him, but it was no good. He couldn't understand." Gallagher was not sure what it was he had tried to explain to Crispin, presumably in the car park at Campion Lake, but it was somewhat academic. Rupert moved another half step closer to her. She shuffled along the wall to keep her distance, while being acutely aware of not allowing herself to be edged into a corner.

"Are you going to kill me now?"

"I'm sorry, Bethany. You don't mind if I call you Bethany? I have to uncomplicate things and then Madge and me can be on our way." She was not sure for how long they stood facing one another before he lunged at her, but, when he did, the room became a blur of flailing limbs.

She managed to deflect the indiscriminate thrust, but only as far as her thigh. She sensed the spurt of blood before the pain registered. His left palm slammed into her shoulder, pinning her against the wall, while he attempted to wriggle his right wrist from the ineffectively slack grip she had on it, simultaneously slashing at her thigh again and again. He wrested his arm free, raised it high above his head and hurled himself at her neck. She dodged the potentially fatal blow, but at the expense of her shoulder. As he raised his arm again, the instinct for self-preservation took over and she fastened on to his wrist again, temporarily keeping the knife at bay. She attempted to knee him in the groin, but missed her target. Nevertheless, suddenly she was free.

The next thing of which she was conscious, was of being slumped on the floor. Blood was spread across the concrete. Her jeans, around her left thigh, were ripped in several places, with blood seeping into the fabric. She could not properly see the wound to her shoulder, but she could see the blood leaching into the apricot top and feel its warmth against her skin. The acuteness of the pain alternated between her thigh and her shoulder. When she looked up, she saw two men wrestling on the floor. The man on top was Molyneaux but, from the way his right arm was being held aloft, the man underneath was of superior strength. Rupert aimed a punch, with his left fist, towards the head of his foe, then another and another. The other man's grip relaxed and Molyneaux wrenched his arm free. The knife came down. There was a muffled yelp. Molyneaux, momentarily off balance, was shoved back. They rolled over. They were side by side, facing one another. A blood stain of rapidly increasing proportions marked the point at which the knife had pierced the flesh. Gallagher recognised the shirt. Nick had grabbed hold of Molyneaux's wrist again, forcing him onto his back. With his free right hand, Nick clamped Molyneaux's throat, squeezing it; pressing his neck into the unforgiving concrete. Molyneaux's hold on the knife weakened. It clattered to the floor. Nick retrieved it and instinctively, blindly, plunged it into the flesh beneath him. Molyneaux screamed. Nick withdrew it and thrust it in again and a third time.

"Nick!" He had been about to drive it into Molyneaux's thigh a fourth time, but stopped in mid-swing. He was breathing heavily. Blood was still pumping from his own wound. He was staring straight into Molyneaux's defiant eyes. "Enough. Get off him." Nick calmed his breathing. Reluctantly he rolled over onto his back. He slapped the knife down on the floor, securing it with his palm, and felt for the wound in his side. Molyneaux, clutching the lacerations to his thigh and groin heaved himself to his knees. He tried to stand, but his right leg would bear no weight. He glanced towards Gallagher, with a derisive grimace, and crawled towards the door. Nick levered himself up onto his forearm. He and Gallagher looked at each other. Her gashes were still oozing blood, but the pain was numbed by her concern for his wound – and for the left side of his face that was already showing signs of swelling.

"He won't get far. I let his tyres down." He tried to smile, but it faded as quickly as it had come.

"Nick, what…?"

"The back door was open." He eased himself onto his back

again.

"We need to get an ambulance." She crawled over to him. His eyes were half closed. "Nick!" She feared him slipping into unconsciousness. "Can you hear me?" The gash, to the left side of his abdomen, was patently deep. "Shit." She felt utterly helpless. "Stay with me, Nick." She gently lifted his blood-soaked t-shirt clear of the wound, glanced around the desolate room for something she could use as a bandage, then, in the absence of anything, gingerly removed her top, ripped one sleeve off, to later press into service as a makeshift dressing for her own shoulder, and used the rest of it to stem the flow of Nick's blood, placing his hand over it to keep it in place. She kissed his brow, then crawled back to her bag to retrieve her phone.

XXIV

DÉNOUEMENT

Gallagher had been oblivious to how much time had elapsed before the ambulances and the police had arrived. She had almost been oblivious to her own pain. Her priority had been to reduce Nick's blood loss and to keep him conscious. She had been cognizant of Magenta being in the other room, alone, and speculated about how much she had heard of the commotion across the hallway and how she had interpreted it. Molyneaux had crawled out of the room, substantially incapacitated, and in considerable pain, leaving his bag behind. She had not heard voices and had not heard the front door open and, thus, concluded that he had attempted to make his escape through the back door, abandoning Magenta, which, she had considered, would have been no bad thing.

The police had found Molyneaux propped against the front wheel of his sabotaged car. Magenta had been discovered, fo4rsaken, scared and visibly shaking. Having ascertained that she was unhurt, they had cut her free from her shackles, and escorted her to a waiting ambulance.

Nick Corvino had been stretchered to a second ambulance, accompanied by Gallagher who had hobbled there, stubbornly repulsing assistance.

It transpired that, Nick's repeated assault on Molyneaux's thigh had resulted in the abductor muscles being ruptured, hence his inability to get farther than his car, where, finding it crippled, Wainwright had surmised, he had given up the fight.

Gallagher had been able to defend herself sufficiently such that her injuries, while painful, had been confined to little more than deep flesh wounds, only requiring cleansing and dressing.

Nick had been pronounced lucky. While the knife had

penetrated deep into his body it had missed all his vital organs and, while it had induced a considerable loss of blood, his injuries had not been life threatening. Of equal concern had been the swelling of his face and the multiple contusions that had subsequently developed. Fortunately, despite the ferocity of Molyneaux's assault, he had not sustained any broken bones.

Laura had collected her daughter - still in shock, but having had appropriate medication administered - from the hospital, having spent the afternoon, at home, in a state of high agitation, mixed with a deep sense of guilt and a measure of shame, which had only partially been alleviated by the attentive support of her husband.

Mr. and Mrs. Molyneaux had been informed that Rupert was in hospital and had rushed to his side, where D.S. Bowden had informed them that, when discharged, there son would be taken into police custody where he would be charged with the murders of Casey Hardacre, Carmine Seacroft and Crispin Molyneaux; the abduction of Magenta Molyneaux, the attempted murder of Bethany Gallagher, GBH in respect of Nicolas Corvino and Timothy Bulstrade and possession of a bladed article. At the earliest opportunity David Molyneaux had phoned Laura Seacroft and the pair had exchanged sympathies and commiserations. Laura had proposed that it might be prudent if they maintained a discreet distance for the foreseeable future.

Nick was recuperating at home, having been thoroughly examined at the hospital, the wound appropriately sutured and, thence, duly discharged. Against all good and solicitous advice, Gallagher was in her office on Monday morning. Before ascending the stairs, which she subsequently did with a considerable measure of discomfort, she had paused to gaze up at the office directory in the foyer of the building. The words 'Bethany Gallagher' had appeared to her to have lost some of their shine. Despite having chosen apparel that would conceal the bandaging to her shoulder and thigh, no one could have failed to notice her revealing hobbling gait.

"What the 'ell are you doing 'ere, Ms. Gallagher?" Clematis

251

could not contain the outburst when she saw her boss enter the office.

"Excuse me?"

"I do watch the news. You should be at 'ome."

"I don't need lecturing, Clemmy." Gallagher continued towards her own office.

"What 'appened in Gissington? What were you doing there?"

"My job. Make me some coffee. Please."

When her secretary entered her office with the coffee, Gallagher was sat in her chair, swivelling back and forth, absently coiling a lock of hair between her fingers, absorbing her surroundings, as if they were completely alien to her. Clematis noted that she had not turned on her computer.

"You don't need to be 'ere, Ms. Gallagher." She set the 'Mine's a Latte' mug on the desk, thought about sitting down, but then reconsidered.

"Am I getting too old for this?"

"Old?"

"I'm forty one."

"Maybe you should go 'ome."

"Nick could have been killed. I should never have got him involved."

When D.I. Wainwright entered the office, Gallagher was stood at the window, staring out over the familiar view of the canal. Three dog walkers had met on the towpath opposite and stopped to pass the time of day. A pair of swans, trailing a gaggle of cygnets, had glided out of view. She did not turn round for several seconds after she heard the door close. She knew it was him; he had called earlier in the morning to say he would be coming. She guessed it would not be entirely a sympathy call.

"We need to talk, Beth." When she did turn to face him, he had already made himself comfortable on the chair most usually occupied by clients.

"You can save your breath, Danny. I don't think I can do this anymore."

Printed in Dunstable, United Kingdom

63446078R00150